Cities at Sea

Cities at Sea

Martin Simons

SCI
FIC
SIM

Rev. date: 01/27/2016

To order additional copies of this book, contact:
Xlibris
1-800-455-039
www.Xlibris.com.au
Orders@Xlibris.com.au
732873

1

As she left the Shanghai Space Museum, Sal did not notice, among the bustle of the jostling crowds, the quiet, slow approach of a large, dark, enclosed vehicle, accompanied on foot by two burly men. Lost in thought, she had almost made up her mind to join Jezzy's fascinating but rather scary project. She had a few more questions to ask but hardly doubted what she would finally decide. It would be a great adventure with the prospect of even more exciting things to do in the longer term. She looked for an unused open-topped robocar to take her back to the laboratory and was about to touch her wrist terminal to make the promised call to say she was on the way there. All the cars in sight were busy so she walked a little way looking for an idle one to pick up.

'That's her.'

She was seized from behind. She struggled fiercely, lashed out; kicked and scratched, feeling her finger nails digging into someone's hand. A strong girl, she knew something about self-defence but more hands gripped her and she was unable to break away. She screamed, continuing to fight, trying with her feet to trip whoever it was who had attacked her. An arm came round under her chin; her arms were painfully forced back and held firmly. None of the passing crowd came to her aid. A hand clamped over her mouth. She bit it hard, kicked back and made solid contact with something, twice.

'Bloody hell, you little demon.' She found herself lifted bodily off the deck, both her feet were held. 'Stop struggling or I will stun you.'

She let herself go slack, hoping the grip would relax so that she could break away, but bands were quickly pulled tight round her arms, wrists, knees and ankles. She was carried into the vehicle, dropped and strapped down into a restraining capsule with a man on each side.

'You are under arrest.' Only then did she see that her two assailants wore the uniforms of the SMC, Sydney Marine Corps.

'*Back to base, fast.*'

The van obediently began to move.

'Why? What am I supposed to have done? Why?' she shouted. 'This is a mistake. Let me go'

The man on her left, glancing at his wrist, read out her ID number: 'BY2405263. That is you, isn't it?'

'Yes, but….' Sal was confused and afraid.

'No mistake. If you make a fuss it will the worse for you. Shut up, be still and behave yourself.'

'What have I done wrong?' There was a momentary silence. 'You're supposed to tell me, aren't you?' she yelled.

'What has she done, Sarge?'

'Buggered if I know. They didn't tell me. Pick the sheila up and bring her back pronto, they said. Captain's orders. Whatever it is, they are in a devil of a hurry. Mutiny, I guess. They'll maroon her.'

To be marooned meant being left alone somewhere on land, unprotected, with minimal food and water. It was a death sentence. Sal trembled at the thought of the land. She was not a mutineer. How could this be happening? She wept bitterly and angrily. The van swept smoothly and almost silently at high speed through the heavy traffic, guided infallibly by the auto control. Passenger-carrying robocars picked up the electronic warning signals and swerved clear to let them through without possibility of error or delay. In the unfamiliar city, Sal had no idea where they were going.

'Where are you taking me? What is this? *Abduction?*' She asked, desperately.

'*Extradition.* Shut up.'

'How can that be? What do you mean? I have a valid pass. I've only been away from home since yesterday.'

They did not bother to reply. Sal was utterly bewildered, unable to see out clearly but aware that other vehicles were rushing by in both directions. The tall buildings on either side of the road were a blur as their vehicle passed in and out of their shadows making the light flicker.

The van stopped at last and the door opened. The men undid the capsule restraints, carried her out, trussed as she was, and dumped her roughly on the deck. There were distant exclamations and a sudden angry altercation that she could not fully hear. She gathered that the two fellows who had grabbed her so suddenly and violently were in trouble. The sergeant hastily released the straps that held her arms and legs and helped her to stand. She stumbled a little. Her legs were stiff.

'Not our fault', the man muttered in self-justification. 'Fought like a little demon. How were we to know?' Her instincts now were to break loose and run but he held her arm firmly.

Utterly wretched Sal realised they had arrived at a chopper pad. A young woman, wearing the insignia of a pilot, came to her.

'These two louts had no right to treat you roughly,' she said. 'They should have spoken to you first and explained. Nemo has sent for you. You must come with me. Don't resist, there's no need. You won't be harmed but you must come. Understand?' Through her tears, still shocked and trembling, Sal nodded.

'Calm down. Nothing terrible is going to happen. We are ordered to get you to him as soon as we can, that's all. Here, dry your eyes.' The woman, sympathetically, gave her a clean tissue. 'Bad luck, kid.'

With little ceremony, aching and bruised, she was helped aboard the chopper. Here there were more straps but when she protested the smiling pilot explained they were only to prevent her being thrown about by air turbulence. The woman tied herself also down firmly.

'Ready?' There was no one else on board. 'Have you flown before?' Sal, shaking with fear and rage, shook her head.

'It's nothing to be afraid of. Calm down. Take the chance, have a good look as we go. You probably won't ever see Shanghai from this angle again. It is a fantastic sight when you have the opportunity, so much bigger than our raft.'

'Lift for Sydney, angels 2,' the woman said to the machine.

Monitored but not interfered with by the pilot, the chopper came to life. The rotors began to spin and they lifted off smoothly. Sal was too disturbed to take as much notice of the new experience as she would normally have done. They ascended vertically from among the enclosing spindly city towers, some over 1000 metres tall with masts and forests of turbines. They cleared the highest of them by a substantial margin. The great city raft, Shanghai, completely surrounded by the mighty expanse of the ocean, was elliptical, occupied entirely by buildings, streets, wide parklands and sports stadia. It was fringed by marinas with yachts and boats of all kinds. A ferry, looking from above like a long, narrow, gleaming fish, was just leaving the dock as another, loaded with tourists, moved in ready to take its place. Yesterday morning Sal had been a passenger on one of those vessels. Agitated though she was, she could pick out the laboratory area, far away on the distant side of the city. The buildings there were generally lower but there was a standard type hydroponic tower among them. The usual arrays of whirling turbines and solar collectors, glittering in the sunlight, were visible. Torva had described the lab district as Jezzy's private empire. That was where she had intended to be; where she should be now. What would Jezzy think when she didn't arrive?

From two thousand metres even Shanghai began to look small against the ocean. The chopper turned, tucked its nose down and sped away. The acceleration forced her back into her seat. Sydney was below them in a very few minutes. She had a good knowledge of practical navigation. It was coincidence that the two cities had drifted close enough to allow exchange visits. In a few days they would be well apart again.

By comparison with the much greater city the Sydney raft was less impressive. From above it appeared as a large, complicated and ponderous piece of flotsam with vertical masts and towers resembling the strange and intricate spines of a huge oval sea urchin. Sydney was twelve nauticals along the major axis but seemed small from this height.

The seat seemed to fall away from under her as their descent started suddenly. They began to drop rapidly, she felt dizzy and her ears popped. She braced herself, expecting a mighty crash. The fall slowed rapidly and now she was pushed down into the seat. The pilot glanced at her, grinning. The touch down was feather light. The rotor slowed and stopped. Chuckling, the pilot helped her out, supporting her when her knees threatened to give way. After a few steps she regained her balance and usual poise.

A grave, tall staff officer met them, politely but solemnly. As if to emphasise his elevated status he wore a plain dark blue uniform with no decorations, epaulets or insignia. The severe simplicity of his clothing distinguished him from the rest of the citizen crew, all of whom, during duty hours, wore badges of rank showing their function and status. Sal understood that this man was one of the highest elite, near to the Captain.

For a moment she was not restrained by anyone and contemplated escape. Before the thought was fully formed Sal changed her mind. There was nowhere to run. Cameras covered every small space in the city. Each person was perpetually within vision, all the way down to the schoolie capsules, crèches, nurseries, insemination clinics with their birthing wards and banks of Huxley incubators feeding human embryos; all were observed and automatically archived. Every individual's behaviour and every event, however trivial, was recorded and relayed to the memory banks. No human bothered to look at the archives unless some crime was committed or contemplated, but the records were always ready to be studied.

Nobody and nothing could be missed. Not even the most obscure corner of the city or the smallest event was lost to the machinery of surveillance. Sport decks and stadia, gymnasia, running tracks, swimming pools, toilets, citizens at work or on leave, sleeping, embracing, lying together, mating, all were observed. The marathon runners (once round the main deck, 26 nauticals), boaters and swimmers, hang gliders, base jumpers, every action was seen and archived. There was no escape other than being marooned on the land and so cut off from everything, including supplies of food. On Sal's wrist was the monitor that transmitted her location every few seconds. It emitted a steady, identifiable signal enabling the wearer's location anywhere within a wide radius to be found immediately. The wrist terminals were also universally used for inter-personal communication and connections to the global net. All messages could be and were intercepted. To interfere with a terminal was an offence. It was not worth the effort. To try to switch, damage or attempt painfully to cut it off, brought swift retribution.

'What is this about?' Sal asked, desperately. 'Why have I been brought back? I don't understand. What does Nemo want?'

'He will explain when you see him,' said the officer. 'There will be a tribunal, an enquiry into your behaviour.' What, Sal wondered desperately, could an insignificant *middy* like herself have done, or thought of doing, to concern the Captain? What bothered him enough to have her extradited and dragged into court?

'Listen very carefully to everything; answer the questions, be honest and straightforward. I assure you he will be fair. Nemo is a good man. Your counsellor Calpurnia will support you.'

Calpurnia *support* me? Not likely. This must be her doing, Sal thought, hurt and furious. She had been betrayed. Months ago Cal had come across her when she was viewing a programme describing the experimental work being done by the Shanghai *biotech* group. Sydney and Shanghai then were half an ocean apart and the possibility of a visit seemed remote. Cal had showed minimal interest amounting to indifference at the time but Sal thought now that had been deliberately deceptive.

To reach the Bridge where Nemo had his offices, they had to ascend on the escalators to emerge soon on the highest deck. From here three days ago she, with the boy Neppy and thousands of others, hoping to tour Shanghai as visitors, had stared across the sea to see the mighty raft drifting nearer. Sal did not count herself as a tourist. Except for that careless remark to Calpurnia, she had told no one of her true interest.

When it seemed likely the two rafts would drift closer together, close enough for day trips, Sal's interest had intensified, occupying more of her attention. Cal had evidently noticed and probed further. Cal had probably seen what she had been learning and it was a counsellor's duty to report anything if she thought it necessary. Cal, officiously as always, had overdone her duty. This should not have surprised Sal but it infuriated her. There had been no need to draw her to the Captain's attention. She was *not* a mutineer. Mutiny was far from her dreams. *Damn Calpurnia*, she thought.

The staff officer now guided her through a very ordinary automatic door into a large cabin provided with tables and the plainest of capsules. These were little more than comfortable couches without the usual gaming screens or access to entertainments. The man showed her a bathing alcove where she could pee, wash and remove the signs of her tears. He advised her to rest and wait. The Captain would call for her when he was ready. Sal did her best to smarten her appearance and afterwards sat on one of the recliners. She was suddenly very tired, lay full length, and closed her eyes.

She opened them at a touch on her shoulder and found a grey haired man standing next to her. It took her a few moments to recognise him. It was the Captain, whom she had previously seen only in formal public holograms wearing full uniform with braid, insignia and cap. In astonishment and alarm she sprang to her feet, losing her balance momentarily, to be supported by his firm hand. He was smaller than she had imagined, hardly any taller than she was, and dressed informally. Face to face, he became an ordinary middle-aged man, seeming full of concern for her. He smiled. She knew his official rather pompous speaking voice but his manner now was gentle.

'No harm will come to you. I told my staff to get you back here as quickly as possible. I failed to emphasise that I wanted you treated with full respect. I apologise for the way the marines behaved. It was partly my fault for not giving my instructions clearly enough. Will you forgive my carelessness?'

Sal was amazed. This man was the supreme authority on a raft carrying seven or eight million people; the most powerful person she had ever met. If he chose, he could issue the order to maroon her. Now he seemed to be apologising. Could he be sincere?

'I did fight. I was surprised and I struggled. They didn't hurt me much, but I don't understand why I am here. What have I done wrong?'

'You have done no wrong, at least, not yet. No breach of the law will be entered against your number. Calpurnia was afraid you were going to make a hasty decision that would cause a lot of trouble. You have made no formal application but it is your right to do so if that is what you wish. Officially, I will record this incident as a request by you to leave us and join the crew of the Shanghai raft. Even so, from what I am told, you were behaving rashly and without proper procedures. I will not simply release you without considering the whole situation. We will talk about this in a little while, with some of my most trusted officers. Do you understand?'

Sal nodded.

'Just so. Now, I know you have had nothing to eat since breakfast in the capsulery where you spent the night.' Sal knew her circumstances would have been advertised by her wrist terminal. 'We will have a meal together. Calpurnia is waiting too. Afterwards we will have our conference.' He took her arm gently and led her towards a rather grand, old-fashioned double door that glided open as they approached. Before going through, he paused and pointed to an inscription above the lintel. It made no sense whatever to Sal. It looked like words, but although there were a few letters she recognised, most of them were strange.

'That is written in a very ancient language that only a few scholars now understand. It is called Greek. The Greeks were a land-dwelling people in a small, mid-latitudes mountainous region. Almost all the land where they grew their food crops and kept their animals is below the sea now. They spoke that tongue more than four thousand years ago. In *Raftunglish*, it says: *The ship's Captain pays attention all the time to the welfare of his ship and his crew.* The writer was called Plato. You are a member of my crew and I am concerned for your welfare, as well as the ship, or I should say, our raft. Now, let's go in and have something to eat.'

The hall they entered was too large to be called a cabin. It had several couch capsules arranged in a circle, with small tables conveniently close, but no gaming screens. Calpurnia was reclining on one of the couches, casually eating from a dish of fruit. She was a tall, elderly, rather bony and angular woman with an unsympathetic face. She came to her feet quickly when they entered. Sal went to her and held out both her hands. They were not taken. Calpurnia looked sternly at her, unsmiling.

'Are you well? I saw the men were a bit rough with you.'

'I didn't expect them. I scratched one of them, and kicked' Sal replied.

'So I saw. That was stupid.'

'I am all right now,' said Sal. Calpurnia tossed her head and turned away abruptly.

'Well, well,' said Nemo, frowning slightly at this. 'Take your place, Sal.' He pointed to one of the couches. 'There's fruit there, help yourself while we are waiting for the main course.' Sal went to the indicated capsule. Calpurnia and the Captain reclined also. He touched the pad on his armrest and spoke.

'Turbot with salad and lemon juice, all the usual trimmings, for three.'

'The curious thing about those Greeks, Sal,' said the Captain, filling in a little time, 'as my learned friends have explained, is that the way they lived is quite similar to the way of our rafts. Each independent city-state had its own customs, officers and citizens as we do. They were confined by high walls on land. We are confined by the sea. The great difference was, even though like our modern cities they all spoke the same language, they were primitive, always quarrelling, fighting and killing one another. There's no reason why rafters now ever should fight like that. The oceans are big enough for all of us. There are no conflicts of interest.'

The meals rose up now out of the tables, with all the necessary utensils, drinks and tasty morsels. The Captain smiled at Sal benevolently and nodded. Sal was desperately hungry and set to work immediately.

There was no conversation. When all were finished, the Captain touched his pad again. The used dishes sank down into the tables and disappeared.

'Now we must be serious,' he said. 'We are going to hear your application formally, discuss it, and afterwards I will make a decision. I will be helped by three of my younger officers and Calpurnia, who knows you well. Whatever is ruled, you must abide by it, but you need not be afraid. The worst that can happen, if I decide so, is that you will stay with us in Sydney, to continue as you were before.'

'I'm not to be marooned?'

'No, child, no, certainly not, that is quite beyond possibility. If we approve, you will be free to go to Shanghai if that is what you still want. You must, however, consider most carefully, as I think you have not yet done, before you take that course. If you leave us and go to Shanghai, you will be wholly committed to something that may turn out to be dreadful. You may prefer to withdraw your application. I am assured by Jessy herself, there can be no going back once the matter is decided.'

So Jezzy had been in touch directly with Nemo, Sal realised. She must have heard immediately when Sal was arrested.

Sal dared not correct the Captain's pronunciation. Jezzy was correct, Jessy was not.

Sal's visit had never been a mere tourist excursion. On the spot she had almost committed herself to joining the research team. It would mean a complete change in her life, a change in herself. It still surprised her that the Captain thought it worth taking so much trouble over her. Was her future so important to him? How extraordinary. Why should he care? Had he nothing more serious to do?

2

Nemo touched the communication pad again and said: 'Advisers, please come in now and take your places.'

The door opened to admit three officers, two men and a woman, all of mature age, dressed plainly but very smartly as Captain's staff. They looked solemn, bowed briefly as they entered, and disposed themselves in empty capsules. Two marines in their black uniforms took station beside the entry door.

'The tribunal is now in session,' said the Captain. 'The proceedings will be recorded for immediate broadcasting and filed for reference as usual.' He became more formal in speech and manner.

'Captain of the Sydney city raft, ID BY2966/6235491, I, Nemo, preside.'

BY stood for birth year. Nemo was 135 years old, in the prime of life. He glanced at his wrist. 'We are here to consider an application by ID BY3083/2405263, this young female citizen, who has chosen to call herself informally, Sal.'

'Present are Tribunes Jake 438, Hanna 512 and Mitch 209, and Youth Counsellor Calpurnia 632.' Each nodded as their names and last three were given.

'263, Sal, is applying to leave Sydney and take up a special laboratory post as a crew member in Shanghai. Her admission to that city is sponsored by the notable research scientist, Jessy, whose name I am sure you have all heard, whether or not you know the direction her most recent work has taken. Jessy has need of special assistants. She informs me that Sal is eminently suitable for the work she will be doing, if we release her, and if she still wishes to join Jessy's *biotech* group. We must decide not only the matter of whether we in Sydney can afford to let her go, but more importantly for her, whether it will be in her own best interests to do so. It is not, as you will discover, a simple matter.' The Captain paused and looked round the small assembly.

All were staring at Sal.

'So, friends and advisers, what are we to do? I should mention at once that 263 has been doing exceptionally well in her Nav studies.' He nodded to Calpurnia. 'Her counsellor and I are confident that if Sal remains with us she will become a successful member of our navigation team. If we decide she must stay she has a bright future.'

Calpurnia raised a hand. The Captain, not pleased by this unexpected intervention, nevertheless waved to indicate she was free to speak. The woman seemed driven by a surprising passion.

'I have known Sal since she left the crèche. I confirm that she is talented and very high-spirited, too much so indeed,' said Calpurnia. 'She has a mind very much her own and is inclined to be rebellious. If she will settle down and stay with us, she may become a successful and *useful* citizen, a navigator and a *full member of our raft community.*' The emphasis was inescapable.

'Unfortunately I find her application wholly repulsive. The famous, I would say notorious geneticist Jezzy, in the name of research, selects and operates on *impressionable* girls and boys. She calls them volunteers. If 263 goes to Shanghai Jezzy intends make a radical modification of her body. This amounts to criminal abuse. We should not allow any child from Sydney to be experimented on in such a way.' Sal felt angry. At 17 years old she was no longer a child.

'What exactly is proposed?' asked Tribune Mitch. 'If it's genetic modification for cosmetic reasons it should have been done before decanting.'

'It is far from pre-birth cosmetics. It involves making her grow gills like a fish, enabling her to swim under water. You must imagine for yourselves what the results will look like. This wicked woman locates and *entraps* her subjects before they have finished growing. I do not doubt there are grotesque results. What happens if her manipulations go astray I can only imagine.'

The tribunes were obviously disturbed.

The Captain interrupted, a little impatiently; 'Jessy assures me that her work has passed beyond the experimental stage. The subjects are truly volunteers, carefully chosen and screened beforehand. If unsuitable, for example, fully mature and beyond further growth, they are not affected at all by genetic changes so are not accepted for Jessy's project. However, already there is a small handful of youngsters still growing who have been successfully modified. They are all in good health and happy. They can and do swim for extended periods under water, but they also emerge to breathe air when they choose, truly amphibian.'

Tribune Jake raised a hand.

'I am astonished that apparently this work and its results are unknown to most of us. Surely everyone should know about it.'

Tribune Mitch raised his hand. At a nod from the Captain he spoke.

'I have been aware of the Shanghai genetic project for years, though I have not kept entirely up to date. I did not know that Jezzy had progressed so far with it. The reports are available to anyone who looks for them. The work has been presented regularly in the relevant Biotech videos. You only need to look at the global index to find them.'

The captain spoke again.

'I can confirm this. I have located several of the reports myself in the last few hours. There has been no deliberate attempt to hide them, but, as with much of what goes on in research laboratories around the oceans, the results are known only to those who specialise in the relevant areas. It seems that the Shanghai biolab is the only established centre where this very sophisticated kind of work in genetics is going on.'

Calpurnia was obviously agitated.

'Well, Calpurnia, you may continue.'

'Sal wants it *only because she thinks it would be fun.*' The woman looked round the group. 'The truth is, it would be a mutilation, a horror not only for her but also for everyone who might come into contact with her. She should be positively prevented from submitting to these ugly operations.'

'Do you deny that Sal has the right to do whatever she wishes with her own body?' asked Tribune Hanna, with a touch of asperity.

'That is not the question; I have more serious concerns beyond individual rights,' Cal went on. 'This is not merely a matter of giving a silly child a shorter nose or the ability to play games under water.' The woman paused to give emphasis to her words, and glared round the group.

'If, as Jezzy claims, the manipulations succeed, the resulting distorted creatures will breed. It is much more serious than modifying a single person or a handful of unfortunate kids. If that dreadful old hag is allowed, even encouraged to continue with this project, she will bring into being a new species of humanity. I suspect that is her intention. That is the real issue today.'

Nemo was about to speak again but Calpurnia was not to be silenced.

'She hopes to create *a new race. She must be stopped.* Not only should 263 stay with us, but also we should demand a full, global intercity conference and a decision to bring these eugenic experiments to an end at once. Jezzy and her so-called team should have been arrested and marooned long before this. There must be an ocean-wide concerted move to stop this infamy before it goes any further.'

The Captain raised a commanding hand, not to be ignored. 'There is no possibility of a global intercity parliament and ruling. It would be unprecedented, extremely difficult to arrange. In any case it would have no power to interfere with individual scientists or groups pursuing whatever line of enquiry they choose. Jezzy has licence and full support from the mandarins of Shanghai. Rightly or not, we cannot interfere.

We have no power.' Calpurnia attempted to speak again, but the Captain suppressed her with a frown and hand gesture, palm down.

'Shanghai and Jezzy's laboratories on that mighty raft are not within my, or any other city's, or combination of raft cities, jurisdiction.'

Mitch raised a hand. The Captain nodded to him.

'This seems like something new but we should recognise that the critical steps were taken long, long ago, soon after the turn of the *Second Millennium*. Humanity has already been modified. We, all of us, are products of genetic engineering that has been going on for hundreds of years. All citizen rafters on the oceans are the result of the established procedures that replaced the ancient uncontrolled random breeding habits of humans as they used to be. Matching and selection, sometimes loosely termed the *mix and match* system, were applied to all of us before our conception, incubation and decanting.'

'There were people born by the ancient processes who had serious, genetically preventable deficiencies, undesirable mutations, cerebral palsy, dystrophies, syndromes often resulting from disorderly insemination procedures and the dangerous processes of old style pregnancy and birth. Many small genetic changes have been introduced over many generations. Each seemed insignificant at the time and was greeted with little or no objections, often with rejoicing. The cumulative effect has been profound.'

Sal noticed both Hanna and Nemo nodding slightly.

'Groups of people also used to differ in such superficial things as, skin, hair and eye colour leading to insupportable discriminations, so-called racial prejudices. None of us here would be what we are if there had been a restriction on the kind of work Jezzy, and those many before her, have been doing for more than a thousand years. We must not try to stop it now'

Calpurnia was furious. 'We who live on the oceans now are at least *all one homogeneous race.*'

Nemo held up a hand. 'Indeed, Counsellor, that is so. But I cannot allow an extended argument now about issues that were, whether everyone approves or not, irreversibly decided two thousand and more years ago. Perhaps you, Calpurnia, believe fundamental answers to these and many other ethical questions have never been fully worked out. Maybe they never will be. So be it. We are not going to attempt them here now. We have not the power to interfere.'

Hanna raised a hand. The Captain nodded and indicated she should speak.

'I have heard accounts before about Jezzy's work and her ambitions. A few scattered presentations have appeared in popular visimags. The detailed reports Jezzy has produced are in the most elevated scientific language. They prove difficult to penetrate by the non-specialist. I have not followed up with serious study but we have access to some definite information that we can all understand. I support the project. We took charge of our own evolution long, long ago and should continue to direct it along desirable paths. We are creatures of the ocean, depending on the sea for everything, food, energy, raw materials and minerals. It is a major defect of our species that we cannot move freely in the medium that supports us. The addition of gills is a highly desirable adaptation in our development.'

Jake raised a hand, and was allowed to speak.

'That's all very well, but I don't think it is going to be a very simple matter. I hope 263, young Sal here, realises it. She is not going to be turned into a fish…. girl-fish…mermaid…whatever we want to call it, overnight. I know something about the process of extracting oxygen from seawater. The best result to be hoped for is likely to be a limited extension of the time she will be able to swim underwater. Maybe Jezzy has found some way of making gills extra efficient, but I am sure it is not a simple matter. Sal 263, do you fully understand what you may be letting yourself in for?'

Sal knew she did not. This question had been in her mind when the marines assaulted her. She had not met any of the young people Jezzy had modified. She must do this before going any further. She was trying to think of an answer that would not make her seem an idiot in front of these brilliant and articulate seniors, Hanna interrupted.

'Maybe it is a mistake to think of gills anyway. It might be wiser to aim at something like the dolphins. They come to the surface to breathe every now and then.'

Jake shrugged, and continued.

'Gills are less efficient than lungs. There is oxygen in the water, it's true, but the proportion is much less than in the air. I can't imagine what the gills are like or where they can be grown. They must be quite enormous. Look at the gills on any ordinary fish. Where in the human body is there room? Yes, and there's the matter of pressure too. We've all done plenty of diving and know very well there are limits to the depths to which we can go. We have to be very careful even with the artificial *Botner* gills, about coming up to the surface too quickly. There's osmosis and dehydration to consider too.'

Mitch spoke again. 'Jezzy has found ways round these problems. Certainly trouble can come to divers who breathe ordinary air from tanks. Bottled air contains the usual high proportion of nitrogen. When divers surface too rapidly, the nitrogen absorbed from the air forms bubbles in the bloodstream. This can be fatal. The difference for fish and, I imagine, for Jezzy's … creatures… with gills, oxygen enters the body directly from the water without the usual nitrogen content. If the blood can be purged of nitrogen this will allow deep diving and ascent without the usual problems. If nitrogen isn't in the blood it can't bubble out. I think the old witch knows what she is doing.'

'Yes, yes, all this is very interesting,' said the chairman. 'But we are not qualified to judge.' He looked at Sal. 'We haven't heard much from you, young woman. You are quite free to speak up. Don't be overawed by us.'

Sal spoke, nervously. 'Jezzy said I would not be the first. She has already shown that the gills work. She also said I am young enough to grow them. I am not entirely sure I want to do it, but I do want to find out what it would be like if I do. If I am allowed to, that is.'

The Captain nodded. 'The immediate issue is not the scientific details. I have said already, we have no power to interfere.' He raised a cautionary finger against Calpurnia, who would have spoken again.

'We are here now, not to examine the procedure itself, nor the ethical issues surrounding *mix and match* or any other genetic procedures, but to discuss and decide on a single matter. We have a specific application before us. I must ask you all now to limit your contributions to this. Can we allow this young woman to go to Shanghai? Should 263 be released or should she stay here and continue her Nav studies?'

Calpurnia was sulking.

'Sal,' said Nemo, 'you have heard what has been said here. Perhaps some of the issues we have barely touched on are new to you. You may not have considered them before. I urge you to think again before you make an irrevocable decision about your personal situation. Is there anything more you would like to say?'

Sal was overwhelmed by the solemnity of the situation. What Calpurnia had said, she admitted to herself grudgingly, was partly true. She had a childish fantasy inspired by ancient myths of mermaids. Her ambition had been to plunge into the water whenever the mood took her with no fear of drowning. She had imagined the delights she would experience if she could swim with the fish and had thought only to explore their habitat, see their brilliant colours and move freely with them under the surface.

Meeting Jezzy, learning from her what the dream might truly become, had sobered her. In the few hours she had been in the Shanghai laboratory and afterwards, she had thought more carefully. She still longed to be with the fishes but saw the other implications. Before she had time to ponder more deeply she had been forcibly wrenched away and brought here to face these mighty authority figures whom she had never imagined she would even meet. How was she to answer the Captain? He was taking everything so seriously. She struggled to pull herself together.

'One thing I would like to hear from you, said the chairman, apart from Jezzy's ambitions, is your personal reason, or reasons, for wanting to leave us. I am, ultimately, responsible for you. Are you, have you been, unhappy with life on our raft? Is there something you would wish us to do that would encourage you to remain?'

'I don't know what to say.' She said, nervously. 'Does it matter what I say? Aren't you going to decide anyway?'

'What you say does matter to me, Sal. You must decide. I can refuse to release you from your duties here, but I would do that only if I concluded that you are indispensable to the welfare of the Sydney raft and its people. You are not so. Nobody is indispensible.'

Calpurnia seemed to be smirking a little now, but Sal was far from feeling humbled. She had never had any inflated idea of her own importance and was still amazed that her conduct had attracted so much attention. Hardly anyone, save the boy, Neppy, would notice if she left. The Sydney raft would continue to wander the oceans as if she had never existed. The tribunal waited.

'I have already said, if you stay with us and continue with your studies, we expect you will become a valuable citizen. I have considered your academic and practical record and see that you have great potential. You will become a qualified navigator, maybe a high officer, possibly in time the head of a major department, even Captain.'

Calpurnia looked grim at this prospect.

'Yet you are not unique,' Nemo continued. There are other bright young *middies*. We are not short of talent. If you decide to leave us, Sydney will manage well enough.' He looked quickly around at the other officers.

She could not find her tongue.

After an interval of silence, Nemo continued. 'I will not interfere unless in some way you become dangerous. You are not a mutineer. If you were a threat to the rest of us, you know the ultimate sanction is to separate such offenders from the raft entirely, to put them ashore to survive by themselves if they can. This does not arise in your case.' He raised his eyebrows, waiting for Sal to say something.

Hanna glanced at the Captain, who nodded, inviting her to speak. The woman was kindly disposed and smiled reassuringly.

'Tell us why you want to make this change. Is there anything very wrong with life on the Sydney Raft? Or are you, after all, just out for a bit of fun? Is that all it is?'

Sal's thoughts now found her voice and the courage to speak out more than she had ever dared before.

'I have not been unhappy. Life in Sydney is good. But it is dull. Nothing very exciting ever seems to happen. You, sir, and your officers, make everything so easy and straightforward for us. All of us are very comfortable, I think too comfortable. Hardly anyone ever grumbles. Everything is so tightly organised, all the important decisions are made for us. You and your officers decide where the city will move, which ocean we will drift in, finding the most pleasant climates for us, avoiding the worst storms, hurricanes and so on. You watch over us, protecting us every moment. We live in complete safety, knowing we can never be lost or harmed. If I am to be a navigator I will be directly involved in this and I am not sure I want it. The work is easy, at least I find it so. It is also boring. We never have any real adventures, only games. One day follows another, one week is like the last, one year is like another. The sports and the gaming capsules are fun, but that is all they are.'

She paused to draw breath and gain courage.

'Jezzy has offered something different. To alter anything important would upset most of the rafters. They would feel afraid. I don't want to be like them. I am not afraid. I want to do something that has not been done before. It excites me to think that some day we may be able to alter ourselves radically and change the world. I suppose Cal will say, I only want a new kind of silly fun. But it isn't that. The idea that I, and others like me, may be the start of a new development for humanity, is thrilling and important. I had not thought of it in this way until I was face to face with Jezzy. Now I do see it, I want to be part of it.' She sat back, amazed and astonished at herself. Things had become clearer in her mind as a result of being made to explain herself.

'At least, I think I do,' she finished weakly.

The officers seemed now also to be taken aback. Sal wondered if they were seeing things, momentarily, as she saw them? Or was their apparent lack of an immediate reaction concealing strong, angry disapproval?

Hanna looked at the Captain, who nodded.

'We will not force you to stay on this raft if you really wish to change to another,' she said. 'That is not, and has never been, the way we work. Exchanges of personnel between rafts are not unknown or even very rare. If the prospect was simply to move you over to join the Shanghai crew there would be no serious objection from us and I cannot believe the Shanghai authorities would refuse to take you. This is your decision, Sal. Do you want to have Jezzy change you into something so very different, and so strange? It is your life, my dear. Do you really understand what it is she proposes to do to you?' Sal again found it hard to speak, but she knew what she must say.

'I must find out more. I need to see Jezzy again before deciding. Can I do that, go and talk to her again, find out what she has already done... achieved? Meet some of the people who have already been changed. Also I would like to hear what my personal friends here have to say. Am I allowed to go and talk to them? Maybe to say goodbye?'

The Captain nodded. 'You have just demonstrated that you are no longer a child, Sal. Go and talk to your friend... Neppy, is it? Short for Neptune, I suppose.' Sal nodded.

'Talk to him and anyone else you wish. As for the central question, we all need a little time to reflect. I will adjourn the tribunal temporarily. Come back to see me, shall we say at 1800 hours? I will give you my decision then, either to let you go or, if you have changed your mind, to take you back without penalty.' He rose, nodded to Sal, 'You already know what Cal thinks. She will stay a here with us for a little while, *protecting your interests* while we consider among ourselves.' He looked sternly at Calpurnia, who flushed. 'Go to your friends now and do some more serious thinking yourself. We will meet here again at 1800.'

As Sal emerged into the public deck area, there was a crowd waiting. She was almost stupefied by the babble of voices and the shouted questions that came from all sides. She glimpsed a monitor image high on the wall and was amazed to see that she herself was shown as she stood there, mobbed by the multitude. This scene with herself at the centre was being transmitted over the entire city and might even draw attention on other rafts. The surveillance system worked in all directions.

Nobody, not even the Captain, had secrets. By law, courts were fully open to anyone who cared to tune their terminal to hear the proceedings or watch the public screens. Most minor hearings or trials were of no interest to the general rafter citizens. This was different. Sal's arrest and forceful extradition from Shanghai had drawn attention. Every word, facial expression and gesture, from the moment the Captain had declared the hearing open, had been transmitted and made available to anyone who cared to attend to it. It seemed nearly everyone in Sydney had indeed watched and listened, and were doing so still. Sal was suddenly notorious, which frightened her.

As she struggled to take this in, she found herself face to face with Neppy. He put his arms round her, hugged her and tried to place himself protectively between her, the rabble and the surveillance instruments. She welcomed his embrace, buried her face on his shoulder. Neppy, holding her close, forced a way through the crowd, swearing angrily and pushing at those who obstructed. He supported and guided her down moving ways, along corridors, the rabble following, until at last they reached his own capsule. They entered and, thumping at the would-be intruders, he closed up the entry. No one could follow them here. They were by themselves as far as it was ever possible on the raft. They embraced, but did not join sexually as they usually did when here together.

'Sal, Sal, what has happened to you? I don't understand. What is all this about? Are you going to leave us? Tell me, what's going on? Come on, Sal, explain, please.'

Sal hesitated, but after a few moments, decided she did need to talk to someone and Neppy had a right to know.

'You remember that day when we had the news about Shanghai coming so near?'

'Yes. That was the day before you dashed off to the ferry.'

'Before that day, before that day.'

3

Sal, Neppy and Brand, teenaged middies, *midshipmen* in the ancient naval parlance, had been taking a break from their Nav 3.9 studies. With a few hundred other youngsters they were now occupying gaming capsules in Recreation Hall 32. Sal, after the early morning callisthenics session that was obligatory for them all, had finished her singing lesson. Neppy was interested in T'ai Chi. Brand was not much interested in anything. To their irritation, all the games suddenly died and the lights dimmed. Exasperated by the interruption, slipping their lightweight VR helmets off they lounged, fidgeting in sudden inactivity. They guessed what was coming. The Captain had one of his announcements to make. They expected a routine chat from the slightly pompous figure, Captain Nobody as they dared to whisper.

Images of Nemo appeared now in holograph on every capsule screen and on large ones disposed for public viewing down each side of the hall and everywhere else in the city. The gamers chatted, there were occasional bursts of laughter. The dancers in other halls, with music in their earplugs, still gyrated. Nobody was compelled to attend to the old man if they did not feel like doing so. Few did.

'Silly old fart,' muttered Brand. He had been at a crucial moment in his VR adventure. 'We've heard it all before. Boring.'

'Hush, that's mutiny,' said Neppy. Sal grinned slyly. She sympathised with Brand sometimes.

'Mutiny? I'm not a mutineer,' replied Brand, far from scared but glancing askance at the interactive screen. His careless words had already been recorded but in his case he was sure nobody wanted to know.

'Shut up, I want to hear him,' Neppy snapped.

'The only one who does. Oh, you are such a good boy,' the other lad said, *sotto voce*. He was right. Most of the gamers were still uninterested.

'He is a good boy, and very nice with it,' Sal said.

The Captain spoke.

'Citizen rafters, attention please. I wish to explain a discovery made recently by our colleagues on the space stations.' He turned with a snap of the fingers. His image was replaced by a three dimensional view of the globe. It was shown at right angles to the normal west - east alignment with the North Pole central. This was unusual. A few of the crowd turned to watch. The North Polar Regions were in darkness. 'There's nothing there, just black.' said Brand. 'Well, sort of blackish blue. No lights, nothing. What's he on about?.'

Sal looked at him, scornfully. 'You wouldn't expect lights. It's winter up there. Cities never drift into those latitudes.'

Neppy, doubtfully, shook his head. 'Why's he showing this? It isn't his usual guff,' he said.

Brand grimaced and muttered, 'Bugger, another lecture. Waste of time. I can think of a hundred things I'd rather be doing.'

'No-one's stopping you,' said Sal. 'You could log in to Nav School again right away. They never switch that channel off. That's something you could do. You might even catch up a bit'

'*Oh yeah*,' was the disgusted reply

'Quiet.' said Neppy.

'Please watch, there is something new,' said Nemo's detached voice, almost as if he had overheard. Perhaps he had.

'Look carefully as we zoom in closer.' The focus changed. In the centre of the dark image a small fleck of something lighter became visible. The view expanded further, the lighter blob seemed to grow, occupying more of the screen.

'That's odd,' said Neppy. 'What is it? That fuzzy thing? Sort of…. sort of white-shiny-milky?' The *middies*, including Brand whose attention was caught now, stared. The Captain's cursor appeared and circled several times round the anomalous object. It was quite irregularly shaped. There was a dead, white, flat area edged strangely with a kind of flickering.

'This is not a simulation,' came the voice. 'You are looking at part of the Arctic Ocean in real time. The image comes to us from Orbital 55 which is stationed over the pole.' The noise level was dropping now. People nudged reluctant viewers, pointing.

'What you see is a very large piece of floating ice. This,' said Nemo portentously, his cursor on the object, 'is termed an *ice floe*.' The words appeared on the screen.

Few of the listeners had ever heard the expression. There was a rumble of astonishment and an undertone of scepticism as they muttered among themselves. Dancing stopped now, earplugs were removed. All heads were turning to the screen. There was near silence as the Captain continued.

'I am confident that you have never before known sea water to freeze.'

He was right. The audience was dumbfounded.

'Rafters, remember this occasion. Some day you will be able to tell children about it. This is the first time in more than five hundred years that a measurable quantity of water in the ocean has become cold enough to solidify. Look again.'

Most did so.

'You are perfectly familiar with ice. The fridges in our personal capsules and machines in every bar, freeze water for us. We put it in our drinks. Some of you are expert skaters on the ice rinks. In certain weather conditions you have possibly seen and heard, maybe felt, hail. Localized hailstorms can be reliably predicted but avoiding them is not always possible, as our navigators tell us.'

'Boring,' grumbled Brand, finding his tongue again.

Sal shrugged. Every Nav student, even the backward lazy ones like Brand, knew about hail. Nemo continued.

'An *ice floe* is a large slab of frozen sea water. The flickering margins you see are waves breaking around the outer limits. The reappearance of sea ice is an indication that the northern ocean is colder now than it has been for a very long time. It is so cold that some ice floes have formed. A very few small ones have been detected in earlier years but this example is larger, about the same size as a small city raft. If you were there, suitably protected from the bitter cold in special clothing, you would be able to walk about on it. A heavy vehicle could move safely on the surface. It would be possible even to erect a small building, even one made from ice. It is said that long ago there were people who, at certain times, did make small shelters out of ice blocks.'

'You should be wondering how it can be that such cold conditions exist now where we have not seen them before? The answer seems to be that the earth is entering a phase of general cooling. If so, this is not the first time. The planet on which we live is subject to fluctuations of climate. Many thousands, even millions of years ago, there were so-called *ice ages* separated by warmer intervals called *interglacials*. We have been in an interglacial for the last eleven or twelve thousand years. The icy planet entered a warming cycle. This change was accelerated a couple of millennia ago by undisciplined human activities with the release of large quantities of methane, carbon dioxide gases and other pollutants. Half-hearted measures to reduce pollution failed hopelessly. The subsequent melting of all the ice and the consequent rise of the sea flooded vast areas of farming land. This was at a time when the human population was growing out of control yet food supplies were insufficient and declining. Desperate attempts to extract ever more food crops from the decreasing areas of suitable land defeated their own purpose. Fertile soils, over-exploited and robbed of plant nutrients, became impoverished. As the climate warmed arable and pasturelands were reduced to arid dustbowls. In desperation the devastation became even worse as opposed tribes fought bitterly over the remaining areas of usable land. As you know, civilisation on land collapsed.'

'As you also know, the major coastal cities, seeing doom approaching, saved themselves. They put to sea. Some landlubbers remain, but those few disorganized tribes now surviving live in wretched conditions.'

'The city rafts are entirely self sufficient, adding no waste products or undesirable substances to the oceans or the air. Sea and marine life have largely recovered now from the destruction they suffered. The human population, with universal use of artificial insemination and incubation, is now under strict control, as you are well aware. Our population is closely matched to our ability to grow food crops by hydroponics.'

The view changed. 'Here now is an image taken some years ago of those awe-inspiring, inhospitable highlands that the few surviving land-living tribes call the Emaliya Mountains. Many centuries ago there were great areas, whole regions of these high lands that were always covered in snow and ice, even in the warmest seasons. Snow, which you have never seen, is frozen rain, that is, flakes of ice. In this picture you can see no trace of ice anywhere. However, for several decades now, each year on the mountains a little more snow has fallen and a little less has melted in the warmer seasons. New snow falls on places where some un-melted snow survives from the previous cold season. The snow accumulates and in time becomes ice.'

'Here is a new image, only a few months old. This is the Emaliya region as it is now.'

The fingers snapped. Scattered white areas appeared on the projected image. 'You see, there is again some snow cover on the highlands.' The Captain snapped fingers several times, switching from one view to the other, emphasising the contrast. The audience collectively gasped in astonishment.

'There is no doubt that the globe is cooling.' The projected image faded and the Captain's personal hologram reappeared. He waited to allow the audiences all over the city to settle down. There was no mistaking the ripple of alarm.

'The global climate is slowly returning to what it was before. The ice floe we now see is an indication of what will happen in the next millennium.'

'You need not be alarmed. Our raft cities have nothing to fear. As cooling continues, even if another full ice age develops, it will take several millennia. Most of the planet surface, well over two thirds, will remain covered by the oceans as it has been since before life on Earth began. Our science and the art of navigation, guiding the drifting movement of all the cities, will keep pace with the changes as they happen. Currents and winds will alter but trained navigators will continue to keep the cities always within comfortable zones. City raft life will continue safely as it has done now since we cut ourselves loose from the barren land. Humankind will adapt. The civilisation we are all accustomed to will continue.'

Nemo was closing his address. 'Those humans who survive on land will, in the coming colder periods, have more problems than ever. Perhaps more of them will escape from the land as our ancestors did, and come to the cities. If they seek aid, we will accommodate them, as long as they agree to become rafters, making themselves useful and conforming to our discipline.' The screen faded.

The audience resumed talking.

'Snow, he said, didn't he?' Neppy remarked. 'I can't really imagine what that can be like. Like a sort of soft hail, isn't it? I've seen hail sometimes. It won't be much fun for the lubbers if they all get covered in ice.'   ·

'Living on land can't be fun any of the time,' Sal replied. 'I can't imagine what it is like for them. It fills me with horror to think of living on the land. Eating stuff that grows in the dirt. It's filthy. They spread shit on the… growing places. What do they call them? Fields? Why do they go on doing it?'

'Yes, farm fields. They say shit makes stuff grow. They call it *organimure*, or something. I know what you mean. They clean the outside but they can't have any control of what gets into the stuff.' said

Neppy. 'And they have to keep scratching at the ground all the time, getting rid of what they call weeds, I think.'

'They actually do eat things coming out of filth. It's revolting,' remarked Sal. 'No wonder they have diseases and die early. Why can't they use *ponics* to control what goes into their food? Apart from that, can you imagine what it must be like to live in one place, stuck there on the land all the time and never moving? And it's so dangerous. I've seen on the old sims. Whatever hits the place, they are caught. Droughts, cold, hot, tornadoes, tsunamis, fires, quakes, floods. In some places there are landslides and mudflows. People get buried alive. Volcanoes and earthquakes. It must be awful. It scares me just to think of it. And now there will be snow as well. They can't move into better regions like we do. I've never met a landlubber. Why don't they build rafts?'

'Perhaps they will, eventually.' replied the boy. 'Or they could come to the cities as refugees. Quite a lot do, I believe, if they get the chance.'

'A thousand, two thousand years late.' Sal said. 'Maybe the snow will make more of them see sense at last.'

Neppy added; 'There are all those nasty animals on the land as well. Not just the ones they eat, but creepy crawly, buzzing and biting things and those nasty, filthy little… what are they? Rodents? Mice, rats, rabbits, roaches, whatever they call them. And slithery things called snakes and spiders with poisonous bites,' Sal shuddered.

Neppy gave her a small, reassuring hug.

'Its all right, they can't reach us here. Give me the ocean any time. The sea is clean now and we don't have any rodents or snakes. The sims say the rafts did have rodents at first but they got rid of them in a century or two.'

'They can't get at us, so long as we keep well away from the land,' Sal replied, cheerfully. 'Oh, damnation. Look at the screen.'

There was another person, a woman, Marguerite, visible now in the hologram. Sal braced herself. This doll-like female always infuriated her.

'Hallo all you happy rafters,' Marguerite cried with artificial gaiety, 'Well, you just heard, we aren't going to be frozen for a few thousand years, so there's plenty of time Have you looked at the Navlog lately? I hope you have.' Sal had been looking studiously every day for a month. Despite her dislike of the messenger, she was all attention now and sat up straighter.

'You really should keep up with what is going on, you know Now, my dears, you must all arrange to take some leave in the next week or two. You are going to need it.'

'Rio, the fine city to which we were close for much of last month, and the Bristol raft which we saw earlier in the year, have drifted away now. Many of you visited them. Now there is something even more exciting. Shanghai, rafters *Shanghai Shanghai is a mighty raft,*' she crooned the chorus line of a well-known, overplayed, song.

'Sydney and Shanghai have been drawing closer together for several weeks. Our rafts are now only some forty nauticals apart, and getting nearer. What? You hadn't noticed? Dear oh dear, what have you been doing?'

Sal had watched the charts assiduously.

'*Mudfish. Get on with it, woman,*' she swore, 'She sets my teeth on edge.' When cities came near one another they often diverged again before getting close enough to be seen or easily visited. Neppy reached out a hand to touch her but she did not respond. The woman in the hologram wasn't finished.

'We are set to be close for the next couple of weeks, approaching to within a mere ten nauticals.' Sal relaxed. This is what she had hoped for. There was a ripple of interest among the crowd too.

'Sydney will never be nearer than this to another city. I am told by those who know that to approach any closer is inadvisable.'

There was a legend that two cities had once collided and both had sunk. Impossible, the engineers swore and no one really believed the tale. Not only was a collision highly improbable, if it had ever happened the underwater structure of the rafts could not be seriously damaged. The cities floated on vast honeycomb structures of the most advanced reinforced/plastic materials. Even so, keeping clear was a commonsense precaution.

'Many of you I am sure will wish to visit the largest, most developed of all cities on the sea. The Shanghai raft is more than 30 nauticals across, and longer on the main axis. How about that? There are over a hundred full decks, not counting the towers, and more below the waterline. Are you listening? A *hundred* decks and *thirty million rafters.* Did you hear me? Already this afternoon if you look you can see faint reflections and mirages far away in the distance. Go to the higher decks later tonight. You will be able to see the multi-coloured lights of the Shanghai towers. At dawn you will see those same towers glinting in the sunlight with flickering reflections from a great multitude of wind turbines above them. Gradually through tomorrow the great city will come near enough for individual buildings to be picked out and identified. I assure you, Shanghai is extraordinary. You are encouraged to visit. There are exciting things to do and brilliant people to meet. Girls and boys, I promise you'll find some lively partners there, every variation you enjoy and some erotic games you have never dreamed of. It is easy to arrange a visit.'

'Many of their people will be coming to us here, as usual. We are organising the ferries immediately, one will be ready in the dock to accept passengers at first light. The crossing will take only a couple of hours. You can spend a few days or a week away, supposing you have so much time free from your duties here. Citizens are already flocking to collect their passes. On the Shanghai raft doubtless the same thing will be happening. Don't delay.'

'Inter city vouchers are valid in Shanghai. The exchange rate is 1.6, not in our favour but good enough. Your work status will be checked, just upload your ID and you will be given a pass date and time to board the ferry. Make the most of this opportunity. It will be many years before we draw so close to that mighty city again. Rafters, *I'll see you in Shanghai,'* she chortled again from the awful song, and waved farewell. The hologram vanished, the main lights returned. The three young people looked at one another in some excitement. The gaming screens came to life again but they were not interested now.

'Come on, let's go and look.' said Brand, jumping out of his capsule and hastening to the up-going ramp where other people were already crowding, ten or twelve abreast. Sal and Neppy followed more slowly and thoughtfully. The distant lights were amazing. After an hour admiring them they spend the rest of the night together in Sal's capsule.

Next morning together they ascended companionways and crowded elevators, deck after deck, until they reached the uppermost. Above was only the turbine level, where rows of spinning vertical *Flettner* rotors generated power. Cooling and hydroponic towers poured out moist clouds, water that evaporated a few score metres from their origin.

Between each pair of rotors were wind vanes. Sal knew from her Nav studies that these served a double purpose. They were normally positioned to deflect the flow of air onto the turbines to improve their efficiency. When the navigators required it, their angles could be adjusted to catch the wind and provide some directed pressure to rotate the city. The raft was far too large for the vanes to drive it at any appreciable rate forward but it could be trimmed to a new orientation. Rotating the city was a useful dodge. The engineers could set the orientation to catch the sunlight as it was needed on this side or the other. Every available place above the waterline carried solar collectors.

The fusion plants, deep in the lowest decks, drove underwater propellers and jets to drive the city forward but were used only when needed. Most of the time the rafts drifted. At places of oceanic convergence and divergence, they would shift to a preferred current. Established in the flow, power down, the rafts were carried towards the best conditions chosen for the season. When Sal and Neppy qualified by passing Nav 4, judging and using the currents would be a main part of their duties. Lazy Brand's future was not quite so secure.

When they reached the high deck, there were already many hundreds of people staring to the southeast. There was a brisk wind. Several hang gliders were soaring high above the windward side of the raft. Their extra elevation gave the pilots a wider view. Among them were wandering albatross that did not stay, and flocks of resident soaring birds that followed the city wherever it drifted. These nested where they could find suitable niches.

The distant rotating blades of Shanghai glittered in the sun, row upon row of flickering reflections.

'It's huge' gasped Neppy, staring across the sea like everyone else. 'There must be hundreds and hundreds of turbines. It's a lot bigger than Rio.'

Sal and Neppy together had visited every other city that had floated within reach during the past few years. Shanghai was far beyond anything they had seen before. Sal had made up her mind long ago, when she had seen how the currents were converging, what she would do if the chance came. She had not told even Neppy of her dream. In a city of no secrets, this was hers.

They made their way through the multitude to the edge of the viewing platform, prevented from falling off the edge by an elaborate system of barriers and nets. 'Look there,' Neppy said, 'There's the first ferry loading.' Far below, long and narrow, was the ship in dock. They could see many small figures as people filed up the companionways.

'Will you be going?'

'Just as soon as I can,' said Sal.

'Trust you. Hoping to find some new boys? They're supposed to be very sexy.'

'What else would I go for?' said Sal. He didn't have an answer for that. She knew Neppy had a special affection for her and she would gladly lie with him whenever the mood took them both, as it often did. To her it was pleasant and exciting but no more. Brand or any other lad Sal fancied for a few minutes, could couple with her. Neppy lay with other girls too. It meant little to any of them.

'I didn't find anyone very exciting in Rio,' she said, 'Not as nice as you, anyway. But this is different. I'm going to make my reservation right now.'

She touched the device on her wristband and spoke to it: 'For Shanghai'. The terminal automatically forwarded all her details. She touched the gadget once more. 'Will you come?'

'I don't think so this time', the boy replied. 'I don't like the ferries. They pitch with the waves. You remember, it made me sick on that rough day when we went to Bristol. Those ships are only about one nautical long and very narrow. They do roll from side to side. Just look at it, down there. It's quite scary. You can see how small and flimsy it is. The others are exactly the same. They are cockleshells with thin skins, like birds eggs. I like to feel a solid deck under my feet.' He stamped to make his point.

'They aren't really small when you get on them and they are stable in all but the roughest seas,' said Sal. 'Anyway if you get sick on the water you could get a chopper flight.'

'They say airsick is worse than sea sick,' said the boy, 'and choppers cost a lot of credits. I suppose you will go whatever I do.'

'Yes, I will. I've got leave. See, there's a reservation already for me tomorrow.' She held her wrist out for him to look. 'I am glad I called in quickly.'

'I'll let the Shanghai girls come for me. It'll be a change.'

'They'll do that, for sure. You're a lot of fun.'

'Let's go for a swim' she said, after a few more minutes looking into the distance. They descended through the decks, down and down again to waterline level, raced to the bathing area, stripped off all their clothes and plunged in naked, joining many others. Sal swam beautifully, spending as much time as she could under water, admiring the small fish that joined them. Neppy dived with her but had to come up, gasping. The girl popped up some time later when he was beginning to feel alarmed about her.

'You frighten me sometimes, Sal. You stay under too long. That must have been nearly five minutes.'

'I have trained myself for it Neppy, you know that. I won't drown. I just love to be there with the fish, they are so beautiful and friendly. I think some of them know me now, they come up so close'

'That's rubbish. We are always moving into different water. They must be different lots of fish every time,' he said.

'Some of them stay with us. I am sure I recognise them, week after week. They come up to me and stare, as if to say: *How do you do Nice to see you again.* They breed in our safe swimming areas and forage underneath the raft when they want to, you know, like the pilot fish that go round with whales. They know when they are on a good thing and they swim along with us like the birds do in the air.'

'Sal, you have such lovely ideas,' said Neppy. '*I do like you*'

'I *like you* too,' said Sal. That was enough. They coupled joyfully in the shallows, as many others were doing.

'I wish I could spend all my time doing this and swimming and diving,' said Sal afterwards. 'I do enjoy playing in the water. I wish we could go deeper and stay under longer.'

'Well, we can, can't we? Get some *Butner* gill gear and we can dive for half an hour at a time if we like.'

'It isn't the same. The masks and harness get in the way. I want to stay down longer and go out further, beyond the barriers, without those clunky-bubbly things on my back. That would be an adventure.' Neppy frowned. Beyond the nets was danger. She didn't fear sharks, but he did.

They had work to do. They dried, donned their uniforms and returned to the Nav School.

Among the most sought-after positions in the crew, the navigators were most prestigious. Those who wanted to succeed needed no supervisor to force them to study. Once judged fit to start Nav training, very few ever failed. Advanced courses were also available for research scientists, computing and laboratory staff and robot engineers. Personal assistants for senior officers, teaching programmers and game developers, fitness and sports trainers, medical specialists and physiotherapists, child carers were needed. Anyone who dropped out some higher level of training was allocated work in a less intellectually demanding department. There were controllers of the maintenance machines and cleaners and for turbine and wind vane adjusters, and every other aspect of the enormously complex city organisation, including marines. Every individual had work to do; everyone wore an appropriate uniform. Routine tasks were done by machines.

4

❊

Next day Sal, with five or six thousand others, boarded the ferry. The sea was calm, the ship hardly rolled or pitched at all as it sailed. She had left Neppy still sleeping in her capsule. She knew his excuse of seasickness was no more than that. They were fond of one another but he had plenty of other girl friends and would enjoy himself with the visitors. She too expected to find a few boy friends during her visit to the other raft but that was not her chief motive.

The Sydney and Shanghai ferries did a two way shuttle service crossing and re-crossing several times each day. Propelled by powerful hydrogen-fuelled motors, the ships cleaved the water as no city raft could, creating sharp bow waves and leaving foaming wakes. As they passed ships going the opposite way there were loud siren hoots and whistles. Passengers waved and cheered. Standing on one of the open decks Sal found the usual strong wind created by the ship's motion. This was exhilarating and quite different from the gentle movements of air when the raft was drifting. For a little time she rejoiced but soon found the air was chilling. Rather than go below she found a place near the stern where there was shelter. From here she looked back at the Sydney raft as it receded. It was festooned with greenery. Plants bright with blossoms, fed hydroponically, spilled over the edges of the decks. On previous excursions, such as to Nyork, Rio and Bristol, she had viewed her home raft from this aspect.

As she stood, a man and a woman, well wrapped up, joined her, to lean on the guardrail looking at the wake and admiring the great birds that followed the vessel and soared above them.

'Isn't this great?' said the woman, to Sal. 'It is so exciting. Erik and I always come out here when we get the chance.'

'It's thrilling.' Sal's attention was caught by a school of dolphins. They swam alongside, plunging and rising in an undulating motion that she imagined herself imitating. 'Look at them,' she said, pointing. 'What fun they are having. Wouldn't it be wonderful to sport with dolphins?' There were flying fish too, which she had seen before. They swerved and turned in the air, their fins vibrating rapidly, before plunging into the water again after half a minute or so. How marvelous it must be, she thought, to leap from sea into the air, fly and dive back again.

'Erik and I love these ships,' said the woman, who introduced herself as Myra 785. 'Every chance we get we go on a ferry and then back again straight away. Whenever they are running trips between two rafts, we spend our time this way. We got on the first ferry yesterday morning in Shanghai and we haven't been off it since.'

'What, didn't you get off to look round Sydney? Not at all?'

'No, we can't be bothered with all that. We come for the ferry voyage.'

'But… the whole idea is to visit other cities'

'That's a waste of time,' said Erik. 'Seen one, seen them all. All the city rafts are much alike, you know, there's little to choose between them. Of course Shanghai, where we belong, is very big, but it's only like your Sydney five times over. We live on the ferry for days at a time. We do this, whenever we can.'

Sal thought this very strange. 'Can you sleep on the ferry? There aren't enough capsules.'

The couple smiled. 'You don't need them. You can lie down anywhere and snooze. There are lots of places, gaming halls with the helmets off, or in the restaurants, without eating. It is quite comfortable,' Myra nodded. 'There's other places too. The robots don't bother us.'

'We treat the ferries like cruise liners. We take our holidays on them,' Erik added.

'Cruise liners? What do you mean, cruise liners?'

'Haven't you heard? That's how the city rafts began, or so they say.' He laughed a little. 'In the landages there were ships called liners. They used to carry people across the oceans, sailing from one place to another all the time. They burned coal or oil for fuel. None of them were as big as these ferries.'

'Erik's made quite study of these things. It's his hobby. You know what coal and oil were?' asked Myra.

'I have never actually seen any, but I learned about them when I was a schoolie.'

'The liners were a bit like ferries, but a lot smaller.' said Erik. They would sail about slowly, that was called *cruising*, for weeks or even months at a time. They would visit a lot of different land cities. When they got to land everyone used to get off.'

'Why? Ugh, that's horrid. Couldn't they stay where they were safe and clean, on the ferry... I mean the *cruise liner?*'

Erik smiled. 'People often wanted to visit other places, to see if they were different, to discover if there was anything their own place didn't have. A cruise liner was like a small city. They had boxy places called cabins, not proper sleeping capsules, but they had everything else, dancing, concerts, parties, gaming, luxurious food, lots of sex partners.'

'What did you mean, that was how the city rafts started?

Erik chuckled. 'Well, there is an old yarn about a cruise liner that ran out of fuel in the middle of the ocean, or maybe it was the engines that broke down. It just drifted. The passengers thought it was great and they didn't want to go back to land, especially when the land cities were all getting flooded. That was the first city raft, a broken down cruise liner.'

'It's a silly story,' said Myra, 'but to live on the water is an ancient idea. There's a much older tale. Erik says it was written on clay tablets six or seven thousand years ago. There was a man called Gilgamesh in a city called Shurrupak where there was a great flood. He had a huge raft built, big enough to save his people and all their animals.'

Erik could not remain silent.

'It was really a raft, you see, not a boat; *let the beam be equal to the length*, was what the tablet said. It had seven decks; *each side measured one hundred and twenty cubits*, making a square. A square raft about 60 by 60 metres, I think. They took enough animals and people for breeding. Obviously they couldn't take every human and every animal, there wouldn't have been room.'

Myar added; 'It would be a bit like a very small city. There are lots of old legends about flooding and escaping; Gilgamesh's story was the first to be written down. But let's go and find something to eat.'

The couple took Sal to a restaurant hall where they encouraged her to taste some Shanghai specialities that were new to her. They called up the menu on their screens and touched the recommended dishes. These emerged a few minutes later from side tables that automatically carried everything needed smoothly into comfortable positions for eating.

'You know,' said Myra, 'the robots still make some of the Chinese dishes they used to have in the old Shanghai, when it was on land. It is amazing that the recipes have survived for so many years.'

'Like music,' said Sal, who loved to sing the ancient songs.

'Oh, yes, perhaps so.' Myra's offhand tone suggested she knew and cared little about music.

'What do you mean, *Chinese*?'

'Haven't you learned about the old land places?'

'Yes, but Chinese? What does that mean?'

'It is very simple. Shanghai was a city on the Asian continent. You do know about continents?'

'Of course I do, I'm a *nav-middy*,' said Sal, a little impatiently. 'Navigators have to know where the land is, to avoid being swept and blown into it.'

'Well, a very big part of Asia was once called China,' said Myra, patiently. 'Shanghai used to be a very important land city of China, it was *Chinese*. It was right down by sea level so it was one of the very first places to be flooded and it was probably the first to start moving onto a raft. That was a brilliant answer to the problem.

'Wasn't it obvious?' said Sal. 'If your city is being flooded, you build a raft and float onto the ocean.'

'No, not so simple It didn't happen like that at all. The flood didn't all come at once.'

'Well, how?'

'I'll let Erik tell the tale.'

Erik was glad to show off his expertise. 'Long before the flood, very early in the land-ages, people made boats. They were very tiny, big enough for one or two people. They got bigger; carried more people, some were used for carrying heavy things around. They were improved to become what they called barges and ships. Most of them took cargo, that's stuff like food and things made in workshops called factories, and there was a lot of oil and coal fuel to be carried about for burning too.'

'I have heard of that. It was called trade because the cities couldn't make everything they needed, like we do.'

'They didn't have much scientific knowledge. There were fishing boats but everything else had to come from the land. There were also some small rafts called houseboats with cabins and sleeping places. People could live on them and move from place to place, wherever there was enough water to float. That was another part of the city raft idea.'

'You mean, cabins like the yachts we use for racing?'

'Yes, but houseboats were rafts for living in, not racing. There was a place called Ongkon where thousands of people lived in little boats, all tied together in one place so you could step from one to the other. They began joining their small boats together to make bigger ones. You could link two or three into a proper raft for a whole group. When the sea started rising,' said Erik, 'it was quite natural for those Ongkon people to go on living as they always had done, on the water.' Sal nodded.

'As the sea level rose, some people started building proper shelters on rafts. They kept them tied up in docks at first but they could move them somewhere else if they wanted. All the ideas started coming together. They didn't think of it all at once but when all the big land cities were drowning the answer was there.'

Erik rambled on. 'There was a man called Otto Neurath who had the idea, even before then. You can rebuild a boat, bit by bit, as long as you keep it floating; do some repairs, add a bit here or there, improve this bit, rebuild that part, scrap that section, extend it, add a new deck, and so on. Go on for a thousand years and you get a raft city. Neurath's boat was never actually built, they say he was really talking about something quite different, but the idea was there. You know, there is not a single piece of the old Shanghai city left now. Every tiny bit has been replaced, improved, re-designed, a little at time, and it is still going on.'

'And after all that you can divide a raft it into two or three pieces and let them float separately,' Myra chipped in quickly.

'Why would anyone do that?' asked Sal.

'Some people want to do it with Shanghai,' said Erik. 'There is quite a big fuss about it. Our raft has grown, you see, with extensions over the last few hundred years. It is getting too big to navigate, takes too long to turn round. The fusion plants have to work very hard to drive it. If the navigators ever make a mistake and let us get seriously out of position, it might take months to get us back into the right current.'

Sal, almost a fully qualified navigator, could not believe such a mistake could ever be made. Erik suggested she should visit a museum that showed how Shanghai had been when it was on land two millennia ago, and how the first parts of the raft had been put together.

Their destination now loomed larger, a vast, vast raft carrying a beautiful city rising high above the ocean and spreading laterally until, as they approached, it filled their horizon. The hanging gardens were more colourful and spectacular than those Sal had left behind in Sydney. An extraordinary mixture of fascinating odours drifted heavily across the water. Behind and above the colourful greenery, slender, gleaming towers rose to heights she had never imagined possible. Buoyancy must demand careful planning and design before any new structure was allowed to rise so high above the waterline. Sal knew that the synthetic materials used in building were much lighter and stronger than anything that had been available in former ages. Could there ever be a city raft that was too big, as Myra had suggested?

As the crowds disembarked there were many vivid holograms and virtuals on the dockside, inviting visitors to this or that place. Numerous small, open-topped robot vehicles waited for instructions to transport visitors to any part of the city. Cars were less common on Sydney. Shanghai was so much bigger that mechanical transport was essential. Advertisements and offers streamed into Sal's wrist terminal. There were art collections to be seen, entertainment halls with synthesised and live music and drama, large capsules capable of accommodating erotic groups, restaurants with all kinds of unusual food, sports arenas and stadia. She knew that various inter-city sporting events had been arranged, there would be team games, water polo matches, swimming races and diving, gymnastics, acrobatics, dancing, athletics of all kinds, a few surviving ancient games like tennis, badminton and fives. Base and bungee jumping could be tried; instruction in hang gliding was available just as in Sydney. Tours could be arranged to see the fusion power centres and desalination plants, deep down in the lowest decks. It was possible to visit the food fish tanks and processing plants, ascend the sunlit towers of the hydroponic gardens, inspect synthetic meat factories, taste their products. Concerts of live musicians and singers tempted Sal to divert from her true reason for being here, but she was determined to do what she had set out to do from the first, find the biotech laboratory.

As Myra and Erik said, one city was much like another but everything in Shanghai was bigger, noisier, and more crowded than Sydney. Somewhat bewildered, she needed help and looked around for someone, an official or guide who might be ready to help her. It took no time at all to pick out a man who looked promising. Uniformed and prominent in the mob, unattached to any other girl, he was scanning the arrivals in a systematic way. Sal was not familiar with Shanghai badges of rank, but he was clearly of some importance and might be ready to advise her. He was older than she and seemed a little solemn. For this important-looking man a young female cadet with long, dark hair and a lively look would surely be an acceptable partner for an hour. Sal caught his eye easily and made the appropriate signs, a smile, a nod, and a gesture suggestive of an erotic touch. He responded quickly, pushed through the crowd, stepped up to her and took her hand. This was easier than she had expected.

Had she paused to think she might have suspected that there was more in it than chance.

'I am very pleased to meet you,' he said.

'Shall we get to know each other at once?' She put her arms round him and hugged a little. To her dismay, he fended her off, firmly but gently.

'Not quite so fast, young woman. My name is Torva 549 and you are Sal 263.'

The girl was astonished. 'How did you know that?'

'I have your picture here.' He showed her the terminal on his wrist. Sure enough, Sal saw her own face.

'I don't believe it. How could you…?'

'My boss is expecting you. She gave me this picture and told me to come and find you. You want to meet her, don't you?'

'Want to…? I don't understand this. There is… there is someone I want to meet, very much, but how could you have known? I didn't tell anyone, I didn't know myself I was going to be here till yesterday.'

'Who is it you want to meet?'

'Jessy.'

The man nodded. 'Yes. Well, Sal 263, Jezzy wants me to take you immediately to meet her.'

Sal was amazed.

'I… don't know… I thought… but oh, yes, yes, I do want to meet her. That is why I came. I thought it would be difficult, maybe impossible. Jessy, the great Jessy I have heard, read so much about her, I didn't know how to… how to approach her. I'm only a *middy*, a student, and she is… a great, famous woman. Everyone has heard of her.'

'And she has heard of you,' said Torva. 'Or rather, she knows about you.'

'I can't believe it. Why would she… how could she know about me? I'm not important'

'Jezzy, it is *Jezzy*, by the way, gave me your name and last three, and your picture.'

Sal, recovering from the surprise, pulled herself together. She noticed his pronunciation of the name. Why the difference, she wondered? Perhaps it was just the Shanghai accent. Or the Sydney accent?

'That picture is you, isn't it?' The bewildered girl nodded. 'I will be in trouble if I don't take you to her at once there. Come along, Jezzy is up to something, she always is.'

He called a robocar and told it co-ordinates, deck level and section. It was a relief for Sal, shaken by astonishment and now a little apprehensive, to sit in the well-padded capsule. They were carried swiftly and smoothly through the streets and tunnels of the city with many other cars like the one they were using carrying people in every kind of clothing or sometimes none. Sal caught occasional strains of unfamiliar music and glimpsed intriguing sights but she didn't want to stop. The adventure was happening more quickly than she had ever imagined. They travelled a long way through brightly lit passages, corridors and streets between towering buildings. The car knew the way perfectly. At last they reached a markedly different area. Here was less traffic, fewer people, and not so many tall buildings. At last, on a deck only slightly above the waterline in a deserted passageway, the vehicle halted and they dismounted.

'Wait,' said Torva, to the car.

They were outside a large but almost invisible door which opened at his touch, like the almond shape of the iris of a cat's eye.

'The Iris Door,' said Torva. 'This is the only way in to the laboratory quarter.' They stepped through to be confronted by walls of huge transparent tanks in which Sal saw fish and sea creatures of all descriptions, some familiar but many wholly strange. There was a transparent ceiling above so she could look up as if from the sea floor to see more fish, sea creatures and plants. She was tempted to linger and stare, for these were beyond her dreams of beauty and diversity. A giant ray seemed to fly gracefully above her. Torva now seemed content to let her stay. Having brought her so far in a hurry he now seemed unsure what to do next and reluctant to take her any further. She walked very slowly round and admired the creatures for several minutes, but this was not what she had come for.

'Can we find Jessy?' she asked at last. 'I mean, *Jezzy.*'

'I thought she would be here.' It seemed to Sal that Torva was a little afraid of his boss, or perhaps in awe of her. He led the way hesitantly

through another, smaller door iris into a larger cabin where there were
viewing and music capsules. No one was there. Another tank full of
wonders formed one wall. The ceiling tank continued above.

'I'll go to find her. You'll have to entertain yourself here for a while.
I'll see what she wants us to do.' He passed through another iris. Sal
waited. The fish fascinated her and quite a long time passed happily.

Torva returned. 'Come,' he said, seriously, bowing with a
formal welcoming gesture. They were immediately in another, huge
compartment, surrounded by apparatus that Sal could not comprehend.
It was all totally unfamiliar to her, so strange, complex and frightening
that she felt suddenly that she had made a stupid mistake. This was not
what she had imagined. Here she was an alien in an environment that
was mechanical, threatening and overpowering. One or two distant
people in long coats, helmets and masks, moved about, taking no
notice of her. There were numerous robotic machines of types wholly
unfamiliar apparently performing set tasks and routines. All was silent
except for a faint but pervasive hum and an occasional gurgling or
bubbling. The tanks surrounding them seemed dark and mysterious.
There were no beautiful fish here. She could sometimes faintly perceive
dark shapes and shadows moving in murky water, differently coloured
in each tank, this one dark green, that brown, another blue and so on.
She could make no sense of any of it.

'Here she comes,' said Torva.

Approaching slowly among the extraordinary machines and
equipment, peering here and there, glancing from side to side, her
reflection multiplied endlessly in the glazed walls and ceiling, muttering
sometimes, snorting and occasionally making slight screeching sounds,
was an old, fierce woman wearing a black lab coat that reached the deck.
It was difficult at first to know which was the person and which merely
mirror image in the great tanks. She seemed to have no feet, floating
nearer as if on hidden wheels or somehow, magically, suspended off the
floor. She floated closer. Long, wild white hair framed a face lined finely
with wrinkles. She had a prominent nose, narrow, dry lips, the hint of
beard on the pointed chin. Her eyes were hooded under incongruous

dark, shaggy eyebrows, but they were bright, piercing. She wafted closer and closer staring fixedly at Sal, and stopped a few paces away.

'This is Sal', said Torva, nervously. 'Sal, Meet Jezzy.'

'Come closer, child,' croaked Jezzy.

Sal, trembling a little, stepped nearer. Those eyes bored into her.

'Sal is not your name.'

'It is 263 Sal. It is my name.' She did not feel like revealing anything more to this terrifying creature.

'I recognise you. I know you. You are 2405263.'

'That is my number but we have never met before.'

The old harridan stared long and hard. Her mouth formed slowly into a grim, crooked smile.

'What is your *chosen* name? What name did you *choose*, girl?

5

Sal dared not speak. How could this terrifying woman claim to know her, and know she had a secret she had never revealed to anyone?

'So, nameless one, what do you want from Jezzy?'

Sal hardly dared to reply. A meeting was what she had hoped for but this was not at all what she had dreamed.

'Tell me directly now,' the creature snapped.

With a great effort, Sal pulled herself together.

'I… I saw something about your work on… on the interraft net. It was…. It said you were… researching fish and… m…m…mammalian… embryos…' Sal gulped.

'Hee,' the old hag cackled, *mammalian*? Hee, hee. Why not say it? *Human embryos* Yes, yes. You dug it out. I knew you had. You've been digging away, haven't you, brave girl, exploring where very few ever dare to venture. I knew you were.' The grin now seemed approving and there was a twinkle in those dark eyes.

'I have learned a little bit about stem cells… embryology,' Sal said. 'And the later stages the foetus goes through. Developing humans go through earlier forms, don't they? Your report said you could re-awaken undeveloped organs…to make them into…'

'Yes, yesss?' the hag hissed. Sal recoiled.

'Gills.'

Jezzy raised a withered hand and spoke sharply.

'Enough. We will talk later, hee hee hee,' the old woman cackled. 'I will find your name.'

'It is Sal.' The woman shook her head, but grinned.

'You do not know my true name either. Or perhaps you do? I think you do.'

Sal shook her head.

'You will sing for me later. Hee, hee.'

Sal was shaken.

'Torva, take her round the laboratory. You know the limits. I will consider what else she should see later. I will call you when I am ready.' The monstrous old woman turned from them and floated away. An iris door that Sal had not noticed opened swiftly for her and she passed through. It closed so smoothly and accurately that Sal could barely see where it had been, almost as if the old woman could pass through walls. The child, for she felt suddenly like a very young child, shivered. She had an urgent need to sit down and collapsed on to a nearby bench.

'There's some secret about you that she likes,' said Torva, seriously.

'Likes? It's a strange way of showing it. She terrifies me'

'She is terrifying when you first meet her. A lot of it is meant to be a joke. You will come to love her when you join us here.'

'When I join you? I didn't say I was going to stay.' No, she had not said it but why else had she come?

'What was that about my name? Why did she ask for my chosen name?'

'It is the only thing about you that she does not know already.'

'Know already?'

'Sal,' said Torva with a hint of pity, 'don't you understand? She's downloaded you. You are in the archives like everyone, every smallest detail, backwards and forwards, right through from the day you were decanted. Even earlier. She has checked you out. Everything except that name. She knows everything else.'

'Why? Why would she go to all that trouble?'

'You will understand if you think about it. Does it matter to you? I am sure she will find the name too.'

'She could have found out everything except that in the archives, I know, but why would she bother? I don't care about the name really but she won't find it. It was never archived.'

'Did you never tell anyone?'

'Oh, when I was eleven. I may have told one or two other kids what I was going to choose. They started calling me Sal. It was easier to say. That was years ago. They will have forgotten by now.'

'She will find it. She must have a reason.' Sal was about to speak but he put his hands to his ears.

'Don't tell me. She will know at once if you do. She's weird, isn't she? But quite brilliant, I admire her enormously and so do all her staff. She can be scary. It is an act, she isn't serious with it.'

'But when she is serious, look out She is always a few steps ahead of everyone. She directed me to go to the dock to pick you up, a girl who looked like the picture. I wouldn't have been there at all if she hadn't sent me. She required me to find you and bring you here.' He paused for few moments, pondering. 'She always has her own agenda.' Before Sal could speak again he said: 'You too, apparently.'

'What?'

'You have an agenda. She knows it.' He frowned. 'Do you want to see the lab?'

'Yes I do.'

They began with the fish tank Sal had already seen in the entrance room. Torva pointed out some species that Sal had never seen before and explained; these were a few of Jezzy's best-known developments. They had been genetically modified in the egg and now were breeding true. They had important advantages in terms of food value and disease resistance. There was now a flourishing population of the best of them in the food fish tanks deeper down in the Shanghai raft. Most other cities too had profited from these developments.

They moved into another large laboratory. Here were many more tanks tended by robotic devices and monitored constantly with results displayed on screens. There were instruments sampling fluids, data collectors quietly displaying numbers, monitor lights, everything eerily silent. Sal was bewildered although Torva said there was nothing very unusual here. Occasional white suited technicians, not in helmets, bowed deferentially to her escort as the pair went by. They were busy checking figures and giving instructions to the machines via touch screens, or verbally.

Torva explained, as they moved along slowly, that the dark and strangely coloured tanks, apparently stagnant, contained algae, the subjects of experiments. Algae, Sal knew, were used for many things from food production to waste disposal and almost all between. They could routinely be made to produce oils. More importantly, raw materials for fabrics, plastics, synthetic foods and so on were made from them. These laboratory tanks, the man said, were where new cultures began.

New types of water plants and animals were constantly under development. Improved benign species, when proved to be useful and breeding true, would multiply. When a useful product resulted, a new industry might begin. Other major cities were working in the same areas, but Shanghai, Jezzy's department, was in the forefront. If a desirable species did not exist, Jezzy could construct it. Details and gene samples would be circulated to all the other cities. The global inter city web without restriction was constantly receiving news of these and other discoveries. It was important for every raft to keep up with what was going on. Exchange of information was entirely free. Sal began to understand the implications.

Torva led her next into sterile areas, first ensuring that they donned the elaborate special clothing required, suits, masks and gloves, helmets. This laboratory was concerned with developing new possibilities that might, or might not, prove useful. The work here was concerned with bacterial cultures. If there was something algae could not produce, bacterial agents could usually be devised to do the work. Seawater contained traces of every substance known to humankind. The tiny unicellular life forms could be designed to seek out required molecules, secrete them and deposit them conveniently for robots to scoop up and pass on for engineers, doctors, chefs, to use. Three vast decks of the main Shanghai city raft were engaged in the resulting industrial processes.

At another step in the biological scale, viruses were cultured, examined, used and, sometimes, attacked and eliminated.

'They morph into new forms,' Torva remarked. 'They could be very dangerous. If a virus turns nasty it can cause disease. We keep a very close watch.'

'Bacteria and viruses are always evolving so there are always new problems,' he went on. 'A new disease could spread through the population of a city in no time. We know how to anticipate and deal with that sort of thing and we report the information to everyone at sea,' he said, 'and to the landlubbers too, if they will pay attention. They still have the old problems, only they lack the organization to deal with them when a new plague breaks out.'

They moved past another, smaller department where there were some humans apparently undergoing treatment. Entry was restricted but a few solitary individuals could be seen through windows lying in capsules, sometimes merely sitting quietly, perhaps gaming, each individual scrupulously isolated from the others.

'Is this a hospital?' asked Sal. On the Sydney raft, hospitals and therapy centres were on high decks with views of the sea or open decks. People still had accidents, cut themselves or fell and broke bones, even had limbs smashed or cut off. Some of the popular sports involved dangers. For injuries that, in the landages couldn't be repaired, arms, legs, failing organs were re-grown, nerves regenerated. Stem cells made from samples taken directly from the injured person were used for this with total success.

'No. We don't do those routine things here,' Torva remarked. 'This is research. I am in charge here, under Jezzy. We are learning how to help an injured brain to regrow. We can implant stem cells to repair damage but we can't yet replace memories and acquired skills. If they have gone they have gone. Everything missing has to be learned again. In here we are finding ways to bring back lost memories more directly, to reconstruct what has been lost. It is fascinating. This is my special interest.'

Torva guided her to another series of small chambers, where a few apparently ordinary women were visible. Torva explained these were all in some stage of what was once called pregnancy. 'Every now and then, perhaps one in two or three hundred thousand, there is a fault in the insemination control and a human embryo begins to develop actually within a woman. They come here and we find out what has happened and put it right, if possible. Or if it.....' Torva stopped abruptly. 'I must not tell you too much about it. As soon as these people's treatments are finished they will return to their raft and their embryos will join the others in the incubators.'

Sal guessed he had almost revealed something she was not supposed to know and she had an inkling of what it might be, but respected the taboo.

'You can ask Jezzy, when she calls for you. She will tell you what she wants you to know. If she doesn't think you should hear, it won't be any use asking.' He paused, made a few sweeping arm gestures.

'Now, you have seen all I can show you. The whole of this part of Shanghai is Jezzy's empire. You haven't seen all of it. It is about two nauticals long and one, or a bit more than one, wide. In plan it's roughly crescent shaped, a sort of fringe along the edge of the main raft. Jezzy likes to be as independent as she can from the city. It gives her a sort of freedom.' Sal had noticed he spoke of 'the raft' as if the laboratory area was not part of Shanghai. In a way, she supposed, it wasn't.

'The few residents like me and Jezzy and... and a few others... have our own sleeping capsules and recreation areas here and restaurants, and so on. We feed ourselves from our own fish tanks and hydroponics. Most of the junior lab assistants live in Shanghai itself but the lab has its own wind turbines and solar panels, fuel cells and a few hydrogen motors. A fusion power plant is about the only thing we don't have. We move with the city, naturally. It is very unusual for any visitor to be allowed through the main Iris Door, as you were. I've only known it happen a few times before. Let's have something to eat and we can lie down together, if you like. You are a lovely girl.' They removed their protective suits and dropped them into a chute for cleansing.

He took her to a restaurant, part of the laboratory area. To Sal the place seemed strangely empty. The pair ate a simple meal in a twin capsule. Afterwards they began to get interested in each other sexually, but before anything much could happen, Torva's terminal came to life. Jezzy had summoned them to her personal office.

6

The old woman had smartened herself up. Her hair now was tied back, her long cloak discarded on a hook. In a neat and sparklingly clean green uniform, she reclined in a capsule facing several large display screens. As they entered, she stood up. She seemed to have changed herself from a weird, eccentric wild woman, into a brisk, uniformed, efficient experimental scientist.

'Torva, You have other things to do,' she said. 'Go and do them I wish to be alone with *Rusalka.*' Sal gave an astonished gasp. Torva grinned at her, as if to say, 'I told you so' but he merely bowed and walked out through the wall.

'How did you find out?' asked Sal.

'I know, I know why you chose that name.' Jezzy grabbed her long cloak, undid her hair, raised her hands, crooked her fingers like talons, and was in her weird persona again. 'Now I will tell you mine,' she screeched, 'I am *Jezzybaba*. Does that mean anything to you? It should'

Indeed it did. Sal felt the hairs on her neck stand up.

'The witch, the awful old witch,' she yelped. The old hag grinned and nodded. Sal shivered from head to toe.

'Sit down, child, before you fall down,' said Jezzy. Sal slumped on to a convenient bench, struggling to control herself.

The old woman was laughing at her. 'You know I am not a witch, although perhaps I would like to be,' said the old woman, gently. 'Yes, I would like to be.' She threw the cloak off, tidied her hair, and gave that crooked grin. 'I play the part when it suits my mood.' She sat on a stool, facing Sal.

Common sense prevailed.

'No, no' Sal said, shakily. 'I don't believe in witches. It was only a story. You cannot be the real Jezzybaba because there never was one. In any case, nobody, not even you, can be as old as that. Thousands of years. No, no, it was only an old, old story, a myth.'

'Quite so,' said Jezzy, 'a myth from more than two thousand years ago. I chose my name because when I was at the choosing age, I wanted to be Jezzybaba the witch. And now, as nearly as can ever be, I am she. Hee hee. And you chose Rusalka because you wanted to be Rusalka. I am right, aren't I? And you still want it.'

Recovering, Sal drew a long breath, and nodded. '*The Little Mermaid*,' she whispered.

'When and where did you hear the tale of Rusalka?'

Sal's voice quavered. 'It was the music. When I was very small, tiny, just out of the crèche, I was about six or seven, I think, our child carer used to play old music sometimes and there was this song. It was lovely, a real human voice, not like the synthetic stuff. I couldn't understand a word; it was a meaningless language, not like Raftanglish at all, but I adored the music. It was Rusalka the little mermaid, singing to the moon.'

The old woman nodded. 'I know the song. The language, what they called Czech, no longer exists, even among the lubbers.'

'I never forgot it. Later I played it for myself, over and over. I still do sometimes, and I sing it when I am alone, without words.'

'Yesss. Yessss I know.' How did she know? She had been listening, Sal thought.

'I found the story in a teaching capsule, to go with the song, the story of Rusalka. And you were there… I mean, in the story, Jezzybaba…'

'Yesss, yess, the witch hissed. Go on, there is more.'

'Rusalka was a water sprite.' Jezzy nodded, grinning fiendishly, crowed delightedly.

'And…? Go on.'

'She begged the witch to turn her into a human,' Sal said. Her words poured out, unchecked. 'That was it. But what a crazy thing to ask for. Rusalka was living in the beautiful sea, but she had this utterly mad idea that she wanted to be a human so that…so that she could lie with a man she had seen when he was swimming, what they used to call a prince. That's a bit like the Captain of a city raft, isn't it? Only he was a landlubber. I can't understand her, it seems so ridiculous, to want a fuck so much that you would give up living in the sea with the lovely fishes and dolphins, just for the sake of some stupid lubber prince, when she could have had a hundred men… I mean, mermen…' She ran out of breath. 'If there ever were such things,' she gasped.

The old woman waited.

Sal stammered on, 'Jezzybaba ch-ch-changed Rusalka, b-b-b-but she was very unhappy on the land.'

Jezzy smiled, nodding, sympathetically. 'You remember what happened in the end? Eh?' she asked.

'Singing to the moon didn't help,' said Sal, 'the lubber prince rejected her. The witch cursed him and he died. Rusalka went back to the sea in misery. But how stupid. She should have rejoiced to be there again, where she belonged.'

Jezzy nodded. The expression on her old, lined face might have been triumphant, but she said nothing, staring long and hard at Sal, waiting for her to say more. The girl made several attempts to speak but now was tongue-tied.

Jezzy had to prompt her. 'And what Ru-sal-ka wants now, from the horrible old witch is…..?'

'I want to be a sea sprite. Is it possible? I think… I think you have been doing something like it. I found it in your scientific papers, buried deep in there. It was a report with a very long and difficult title. I couldn't understand it very well but I thought there was… a hint. I read the report. It is there, isn't it? I had to look up a lot of the words. But if it is true, I thought… I don't really want to be a mermaid, not entirely, not the scaly tail. If you could… if you can, give me gills. Like the fish. Just gills, leave the rest of me as I am,' Sal gasped. 'I mean, I… I like being a middy, and lying with the boys. But I want to join the fish in the water too, to be with them, as much as I can. It's so much fun. When I am in the water, I feel that I am one of them. They are my friends.'

Jezzy chuckled. 'Rusalka wants to go back to the sea, *just for fun.*' Sal nodded.

'Sing for me now, Rusalka'

Sal stared at the old woman, who closed her eyes, waiting.

'Sing, sing, to the moon, *little mermaid,*' she croaked.

Taking a deep breath, nervously at first but becoming more sure of herself, Sal sang like Rusalka.

Rusalka to the Moon

O, moon high in the deep, dark sky,
Your light shines on far distant regions,
You roam over the vast wide world
Stealing into human homes.

O, moon be still.
Tell me, oh, tell me where is my prince
Silver moon in the sky, tell him please
That I love him always.

Make sure that for a while
He will remember me
Illuminate his distant mind,
Tell him, ah, tell him I am waiting

If perchance he dreams of me,
May he wake with the memory
  O, moon, forsake me not, forsake me not.

'Ahhh. You have a beautiful voice, a fine voice. You should be a professional singer.' Jezzy, eyes open, was smiling but serious. She opened her eyes and turned them on the girl, who was overcome with a sudden shyness.

'What you ask is possible. What you saw in my report was not much more than a hint, but you understood that hint correctly. There are limits to my powers, but as you have said, no magic is involved. For one with your genetic make up, it would be straightforward. You would fit in very nicely into my scheme.' She raised a gnarled old hand to point to the hidden door through which Torva had passed. 'You would not be the first.'

Sal was delighted, leapt to her feet and turned to where the automatic door was, to present herself immediately for the magic potion, operation, injection or whatever it was that would effect the change. Jezzy did not stand but pointed firmly and a little fiercely to the bench. After a momentary disappointment, Sal obediently took her seat again. It could not be so simple, after all, she thought.

'You already know some of this. At a certain stage, human embryos are like fish. That is our link with ancient evolution. Soon after you were conceived, organs that a fish would need began to develop in you. In the usual human foetus those fishy cells are soon diverted into other things. Yet in you and in a few others like you, unmodified cells are still discoverable, dormant, undamaged but undeveloped. In your case it would take very little to start gills and other necessary things developing. All that is needed is a gentle wake up call. We can stimulate the development that was checked. Within a few months, if you wish to go on, you may be equipped to breathe like a fish. *For fun?*'

Full of excitement, Sal once again made to stand but subsided again at a sign from the old woman.

'Stay there. Do not rush ahead without a great deal of consideration. You imagine this as something that would be fun for you. There are risks. Remember, when she became human Rusalka lost the power of speech. In some versions of the story she could not walk on land without agony. Changing her fishy tail into legs didn't work properly. We would call these side effects now. We can avoid anything of that kind but it is always possible something else could go wrong for you. That would not be fun. *We are not talking about fun.*'

Sal nodded, seriously.

Jezzy continued. She was grim now. 'There is more. Remember, the little mermaid was miserable in her altered state; she could never be fully human. You can never be totally fish. At best you may be part fish and not entirely human either, neither one nor the other. If you choose to change, there can be no going back, as Rusalka did. By Jezzybaba's magic, she went back to her original condition and afterwards was never happy either on land or in the sea. In this world of rafts and cities and nasty but clever old women, if the alteration is made, and if you are wretched afterwards, nothing can be reversed. I do not have the magic spell to turn you back again.'

'I understand,' said Sal, hesitantly.

'I doubt you do fully appreciate what it means. If you continue, you will never return to Sydney. You will become a special kind of citizen of Shanghai, and perhaps not even a full citizen here. You will no longer be a *middy*. You will leave Neppy and Brand and never see them again.'

'Oh yes, I know about them and all your other friends,' said the wicked witch.

Sal was more afraid now, yet strangely excited. She had said to Neppy, she wanted a real adventure. This would be real enough, dangerously so.

'There is no great hurry, you have time to ponder,' Jezzy went on, 'and remember this. My interest in this project is not merely to satisfy the desires of a few restless children. Jezzybaba demanded something from the little mermaid. If you decide to proceed, I will expect something from you in return. It may be, may be, fun for you, but I am serious.'

'There is more you should understand.'

Sal wondered what was coming.

'Our meeting was not an accident. Some months ago my computer noticed and alerted me to the fact that there was a persistent person hacking into and going through my obscure material. Someone had hacked into my pages, not once, but many times, delving deeper each time. You are the second person to do this. Hacking into records also works in the other direction. I was able to reverse the process. I made a search and found you hidden on the Sydney raft among the millions of other young rafters.'

Sal was surprised by this, but began to understand.

'You know that all data from every insemination is automatically downloaded to the central archives on the raft where the work is done. Everything about you, even very intimate details, is there in the Sydney memory banks to be discovered. I knew you would come to me when the chance arose.'

'But... I... I... this was my idea. I came looking for you I only decided to come yesterday. *Doldrums*, did you read my mind? Did you even control me?' Sal was astonished and appalled, but fascinated. 'The cities only came together by accident. You couldn't have known they would drift so near one another. Are you some sort of witch after all?'

'No mind reading or controlling. There is no witchery but there is an element of the little sea sprite in you and it has influenced your behaviour. My search program, fully automatic, found you. The machine was simply doing what I required it to do, searching, finding and reporting, that's all. Your chart matched the DNA sequences I hoped to find. I had the information weeks ago that there was a very suitable girl on the Sydney raft and. I spied on you a little. I know the kinds of things you do for fun, the kinds of holograms you choose to look at, and, *hee hee hee*, the kind of music you enjoy. *Hee hee.*' Jezzy cackled, triumphantly. 'I heard the songs you played and sang to yourself Ru – SAL – ka. I knew of your fascination with fish, and how you taught yourself to stay under water for long minutes at a time.'

'When I saw that we were both in the same ocean I persuaded the Chief Mandarin, my Captain, to bias the drift a little; to bring our two rafts closer. I felt sure you would come to Shanghai when Sydney was close. I constructed a likeness, a portrait, from your DNA. As soon as I saw you were on the ferry I sent Torva to find you, to make sure of you.'

Jezzy smiled again. 'With the co-operation of your Captain Nemo, I could have made contact with you before now, directly. I would have invited you to come to see me. I did this before with another, a boy who, in the same way as you did, drew my attention. If you had not chosen to come to me, I would have sent Torva to find you but I was confident you would come by your own choice. You had made yourself aware of my work. As Jezzybaba I feel an affinity with you, little mermaid.' Jezzy got to her feet and put on her cloak.

'You have a little more understanding now of what is involved. I have other things I must attend to, so I will leave you to think things over. If you decide you do not want to continue, I will be disappointed but you can leave when you wish. The car you came in is still outside where you and Torva left it. You can tell it to take you back to the ferry dock and return to Sydney immediately. If you do so, your life will go on as before. I cannot and will not insist on your staying.'

'Spend a day or two looking round Shanghai. There is much to see and do in the city. Go to a concert, Shanghai has excellent music.'

'Remember, I have a serious purpose in all this, in all that I do. Use your terminal if you want to talk to me again. Speak the word Jezzy and I will answer at once. If you wish to continue with this project, the adventure that you seek, get a car, tell it to bring you to Jezzy and we will continue.'

The old woman pointed to a door behind Sal, turned and vanished through the other wall. Sal was alone. She went to the door Jezzy had indicated, touched it and stepped through as it opened. To her surprise she was again in the room where she had waited before. Was the laboratory like a magic palace with secret and hidden ways? She went to the entrance room beyond and to the passageway. The car was there. Getting into it she whispered; 'Go to main deck and wander round the city slowly.' The car moved off and she let it go where it would. Hardly conscious of what she was seeing and hearing, she pondered.

Sal could not remember any time in her life when she had not wanted to swim and breathe like a fish. Was she internally made this way from the beginning? Was being a fish girl, a sea sprite, built into her brain? If so, would she ever be happy if she went against her inborn character? Wherever these desires came from, she felt sure they would never leave her. Jezzy said she was especially suitable for the proposed transformation. If she returned to her ordinary life, she knew she would still wish to be with the fishes. Would she ever forgive herself, if she did not take the opportunity?

Yet, to leave Sydney, her home raft, to cut herself off from everything and all the people she knew, was a daunting prospect. Never to see Neppy again? She liked Neppy. She would miss him but she had never felt their companionship was very important. He would miss her but would soon forget. No one ever remained devoted to one person for very long; surely that wasn't natural.

Would fish girls….mermaids…. have babies? Neither fully girl nor fully fish. Would there be fish boys? Would the whole clinical business of insemination, incubation and decanting be the same for the altered persons? This whole topic was something that shocked her when she suddenly thought of it. If the change was limited to the gills the rest ought to be the same. Torva had said something about breeding true. The babies might be fish. Who would care for them? Would the babies be in special crèche tanks or might they begin living on the raft and take to the water only later?

These were questions she needed to think about. Jezzy must know the answers.

She almost called at once to ask, but hesitated again. She should talk the whole situation over with someone else. The car wandered aimlessly. Sal stared around as they roamed, but with waning interest after a while. She began to see that Shanghai, so very large, was, as the couple she had met on the ferry said, really very like other cities. She had seen a few rafts, Rio and Bristol and before there had been an encounter with Nyork 2 and Lunnon. They were only other rafts, bigger but not fundamentally very different. There was little to choose between Sydney and Shanghai, only size. Her adventure, if she decided that way, would not be merely a change of rafts and citizenship. It would be a totally new way of living, not just *fun*.

She had no particular aim as the car roved around, did not feel very curious about the innumerable things to see and places to go. She halted the vehicle after a while at the base of a tower, almost unbelievably tall, tapering upwards to a slender column that seemed almost to pierce the clouds. Rides to the top for a view of the city could be taken. From such a high point she expected to be able to see Sydney. In a few minutes the elevator, with a few other visitors reclining in the internal capsules, arrived at the top. Sal walked out onto a broad viewing platform. It was windy here, and cold. The tower was not, she discovered, the highest in all Shanghai but it was high enough. Notices informed her that she was 1000 metres above the sea. A few young people were base-jumping from the platform provided for them, and a paraglider pilot ran forward to take off and soar away. Through the broad windows she could see Shanghai spreading out in all directions but other towers and the ever-present turbines and cooling chimneys cut off any view of Sydney. She could barely even catch a glimpse of the sea.

Everything she saw had been imagined, planned, designed by human builders and engineers and built by robots. All was artificial, all was done by and for the benefit of the human beings who swarmed in their millions everywhere, in the towers, in the smaller buildings, on the deck of the raft itself far below where they moved about like small, busy dots, and down further, deck by deck, to the lowest levels. For a few minutes she felt totally hostile to this world. If she became changed, so that she could live in the sea, the ocean could never be more alien to her than the raft. She remained gazing out over the floating metropolis for a long time until dusk began to fall and the city lights came on. There was beauty in this, yet suddenly she wanted none of it. The ocean was where she wanted to be. She rode the elevator down to main deck.

Sal was tired and decided to stay in Shanghai at least overnight. The option of returning to Sydney remained open. She must call Jezzy with her few questions in the morning, and try to arrange another visit to the laboratory. She seized a vacant car and soon arrived at a small, standard hostel capsulery. Here she could eat and sleep. She had spent few of her credits so the cost was easily met. She slipped easily into the allotted pigeonhole, ate the meal provided there, bathed, dried in the warm airstream, closed up and slept.

On waking she was again full of doubts. If ever there was a time when she should ask for advice, this must be it. Every young person had an appointed, professional counsellor. Sal met Calpurnia regularly. She had received little attention from her. She was not especially understanding and sympathetic and there was no very special affection between them. As long as things were going smoothly Cal's advice had been offhand, bland, always the same; continue to work at the Nav School, mix freely with the other girls and boys, have plenty of sex, keep up with the calisthenics, continue the singing lessons, and eat properly. Sal was doing well; let things go on as they were. This time her counsellor would really have to attend. Sal touched the terminal.

What she had to say was beyond Cal's understanding at first. Sal had to explain in detail everything that had happened and what she was contemplating. It took a long time and several repetitions. Once the initial puzzlement and shock was cleared, Calpurnia was horrified. Jezzy, she said, was planning to exploit Sal for her own mysterious purposes She would be used like an experimental fish. That was appalling but far removed from anything that Jezzy could have intended. Sal felt she had wasted her time talking to the woman. Nonetheless she agreed she must question Jezzy again. There was much more she should know.

She left the capsulery to roam further. Knowing that at any time she could get a car to take her anywhere, she did not care when she became totally lost. At one point she found herself more or less accidentally at the rocket-launching platform. It was rarely used now. There was a small space museum attached. Sal wandered in and spent a little time looking at the exhibits. Some of Neppy's friends said they wanted to be astronauts, and perhaps one or two of them would do so.

There were space stations in orbit and on Mars, and one or two on outer planetary moons. All were totally self-contained and sealed even more perfectly than the raft cities. Sal supposed life in orbit, or in a station on a moon, or Mars, was not very different from life on a raft and even more artificial and rigidly controlled.

How strange, Sal thought, that people wanted to explore the largely empty cosmos, where they could never directly experience anything very different from an enclosed, ordered way of existence within the confines of a space ship or planetary colony. A realm teeming with life and beauty lay immediately below the rafts. She wandered out of the museum. Her pondering was shattered by the two arresting marines.

****

'If they let me go I intend to see Jezzy again tomorrow,' Sal said. 'I will ask her to explain everything she wants to do, and what... what I will look like, if I let her do it. There are others, I believe. People who have had the treatment already. I will ask to see them, speak to them. I won't decide till I have done that.'

'But why bother at all, Sal? What's the point of it?'

'You know, I have always wanted to be with the fish. I love them. This gives me... may give me, the chance to be with them, to learn from them, my friends.'

'I am your friend, Sal. I don't want you to go. You will be changed and I don't want you to change. I like you just as you are.'

'If I go... If I do, Neppy, it will be a terrific adventure. It will be a new world. I haven't really decided yet, but if I do, that will be the reason.'

'Terrific adventure? Terrific, yes it will be, terrifying, it terrifies me. What's wrong with this life, Sal? This is where you belong. Why do you want to leave us, and... and at what cost? An adventure? You can have virtual adventures any time you like. Our pal Brand does.'

'I don't want virtual reality. I want real adventures, Neppy, can't you see? I agree with Brand, this life is boring. Nothing ever happens. Don't you feel it?'

'Things are happening all the time. We have plenty of water sports if you must swim, and we can visit the other rafts too, like we did Rio and Bristol and so on.'

'We spend all our time drifting around, and if the navigators do their job we never have any important disturbances. We don't even have hailstorms if they can help it. That's what being a navigator will be for me if we go on as we are. Carefully directing the drift so that nothing, *nothing*, **nothing** will ever happen Even the big cyclones and eruptions don't affect us, they are just noisy displays far away, if we are doing our job, which of course we always will.'

Neppy shook his head. 'I wish I had gone with you, then this might not have happened.'

'The rafts are all the same, Neppy, boring, dull people, routines, routines, habits, rules, nothing new. The people on the moon and Mars live in artificial cities, self-supporting, closed in even more than we are, changeless, just the same. The ocean waits, just down there. There is a different world down there, waiting for us. We still don't know as much about it as we should.'

'You've made up your mind, haven't you? You will go, whatever I say.' Neppy was much more upset than Sal had expected. She felt a sudden pang of sorrow. She should not leave him without very good and convincing reasons.

'I have not made up my mind. But talking about it is helping me to understand. I can see much clearer now, what I would like to do and why. But I promise you, Neppy, I will not decide until I have spoken again to Jezzy and found out exactly what she intends. I swear.'

'She wants to use you, meddling with your genes to see what happens. Sal, do you want to be used like that? She is a witch, truly, Sal. She is the wicked Jezzybaba as you thought at the very beginning. Don't let her put you under her spell.'

The time came for her to return to the tribunal. Neppy did not come with her. It was a brief meeting. The verdict was settled. Tomorrow she was permitted to take the ferry and visit Jezzy again. The Captain himself would arrange that the old woman would be ready to spend time with Sal and make sure she understood everything that was proposed. If, after all, she preferred to come back to Sydney, she would be welcomed and could continue as before. If she chose to join Jezzy, that would be the end of the matter as far as this tribunal was concerned.

Calpurnia was seething as she escorted Sal out.

'You will be in salt water all the time, do you realise that? Jezzy might be able to give you gills, but you know what your skin is like when you have been soaking in a bath for a while. Sea water can be nasty if you stay in it all day long. What does she plan to do about this? Will you have to grow scales? Perhaps you will have sharkskin. You will develop layers of blubber to insulate you against the cold. What are you going to look like?' What more can you possibly want that you don't already have here?'

Sal shook her head.

'Oh, don't listen to me. You never have, why start now? If you must, then go. At least I won't have to bother about you any more. Go and be damned.'

Calpurnia had never bothered much about her, Sal thought, resentfully. But she had listened this time and the woman's words and images struck home. She was plunged again into doubts, still far from clear about what to do. She wanted to be with the fishes. The feeling was as strong as ever but the price she might have to pay was greater than she had ever envisaged. Was Jezzy indeed planning to change her into an ugly, fat monster with shark-like skin? She did not want that.

'I will ask her to explain everything she wants to do, and what... what I will be like, if I let her do it. There are others who have... had the treatment already. I will ask to see them, speak to them. I won't decide till I have done that.'

7

Torva met Sal off the ferry. Soon they were in the laboratory again and she was escorted to Jezzy's office. The woman looked almost normal, old, wrinkled but smart in formal garb, hair tied back tidily. Yet there was a wild sharpness in her eyes as she surveyed the girl.

'So you are here again after all. You want to ask more questions and I will answer them. I have already said, if you decide to join us there can be no going back. I will not accept you on my team unless you are willing and committed to the programme. What is the first thing that concerns you? Where shall we begin?'

'You told me before, that I was not the first. You have already altered some real people in this way, given them gills. Are they very ugly? I want to meet them, and find out what they are like.'

'I can arrange that, if they are willing. I do not control them, although I am responsible for them. They have wishes, desires and intentions of their own. They may not wish to meet you, an unmodified girl.'

'Neppy says, you will make me into a monster.'

'I know what Neppy said. I heard your counsellor too. She is right. We are creating a new human species, better adapted to life on a planet that is mostly covered with water. The sea sprites, the children, are not monsters, they are fine human beings but they are not the same as they were. They are amphibians, moving freely between land and sea, learning to live in new ways. Increasingly they are becoming adapted to their new life.'

'I need to be sure that the... gills... work properly,' said Sal. Neppy...'

'I know', said Jezzy. 'Neppy said he didn't believe we can do it. Everyone is sceptical at first. We can do it, Rusalka. We carried out many trials before we were permitted to modify our first human. Darien, the first sprite, is out there somewhere, swimming now. He's a bright lad, but tends to act before he thinks. I made him think very long and carefully before he was allowed to undergo the treatment.' She waved her hand vaguely over her shoulder. 'Very possibly he is fathoms beneath us even as we sit here. The others are with him, young boys and girls like you. They have to be young. It won't work with older people.'

She went on. 'There remains one vital thing you must consider. Can you work out what it is? It will be a few months before we can answer the question you haven't asked. There is only one way to be quite sure of the answer.'

Sal stared at her. A few months? What could take months? The answer dawned.

'Are they really a new species? Will they be able to... breed.... to breed true?'

'I have checked everything but there is only one final proof to convince everyone. I am confident they will produce children like themselves. We are waiting for the first definite signs.' Jezzy paused, stared hard at Sal. What was coming next?

'We are not going to use incubation. Do you know what I mean by pregnancy?'

Sal gaped.

'I think so. In the old times... they say... didn't it meant an embryo, a baby, was growing inside a woman. She was called the mother. When it was ready it had to come out... emerge... I don't understand how that can be but I know it used to happen.'

'You will learn. For many centuries, for millennia, that is how human beings and other mammals reproduced. It is the natural process, insemination, gestation and pregnancy leading to birth in about nine months. Giving birth, as they used to call it, was painful and sometimes dangerous for the child or the mother, or both. We arrange it now without distress or danger to either. If you join my group you will assuredly become a mother and give birth. It is central to the project, a most, important, perhaps *the* most, important part of it.'

Sal shuddered and could not speak for some time.

'It is part of the adventure you are seeking, Rusalka. If you stay here with us you will become pregnant and give birth. This will be a very large part of the adventure you are seeking, the real adventure. You will be a *mother*.'

Sal had difficulty understanding but the thoughts that came to her as she tried to grasp the idea became more and more fearful but at the same time exciting, even tempting. Tempting, greatly tempting. This would be not merely an adventure for a girl, a carefree sprite who would enjoy playing with the fish. It would bring other people into the world, babies, children. She would be a *mother*.

At last she was able to speak again without showing her confusion more than she already had.

'I want to meet the… people… the sprites…and to know more, to understand what you will do. Might do…to… to me. To see them and talk to them.'

'I will ask them to come. Before I do that, I will show you something. Come along.' Jezzy rose to her feet, holding a hand out and guiding Sal though one of the seemingly magical doors. This meeting was much less disturbing to Sal than she had expected. Jezzy was very old, and indeed very odd, but today she was businesslike, rational, and in a way, affectionate without making any very obvious display of such feeling. Sal could see that those who knew her well, like Torva, might come to like her even while they were a little afraid of her.

They moved now into a chamber Sal had not seen before. Here was a small tank with some speckled black and brown creatures swimming about. They had short, slender bodies, long tails, four small legs sprouting from the body, and round, slightly wedge-shaped heads with eyes and mouths. They were, over all, about mandrim centims long. Immediately behind the head, where the neck would be if there was one, they seemed to be wearing a ruff, like bundles of feathers.

'What do you suppose those frilly things are?' demanded the old woman.

'Gills? They must be gills.' Jezzy nodded, approvingly.

'These little animals are what the lubbers call newts, or efts, in the immature stage. They will grow into mature adults. There are other creatures with similar arrangements. Suppose you were going to have gills like these, where would they be on your body?'

'Sort of… round here, each side of my neck? But.. wouldn't they.. aren't they liable to damage? They look so fragile'

'The efts manage very well. Put your hands to show me where you think human gills might be.'

Sal raised her hands as if to hold her head on.

'What do you feel?'

'My neck. The top of my shoulders. My hair hanging down.'

'Never mind the hair. What else?' asked Jezzy.

'Nothing… else… Oh, *Poseidon*. My ears. My ears.' Sal stared in astonished realisation at Jezzy, who was grinning at her and cackling.

'And if your ears, your outer ears, were to grow, become softer, feathery, longer, well supplied with capillary blood vessels, do you think they might work like these little eft gills?'

Sal looked again at the swimming animals, stared for some moments. Surely it could not be so simple. They would look very strange. To have such appendages growing from the side of her head would be a terrible embarrassment, awkward, restricting free movement, even creating a lot of resistance if she was swimming. If they worked as gills in the water, wouldn't they dry out when she was out of the water and breathing air? How would she breathe then? Would her lungs still work?

Her ears. Would she still be able to hear?

'Not convinced? Of course not,' said Jezzy, grinning. 'There is more. Come along. I have something else to show you. Have you ever spent time looking closely at fossils? I mean, real fossils, not the one they show you in the simulators.'

'I know what they are, but I never saw any real ones.' The old woman led the way, ignoring more fish tanks until at the side of the corridor they were walking along, they came to some cabinets, a series of wide but shallow drawers one above the other with elaborate locking systems requiring code words and numbers to allow them to be opened.

'These are precious, access is restricted. We do not touch them, they become damaged and worn with handling and we may never be able to replace them. You may look, but do not touch.' She fingered a pad. One of the drawers slid smoothly and silently out and Sal saw it was divided into multiple compartments. In each was what seemed at first to be shapeless lumps of stuff, the like of which she had never seen. She realised after a moment that these were pieces of stone, rocks taken from the land where she had never set foot in her life. All she had known before was what had been presented to her in the simulators and video lessons. Studying the objects closely now she could see that they were impressions of the skeletons of some kinds of animal.

'Here we have an ancient fish.' With a fingernail, Jezzy pointed to a roughly V shaped bone. 'That is an upper jaw. See? Part of the skull.' Sal nodded.

'Here is the spine, where it joins the head.'

'Yes, I think I see.'

'This, here on the side, and this on the other, the shapes match. Can you see that? Then what are these strange little striations in this old fish?'

'Are you telling me, these are the gills?'

Jezzy nodded. 'Gills, yes, and becoming more than gills,' she said. 'They are primitive ears.'

'Ears, do you mean, ears evolved from gills? Is that right?' Jezzy nodded.

'This fish, called *Panderichthys*, was at an intermediate stage. Fish gills in this era were beginning to develop into ears. A fish with gills was able to feel vibrations in the water, to distinguish different frequencies and intensities, to hear sounds. This is what started me thinking. I have already established that in you and some other young humans now living successfully on the city rafts, breathing air, you still have within you what is required to promote your ears to gills.'

'Imagine that your external ears, those parts that you can touch easily with your hands, were much larger, more convoluted, and full of many fine thin-skinned blood vessels. Imagine the water flowing round you as you swim, finding ways through the feathery maze of fine blood vessels. Do you think oxygen from the air dissolved in the sea, would pass into the blood stream from those beautiful, feathery ears?'

'So that's what you do. I can see, it might work. Oh…. It must work that way. That is what you are doing. Oh, Oh *Neptune*' Suddenly, she had a guilty flash. 'Oh, Neptune, Neppy, you were wrong.' She found herself suddenly in tears for no reason that she could imagine. Was it memory of Neppy?

'Yes, yes, Neppy was wrong.' said Jezzy. 'That is what I do, in outline that is what I can do. There is more to it in detail, but you have the essence.'

It took Sal a little time to calm herself. She was suddenly more doubtful, not less, about the project. This adventure meant parting from everything, and everyone, she had known before. What had been a dream would become her reality.

Jezzy continued. 'It is a continuous flow system. There is no breathing in and out. That wastes time and reduces efficiency. In my gills, the water flows constantly through so the oxygen exchange has more time, making up to some extent for the lower proportion of the gas in the fluid. Why are you weeping?'

Sal hardly heard her. She had promised Neppy not to make a hasty decision. Why should her promise worry her now? If she joined Jezzy, she would never see Neppy again anyway. Did that matter, so much? She liked Neppy. It did matter. They were friends, good friends. She liked Neppy.

'Could he… would you…?'

'What? What are you going to ask?'

"If I could talk… talk to him again… I mean, Neppy. He likes swimming. He chose his name after Neptune, the ancient god of the sea. I mean… he …I could persuade him, ask him to come with me? Could he?'

'Ha. Neptune, indeed' the old woman exclaimed. 'Rusalka, I know everything about your Neppy. He named himself for a sea god but he is not, and cannot be so. I have studied his body structures and his genes. He cannot be adapted, cannot be stimulated to grow new organs, as you can. If you come with me, you must leave him behind. Forget him. He will never become a sprite.'

'There is no middle way for you,' said Jezzy. 'Forget Neppy, or forget me.'

Sal pondered, sadly, but faced the issue again.

'I cannot decide. I must meet those people who have been changed. I must talk with them.'

'Then come with me.'

Together, they walked through the wall.

8

The laboratory had its own access to the ocean, separate from the swimming centres for the general population. Jezzy took her to another iris door which opened onto a small, flat deck level with the sea. There was nothing there. Sal was daunted. This place was almost grim, as plain as it could be, devoid of all the usual facilities. The familiar recreational swimming places on the rafts were enclosed with carefully designed protective nets to keep out dangerous fish, poisonous octopus, killer whales and sharks. The barriers also served to prevent foolhardy humans from losing themselves by venturing too far out from the city. There were shallow pools for babies to swim, water slides, areas set aside for adult sports and games, racing and diving. Poolside decks at several levels had spectator seats and couches for relaxing, there were snack bars and restaurants, massage parlours, capsules for couples or triples to lie together, showers, everything a citizen could wish for when off duty. All was enclosed, guarded and watched.

This place was quite different. There was no shelving surface allowing a timid swimmer to wade into the water gradually before running out of depth. There were no steps, diving boards or piers, no safety nets, and most significantly, no people bathing, sitting or lying around. There was nothing but a flat shelf and the regular rhythm of the waves slapping at the edge. Sal was frightened yet thrilled at the same time, a feeling that was becoming familiar. With a few steps, she could step, or dive, instantly into the deep ocean. Dare she do it? She would enter the open sea extending over most of the planet, a realm with no one to instruct and protect her. There would be nothing but herself, the fish and the sea with all its wonders and perils. It was an even bigger field for adventure than she had dreamed of. If she plunged in she would be more alone than she had never been in her life, no one to watch her, supervise, listen and watch, order her to do this or that, possibly arrest her and haul her before a tribunal.

She remembered with a sense of relief, the fish would be her friends, and somewhere, down there, she thought, there were the new humans, sprites, Jezzy's sea creatures, one of whom she might become. They might be, must be, would be new friends for her. She would not be entirely alone. But these creatures, were they ugly, revolting, scaly skinned, fat and monstrous? Would they accept her?

And where were they?

Jezzy stepped briskly to the edge of the deck, as if she intended to take to the water herself. Instead, she stopped, knelt down and pressed one hand onto a small projecting lever or knob that Sal had not noticed previously. As she did so, a hooting sound rose from the water. As this faded, Jezzy worked the knob up and down rapidly. There was an irregular, repetitive buzzing, a series of short and long sounds, with brief spaces between. The old woman continued for a little time, then ended with another extended hoot. Jezzy got to her feet, turned to Sal, laughing.

'They will come. I don't know where they are, but they will come.'

'What were you doing?'

'It is a signaling system, a crude machine but it will do for the present. They can hear it. Sounds carry well through the water. Their ears do still work as ears. We found an ancient code, the *Morse* code, which was once used for the earliest forms of telegraphic and radio communication.'

Sal shook her head, not understanding.

'Ha' said Jezzy. 'Never heard of it? There was a time when the only ways of sending messages over long distances was by electrical pulses through wires. It was called the telegraph. I have adopted the code that was used then.'

Sal was still puzzled.

'If I send out a short sound like this "di", then three longer ones, "da da da", that is the code for the first letter of my name, J, di da da da. Get the idea? Then I wait a little and send out one single short sound by itself, "di", that is E, the second letter. And then "da da di di" is Z and that sent twice is Z again. And da di da da is Y. So "di da da da   di da da di di da da di di da di da da" is my name, JEZZY. Each letter and number, has a code in di da fashion, and the punctuation marks as well.'

'I'm sorry, I'm baffled.'

Jezzy grinned, deliberately teasing.

'What I just sent out, the full message was "JEZZY CALLS COME BACK TO MEET A NEW FRIEND." It goes like this:

"di da da da   di   da da di di   da da di di da di da da, JEZZY,
da di da di   di da   di da di di   di da di di   di di di, CALLS,
da di da di   da da da   da da   di di di di, COME,
da di di di   di da da di da di da di da, BACK,
da da da da, TO,
da da di di da, MEET,
di da, A,
da di di di da da, NEW,
di di da di di da di di di di da di da di di, FRIEND,
di da di da di da, END."

Jezzy leered at her. The witch seemed to have gone mad. Sal could not help herself. She burst into a fit of giggles.

'You will have to learn it … if you decide to stay. We are working on better ways for sending messages.'

Sal was still struggling to keep a straight face.

'Rusalka lost her voice when she came onto the land.' Said Jezzy. 'For you, it will be the other way round. Under water, without a facemask you lose your ability to speak. Your vocals chords depend on air going through the larynx, and your throat will be closed. There will be no air going through.'

Sal sobered immediately.

'Signals under water carry person to person over a few metres but they have much less range and it is hard to read text messages. You have to get out of the water to signal over longer distances.'

Sal did not like this prospect. Jezzy was taking too much for granted. Would she still be able to sing when out of the water? Maybe I should go back to Sydney, she thought. Jezzy seemed to have understood her facial expression.

'The quality of your singing voice out of the water will, I think, be slightly improved, though it is already very good.'

'In air, you will breathe as you are doing now, and speak normally. The code can give a swimmer directional signals, for navigation. That's how my children can find their way back here. The sprites are working out their own ways of communicating under water. They can make sounds, clicks and buzzes, with their mouths, lips, tongues and teeth. And they can use their hands. In the days when some people had defective or diseased ears, there were advanced codes for signalling. They could converse normally as long as they could see one another's gestures. Nobody in the rafts needs them now, but we have resurrected those deaf languages and are learning them again. You will get used to it.'

'If I stay.'

Jezzy stared at her, and nodded, a little grimly.

'If you stay. Now, where are my sprites? They should be here by now.' Jezzy went again to the signalling device but before she reached it, there was a disturbance under the water and a naked man leapt out onto the edge of the deck. He took a crouching position for a moment, spat water from his mouth, swallowed, stood upright, seemed to bow, rose to his full height and took a deep breath.

'Here you are, Darien,' said Jezzy. 'What took so long?'

Sal saw immediately that he was somewhat older than she, tall, athletic and strongly built, handsome, which was normal for a rafter, but from each side of his head, tangled with his long hair, there grew long, tapering, convoluted growths that swept back behind his shoulders. The man shook his head, scattering water droplets everywhere. Somewhere Sal had seen a representation of an ancient, mythical messenger of the gods who had a helmet with wings attached at each side. These gills, for that is what they must be, were something like that, but much larger. She could see they had been ears before the modification, but as the man stood they seemed to deflate gradually so that they sank down behind his shoulders, not reaching quite to his waist. They were like the fronds of a plant. As they softened, she was reminded of the feathery newt gills.

'We went further out than usual, and a bit deeper,' he said. 'The others are not far behind.' The voice was clear but Sal thought it unusually resonant. She supposed modifications to his mouth had caused it to change.

'Come and meet Rusalka,' said Jezzy.

Darien came forward, smiling, and extended both arms to embrace her. She withdrew nervously. He seemed a little slow to understand her hesitation.

'Oh... er... sorry, too hasty'

'Rusalka, I have heard that name before, I think. So you are coming to join us. A new member of Jezzy's family? A new friend. That is wonderful, you are most welcome. I am Darien.'

'Yes, *Darien*, I heard. But... I am doubtful about joining you. I have not decided.'

'Too quick as usual, boy, said Jezzy. 'She wants to see what kind of monsters you are. She needs to talk with you and the others.'

'And here they are.'

In quick succession, two more young men and two girls emerged naked from the water. They went through the same movements, spitting, crouching, swallowing, bowing, stretching and drawing breath. All were handsome and strong, had gills, and greeted her with smiles and enthusiasm. As Jezzy said their names each stepped forward to touch hands with her. The girls were Euna and Alicia, the boys Sistus and Michel. They were close to Sal's own age, Sistus a little older.

'Come inside,' said Jezzy. 'You must all have something to eat and drink. No dehydration? Good. I will leave Sal with you. Look after her and tell her everything she needs to know. She sings, you should hear her. I must go back to the lab to see what the bugs are doing. When you are ready to talk to me again, Rusalka, Darien will bring you.'

She led the way again to the laboratory and into the hall Sal had seen before with Torva, capsules, tables and meal service. Waving casually, she vanished through another hidden doorway.

The system for ordering meals was the same as Sal was used to in the Sydney restaurants and mess halls, and in Nemo's quarters. The sprites, as Sal found herself thinking of them, chose their places and she took one herself. The menu on screen needed only her touch against the items she preferred. She identified some items that the couple on the ferry had introduced to her, others were less familiar. She chose a very ordinary Sydney type of meal, grilled butterfish and vegetables, with a fruit salad and a lemon cordial. As they waited, Sal looked carefully at the others. Except for the gills, and the slightly resonant undertones in their voices, they looked and spoke like any group of half a dozen young rafters, hardly different at all from a similar gang of young middies after a swim, naked and cheerful. Michel was excited, for he had seen something unusual, a small sea creature he could not identify. His description left the others baffled and as she listened Sal knew she had never seen anything like it.

'It was very small,' said Michel, 'no bigger than my thumbnail, with what looked like petals arranged round a central mouth. I watched it for a few minutes but it kept turning this way and that so I couldn't be sure of its shape. It swam a bit like a squid, you know, pulsing in and out, but with petals, not tentacles.'

'What colour?' asked Euna.

'I'm not sure; it seemed to change as it pulsed and turned. The light wasn't good, it is almost transparent and I was quite deep.'

'We can make a data search. Who knows, you might have discovered a new species' said Darien. 'There's plenty of new ones still waiting to be discovered. You will be famous. We'll have to give it a name. What about minicephalopodia michelii?' Michel laughed.

'I have no idea what it is, it could be almost anything, or nothing. Might be a larva of some sort.' The dishes arrived quickly. The sea children were evidently hungry and thirsty, wasting no time tackling the food, drinking fruit juice copiously

'We aren't being very polite to our visitor,' said Alicia, after a short interval for eating. 'Are you going to join us? Rusalka, truly? It is an unusual name. Have I got it right?'

'Yes, but call me Sal, it's easier. I don't know about joining you. Can you tell me more about it? What does Jezzy do to make the changes? And... well... are you...do you....' Sal stopped, afraid of offending them.

'You want to know if we are happy,' said Sistus. 'Do we regret what we let her do? Do we want to go back? We can't, so wanting it would be no good, and we knew it from the very beginning,' said Sistus.

'Jezzy has told me that.'

'Speaking for myself, I am still getting used to it. I remember my old friends and that makes me sad sometimes. Living on the raft, I was on Calcutta, was easy and I enjoyed it in most ways. I was a Robot Master, not just an engineer. It was fascinating work, but they are only machines. There was never one that didn't do exactly what I programmed. I began to feel there must be more to life than robots. One of my favourite games was exploring strange planets in the VR capsules and meeting different kinds of being. I got sick of that too, eventually. It is only pretending. What we are doing with Jezzy is different, a real exploration. I am not at all sorry to be here now.'

'It is an open ended situation,' said Darien. 'I am a bit older than the others.' He explained he had been born a Shanghai rafter and started training as a child carer but became deeply interested in what Jezzy was doing. He became Jezzy's student and joined her team even before his own genetic suitability for the transformation was realised. He had himself discovered what he was and rejoiced, offering himself immediately for the first trial. 'We spent a lot of time together, studying and thinking, arguing. She is a marvellous person. I was with her when she found Sistus poking about in her archives. He was far away on Calcutta in the southern ocean at that time. She sent for him to come. I went into it knowing exactly what was going to happen and understanding the risks.' Clearly, he adored Jezzy and still regarded himself as her special assistant.

'What do you mean, an open ended situation?' asked Sal.

'On the raft, I knew everything was going to go on as before, I knew where I was going to be next week, next month, next year, for the next hundred years. The future was closed, limited. Now there are always new things to do, new ideas to try, new things to discover and think about. The future is unknown, unpredictable. It's exciting.'

This made good sense to Sal. 'I know what you mean. Everything on the rafts is so well organised, so smoothly arranged, it's,'

'Boring' said Michel. He sounded like Brand. He had joined Jezzy's group when the opportunity arose because it promised to be different from anything else he had experienced. This was turning out to be correct, and he was happy. Sal saw in him what she herself had been at the beginning, a child looking for new games to play. There was no lack of fun to be had, he said, but there were serious discoveries to be made too and he was especially glad to be part of this. The change had opened a new world to him.

Born in Nyork, he had been driven from early childhood by a passionate interest in sea creatures. He had imagined himself, and still did, becoming a leading research scientist in this area. As a juvenile he had done some serious, though he admitted, childish research. He had put his results out onto the net and they caught Jezzy's attention. She called up his genetic structure as she had done with many others. At that time Nyork was in the Pacific and Shanghai in the Indian Ocean. She offered him a lifetime doing exactly what he wanted, in a laboratory as big as the great oceans. He had leapt at the chance. Using a long series of choppers, hopping from one raft to another, he had flown half way round the globe to get to her. Said Michel, 'I have seen more strange creatures in the sea now than I could ever have imagined before. Most of them are already known, they are in the data banks, but no one has ever been swimming and living with them as I can. I will be able to spend the rest of my life finding out more about them. There's nothing else I want to do now,' he glanced at Darien, 'and maybe I *will* discover some new species'

'It is quite painless, Sal, well, almost,' said Alicia. 'What she does, she takes a little sample of your body cells. She grows them in a culture

and modifies their genes, making them into *pluripotent* stem cells. Then
there is a further modification to teach them that they are going to be
gills. There's a series of injections and she puts an implant into you here,
and here.' She touched her ears. 'It raises a bruise for a week or two.
There are other implants too, for other bits. You don't notice anything
at all for the first week or two. Then you start to grow the new parts.
Things begin to swell and it is rather irritating. You feel a bit sore in
your throat and mouth, but it soon gets better and you feel fine.'

'After while,' Euna said, 'when the gills begin to show, you realise
you can go on for longer and longer periods in the water and under it.
Your reflexes make the adjustments as you need them, in the water and
out of it. You don't have to think about it, it's automatic.'

'As to why we agreed to all this,' said Alicia, 'Euna and I both felt the
same. We belonged to a group of other girls like us, chatting on the net
about babies and childbirth. We wanted to have babies and look after
them ourselves, and we didn't want to be restricted to only two. Jezzy
found us in one of her searches. She gave us the chance to do what we
wanted.' Sal was quite shocked. Euna saw her expression.

'Well, it isn't so strange, is it? Mothers used to look after their own
children and bonded with them, at least, most of them did. That isn't
possible at all on the rafts now, is it? As we grew up we never knew who
our biological mothers were. If we bonded with anyone it was our carers
and we were just part of the job for them. We want to experience the
old way. There are many other girls who feel the same but there isn't
any chance for them.'

Alicia added; 'We know perfectly well why they have the laws. They
have to control the population of every raft very carefully. You don't
have to agree with us, Sal, but that is the way we feel. The ocean is so
huge and we will be more in the water than out of it. There is no need
for such strict limits. We can have as many babies as we want. Don't
you feel the same way?' Sal shook her head, doubtfully.

'Well, maybe you will change. But there are still lots of wonderful
things to do in the water. That you will see.'

Sal looked carefully at the two girls. Their skins were quite normal.
They were plump but not fat. Not *fat*, not *scaly*.

'Can I ask a special question?' No doubt she looked at the two girls in a way that betrayed her thoughts.

'I can guess what it is,' said Euna, solemnly. 'No, not yet, neither of us is pregnant. We are still hoping because so much depends on it. It's early days still, we haven't been trying for very long, but we are trying. We are fertile, the usual contraceptive implants have been removed. Jezzy is sure it will happen. She tells us not to worry, let things take the course they will. We have to be a bit careful. We can't lie with just anyone who takes our fancy, like ordinary boys. They don't know we are here anyway. We aren't short of partners.' She waved in the direction of the three young men, who grinned. 'We aren't using artificial methods.'

'The usual rules don't apply to us,' said Alicia. 'Jezzy made sure that was agreed with the Captain from the beginning. We can multiply and multiply, the more the better, she says.'

'That's the whole idea, isn't it?' said Michel.

'You mean,' said Sal, 'this truly is an attempt to change the human species?'

'That's how Jezzy sees it, yes.' Darien nodded. 'We still depend on the raft for a lot of things. We will have to submit to the law once our numbers are sufficient to maintain ourselves.'

'She's trying to give the evolution tree another branch, one that will grow and bear its own fruit but still developing from the same roots,' said Michel.

Sal remembered Calpurnia's outburst in the tribunal. 'There are some people who don't like that idea,' she said.

'Jezzy had a big argument with the Captain at the beginning,' said Darien, but she knows him well and he finally ruled in her favour. If he had not done so, we wouldn't be here. What she started cannot be stopped now. We have to produce some children. If we can't do that, the experiment will have failed. We will be a small group of freaks and when we die, the idea will die with us. But that is a long time in the future and I don't think we are going to fail. What else do you want to ask about?'

'Is Jezzy expecting to get more people joining in?'

'Yes, she's searching all the time. She found Marcel and Sistus, and the girls here. Now she's found you. There were a few others earlier who baulked and wouldn't join.'

'If we don't get more, it won't be good,' Alicia remarked. 'We will need some genetic diversity, once we get started properly. So, what about it? Are you in?'

Sal still was not quite decided, and sat, silently, wondering.

'We don't want too small a gene pool, but I am sure Jezzy will work out ways round the inbreeding problem, if it looks like happening. There should be more people coming. If not, insemination is still an option.'

'You can go back to Sydney if you want to, but I think you would feel sorry afterwards,' said Euna. 'Once you have taken the plunge, as it were, you will be glad. Come in, the water's lovely,' she laughed.

'Is the water always lovely? Don't you get cold sometimes? Someone said I will have to grow a lot of fat to keep me warm.'

'The rafts don't go into the really cold areas, do they? They follow the warmer currents. We are with Shanghai always, it is our base. If it is cold we can come out of the water any time we like.'

'Do you ever go out and mix in with the other people?'

There was a silence. The young people looked at one another and obviously hesitated to speak. After a while it was Sistus who answered for them all.

'So far, no. We keep very much to ourselves. I should say, we are kept. Jezzy has been careful to avoid drawing attention as far as possible. If we just walked into one of the common rooms or went swimming with the others, it would be a big surprise. She thinks there would be a lot of fuss and some shock. There used to be a lot of trouble, in the landage, about people with different coloured skins and faces, and eyes. That doesn't happen now because all rafters are so much the same. There's hardly any variation in skin colour, slightly different shades of brown, and people don't seem to notice at all when eyes have this little fold in the corner.' He touched his own eyes. 'There was often violence between the different groups. We don't want that to happen again. Jezzy wants to keep quiet about us as long as possible.'

'I heard about Jezzy and her work, by following the index in the capsule programs,' said Sal. 'It was never a secret. It was hard to find it, but anyone could have done it.'

Alicia smiled. 'Not a secret. Jezzy says if you try to hide what you are doing it just encourages people to investigate to find out what is going on. There are entries in the indexes and anyone who looks finds at least a few references to us. But we are included among an enormous number of files, reporting all the other bio research that is done. Almost everyone gets lost. Jezzy guessed that nobody, or only a very few, would follow up and dig deeper. It seems you did. That was quite something. That's how Sistus found out about it, too.'

Sistus spoke now, seriously. 'Sal, Your experience in Sydney caught everyone by surprise. It has drawn attention to what we are doing. The news will get round everywhere now, in every city. It was sure to happen eventually. There should have been some preparation to get people accustomed to the idea of our existence, and what we look like, before we let ourselves be seen in public. Fortunately you are only one person so it hasn't created much of a stir. Not yet, anyway.'

'If it gets difficult, we can always jump into the sea and dive,' said Michel, chuckling. 'They won't be able to catch us there.'

'It must not be allowed to come to that.' said Darien, solemnly. 'We can't manage without the city.'

'Sooner or later, we will have to be independent,' said Sistus.

Michel smiled. 'Sistus has ambitions,' he said.

'I'm still not sure,' said Sal. 'Do you think I will fit in?'

'Why not? You wouldn't have got this far if you hadn't been attracted to the idea in the first place. I think we all went through the same hesitations and doubts. No one's putting pressure on you,' said Sistus.

'Jezzy said you can sing. Show us,' he added.

Sal sang as she had for Jezzy. The group fell silent and still.

'You will fit in,' said Sistus, quietly. 'That was beautiful. Oh yes, you will fit in.'

9

Sal was sure she ought to be asking many more questions but she knew, or could work out, answers to most of them now. She studied the sea sprites carefully. They made no objection when she asked to look more closely at their gills, even to touch them. From a little distance they resembled long and glossy hair hanging behind the shoulders and were quite soft. Sal felt she would get used to them, if she were so equipped. The others explained that on entering the sea a few seconds were needed for adjustments. Blood was diverted into the gills. They enlarged and became somewhat harder rather like a man's penis when mating. The lungs became idle, the throat closed and breathing reflexes were suppressed until they were needed again. She had seen the gulping and intake of breath to get the lungs working on emerging.

'We can't eat under water. I don't like raw fish so it doesn't matter. We have to surface for our meat and veg,' joked Euna.

Sal felt these were ordinary young men and women with interests very much like her own but with a far greater knowledge of the sea and its creatures than she could ever acquire from the data banks and her short, breathless excursions under water.

They told her they were investigating the limits to the depths they could comfortably dive. They could already go much deeper than scuba divers. Under Jezzy's direction they were studying the problem of rapid surfacing. They had encountered no difficulties so far. They said she should talk to Jezzy about this.

The main problem for Sal remained. Was she prepared to allow herself to be changed and to learn to live with this group of strangers in an entirely new way? The modified youngsters were content, but as Sistus had said, not entirely without regrets. They hoped soon to be reproducing, bringing into being a new species, living as amphibians. Could they ever live independently?

Sistus dreamed of a new kind of raft. As a child he had invented a game called Atlantis. His imaginary city could float on the surface but could also submerge itself. There were already submarine exploration vessels capable of going to the deepest parts of the deepest undersea trenches. Why not, some day, submarine cities? As he said, half seriously, it would not be the first time that a fantasy game had become fact. The ocean would provide everything they needed. The sprites all smiled at this dream.

'You are in the uniform of a cadet navigator,' he remarked to Sal.

'Yes. I have nearly finished the course. I suppose I would have to give that up if I joined you here.'

'No. You could continue with the training. There will always be a need for navigators. There would be no reason to stop learning.'

After their meal and talk, the sprites were anxious to get back into the water. Darius returned Sal to Jezzy's office. Jezzy was not there but, he assured her, would know she was waiting and would come soon. Sal was left alone with her thoughts for a while. This was not a bad thing. She had almost made up her mind. Added to her childish dreams of playing with the fish, now she had the exciting but also rather daunting idea that she, with the other girls, might become, would surely become, the source of a new kind of being, a new race, perhaps a new kind of civilisation.

What would it be like?

Jezzy arrived, in her guise as a serious research scientist but still, Sal thought, a witch at heart.

'Rusalka, have you seen, and learned, enough? I will not try to persuade you, except to say that if you join us in our adventures, you will be very welcome. We need you, and more like you, but I have prospects on other rafts waiting to be approached. It is not essential for us to have you. I will not accept you if I think you will have serious regrets.'

'I have decided. I want to join you, Jezzy.'

Jezzy looked at her with those fierce eyes.

'What you have seen and heard has excited you. I do not want to put you off but you should take a little more time to settle down. Leave here, explore the city again for a day, and talk if you wish to Neppy, Calpurnia, anyone you like. Think about it all calmly. You know I cannot reverse the alterations if you allow me to make them. You commit yourself either to life as you already know it, or to a new way of being. There can be no half measures. Come back to me ready for the injections, or get on the ferry and go back to Sydney. I will say no more now. Go away and think.'

When Sal passed out through the Iris Door, and took the car again to the main Shanghai deck, she was shocked when the car she was using stopped without warning. A red light on the screen was flashing. Had it broken down? Such a thing was almost unbelievable, she had hardly known any machine to fail in such a manner. There was a space on the screen to press for information. The reply was that the car could not proceed at present because there was too much traffic. Sal stared around. There were a few people on foot all hurrying away to hide, it seemed, but the street as far as she could see was empty. There were no other cars in sight. As she gazed about in puzzlement, a phalanx of vehicles did appear in the distance, coming towards her. This was not normal heavy traffic. There were hundreds, and behind the leaders more hundreds and behind them yet more. It was like an incoming tide, they were driving forward steadily, filling the broad street from side to side. Many carried flags and banners on poles. As they came close enough for her to read them, she saw they carried slogans like DONT DIVIDE

OUR CITY, and SHANGHAI IS ONE, another screamed LIVE IN PEACE, NOT PIECES, another; FRAGMENTATION IS FOLLY, DISUNITY IS DISGRACEFUL, and so on. A graphic, painted image showed a human cartoon figure standing on a diagrammatic city raft which was splitting in two beneath him. He had a foot on each as the parts drew apart, so would soon fall into the sea. This was what Erik and Myra had talked about on the ferry.

The multitude riding by was noisy. Voices were raised, some seemed to be chanting. There was a half hearted attempt by some to sing, but the column was so large and so long that those who drew level with Sal and continued past her, could not possibly hear what those far behind were shouting, singing or doing.

Sal touched her hologram screen again, and again, until she found an explanatory broadcast. This showed a crowd like the one that still moved past her, but these had banners and slogans of the opposite persuasion; TOO BIG TO BEAR, SEPARATE OR STINK, TIED IN TAPE, BUGGER BEING BIGGEST. The holo-commentators made it clear that these demonstrations had been organised to express mounting feelings among the ordinary citizens. There was a serious political proposal to cut the huge Shanghai raft into three, each with a population of about 10 million. As the multitude passed by, Sal watched the screen and listened to the explanations and arguments presented. Various people and officials came before her in hologram form. Engineers agreed that the raft could indeed be divided into parts, it was feasible from a practical viewpoint, but though agreeing on what was possible they disagreed about whether it should be done. Already, for convenience and simplicity of management, Shanghai had been arranged in modules, each more or less self-contained. Administrative districts corresponded to major structural members below the waterline. These would be the basis for any division. It could be made to happen. Several separate cities would be freed to wander as their navigators chose, each of them large enough to function successfully. Demographers and engineers showed with diagrams and statistics that a city of ten or twenty million citizens would be comfortable and safe. Sydney itself was cited as an example, still close enough to be seen and visited by many of the citizens.

The opposition insisted, there was nothing wrong with living in Shanghai, so why change? Sal could not follow all the arguments she heard, nor the occasional shouts from the processioners who drove by in a fairly ragged fashion, the numbers gradually thinning until only a few stragglers trailed along. On impulse, Sal instructed her car to start again and join the procession. After some hesitation it moved forward and joined the tail. Sal found herself alongside another car on which rode a young man. He looked at her, smiling, and came closer alongside. Sal decided to speak.

'What's this all about?' she asked.

'Don't you know? Where have you been living? Some people want to divide Shanghai into two or three smaller rafts.'

'I am a visitor from Sydney. I've never seen anything like this. Are they serious? Is this procession allowed, I mean, legal?'

'Legal? Nobody says it isn't. Anything that isn't definitely forbidden in Shanghai is legal. Don't you have demos in Sydney?'

'Demos?'

'It's an old word, it means showing that a huge lot of people want to change something. Or not to change it in this case. I am on that side, that's why I am here.'

'But can't you go to the Captain about it? That's what we do in Sydney, and he deals with it.'

'We don't have captains here. We call the officers mandarins. It's no good appealing to 983 about this. He has to follow the popular vote on an issue as important as this.'

'983?'

'That's his number, Merlin 983 is our Chief Mandarin. I suppose he's like your Captain. He's been ruling this raft for years. His term runs out in a few weeks. He keeps being been elected and re-elected but he says he is going to retire this time. There will have to be an election for someone to take his place and this business of dividing the raft is the main issue. If the vote goes that way we might have to find three new Chief Mandarins, or just find someone to replace 983.'

'What will happen?'

'You've seen the banners. A lot of idiots want to divide Shanghai into three smaller rafts, chopping us into pieces. I think it is a rotten idea.'

'Divide? Why?'

'Why indeed? We are happy as we are. The queen of all cities, the biggest and best. Their only reason is that the raft is too complicated and too big for them to control. Some of the officers are saying it is inefficient to have such a big city. What they really mean is, it's too big for them to manage in the way they want to manage it.'

'Aren't they managing it very well, then?'

'Most of the time the staff are nothing but a bloody nuisance. We'd get along well enough if they just leave us alone. If something does go wrong, like a crime, it's the marine's job to sort it out, and they are quite good at that. There is no need for change, and I don't understand why some want it so badly.'

'I don't think Nemo, the Captain on my raft, wants to change anything.' As she said this, Sal felt a pang of conscience. She spoke of *my raft* when what she was planning to do was to leave it. One of her reasons for wanting to leave was that Sydney never changed.

The procession moved steadily on. Sal soon became tired of it, feeling that the future of Shanghai was not going to affect her much. If she became a sea sprite her life would be different whichever city she was in. Anyway, she might still change her mind and return to Sydney. She instructed her car to leave the crowd. The young man she had chatted with came with her. They spent the next few hours and the night together. The casual relationship was pleasant but meant little to either of them.

The next morning, her mind made up, Sal returned to the laboratory.

10

The injections did not hurt. The fine needles went in so quickly and out again that this part of the operation was over while Sal was still waiting for things to begin. Several days previously Jezzy had taken samples of her body cells for preliminary culture and growth. She instructed Sal in the use of the instruments enabling her to observe the intricate and delicate procedure used to make the cells pluripotent and subsequently to re-arrange their genetic instructions. Manipulation of the DNA was done before her eyes, carefully, and explained to her. The cells were further grown in cultures under carefully guarded and controlled conditions. Sal was amazed to see how rapid their replication was. These leader cells, as Jezzy called them, when implanted, would instruct others nearby to grow with them, resurrecting the old slumbering codes that, till now, had been moribund. It was the survival of these relics in her body that made Sal, and a proportion of other youthful humans, suitable for the coming transformation. The implants following were painless but she became aware soon that something was changing her ears. There was a sensation of enlargement and pressure that seemed to be deep in her head. The feeling took several days to subside, after which she detected nothing more for some time.

Jezzy warned that for a few weeks Sal would be going through a difficult time. She was instructed that during the period of her changing she must be entirely celibate. For some weeks she would belong to no group, not a normal human like those outside the lab, but not yet one of the free swimmers who knew each other so well and who could sport and lie together whenever they wished. It was not known what the effects might be if she became pregnant while her body was genetically in this transitional stage. Later, when she was fully grown into the new form, she must mate only with others of the same sort. The new people would not be capable of interbreeding with the old race.

There was little to do while waiting for the changes to take effect. Sal spoke to Neppy and Calpurnia, to say farewell. Neppy was sad, but did not argue. He agreed, there were other girls. Perhaps he would find someone as lively as she had been. He did not sound sure of this. Calpurnia was short with her, even angry, and uninterested when Sal assured her that she was not going to become monstrous. The counsellor must have reported to Nemo because a few hours later he himself called Sal. She was astonished that he should bother but he chatted amiably with her for quarter of an hour, wished her well and was interested to learn about the others who had already gone through the alterations. He asked also about the likely division of the Shanghai raft into smaller units. The protest demo Sal had tagged along with for a few minutes, had been heavily outnumbered by the other procession calling for change. Influenced by the numerical result, the decision of the assembled Shanghai advisory council, chaired by the Chief Mandarin, was the consequence. There would be three rafts. A minor dispute about names had been resolved amicably. Three cities, Shanghai Alpha, Shanghai Main and Shanghai One would still rank among the largest rafts. All would claim to have arisen with the original city.

Nemo asked if the laboratory would be affected. Was Jezzy's department going to be split up or even disbanded? Could one of the separated rafts contain it all? Sal did not know. She asked Jezzy afterwards. The laboratory would not be divided, she was told. Her department would continue as part of Shanghai Alpha. The other two rafts would have bio labs, though smaller. Jezzy expected to help organise and select staff for them. Torva would definitely head the one on Shanghai Main.

The separation would take some time to complete but work was beginning immediately. Preparatory planning had been done long in advance. The engineering robots began to carry out the multifarious disconnections and re-connections that were needed at the basal level, above and below waterline. Mundane services such as power, water, drainage, sewer and gas pipes, had to be diverted, re-routed and rearranged before anything would show on the upper decks. At every stage, the elaborate systems would be fully maintained. When done, each raft must be entirely self-supporting and fully independent. Communication between all cities would continue as before. There would be two new, separate, fusion power units to replace the one that already existed. Constructing these would be the most substantial effort undertaken and was still going on. There would have to be an election soon to find three Senior Mandarins to become Chiefs

Sal now had her own accommodation capsule in the small residential section of the laboratory. The other youngsters had adjacent capsules. All shared a central hall for recreation and informal meetings. Meals were provided there, on demand. There were some unoccupied sleep capsules similar to her own, waiting, she was told, for newcomers joining Jezzy's sea children as and when they came along. How many there might be was unknown but Jezzy was still searching, as she had searched to find Marcel, Alicia and Euna. Darien, Sistus and Sal herself had in effect selected themselves.

The sprites never ventured out into the main raft community. They were a very friendly group, comfortable but enclosed. Sal began to recognise, they were in a special and strange situation, isolated from the general population. Yet as soon as she dived into the ocean, as she would in a few weeks be doing, she would be free to move out and venture into a realm beyond the control of anyone, even the dominant person of Jezzy herself.

It was several days before Sal realised, with a sense of shock, that there were no surveillance instruments or listening devices anywhere in Jezzy's territory. Nothing said or done could be observed from other parts of the lab, let alone the outside. For the first time in her life, she had privacy. She did not welcome it. It was a strange, lonely feeling which was quite distressing. She had grown up in a world where everything about her was known to everyone who bothered to look and listen. This had been so familiar and fundamental that, like breathing, she had hardly been aware of it unless there was some kind of crisis. Now it was as if she had been cut off from a vital support. *No one was watching now.* She had always accepted that if she needed help it would be there. *Now, nobody cared.* But then, she reminded herself, with all the surveillance, nobody in the ordinary rafts ever truly *cared*.

Darien, to whom she spoke about it, told her Jezzy had insisted on the total disconnection from the beginning of her rule. The lab area was indeed her empire. A law unto herself, she would never have her work supervised. Her results were made known only when she was ready.

'Jezzy and Merlin are old friends, Sal,' said Torva. 'They were schoolies together. I don't know how many years ago it was. He encourages her all the time, lets her have her own way with things. When she started her research and didn't want surveillance, he made sure she was free of it. Better get used to it.' Sistus too understood her feelings at once when she hinted at them. He had experienced the same sense of disorientation when he had come to Jezzy. He admitted that he still did not feel entirely at ease but was looking forward to a time when the sea sprites would belong to a larger society of people like themselves. There would, he remarked, have to be plans for this, everything must be worked out in preparation. He was a very thoughtful young man, almost opposite to Darien who seemed, more often than not, to leap before looking.

It took weeks for Sal to become accustomed to the absence of the watchers. She began to appreciate the situation at last. The others in the group pointed out, in the water where they spent much of their time there was no one looking.

She enjoyed Sistus' company. He liked to hear her sing. They talked a good deal about music when he was out of the water. He had a good bass voice with that little extra resonance that, she knew now, was common to all the sprites. As she herself changed, she sensed that her voice too would soon have the same small extra depth and sense of feeling. They often sang together, trawling through the archives to find suitable duets. She dreamed of a time when they could plunge into the ocean together but that was not yet to be. When she was ready, she thought, she would choose Sistus to be the *father* of her children. This idea was strange at first, but became stronger when Sistus suggested the same thing. They must wait for her to reach her final maturity.

'Are you keeping up with your nav studies?' he asked. Sal was puzzled by the sudden change of subject.

'Why do you ask that?'

'I just wondered. We all need something to keep our brains busy.' He left it there.

Sal understood only half of what she had been told about the transformation of her body but resolved to learn more. While the changes were developing within her, Jezzy began to treat her as a student. She was invited to spend time with the old woman as she went about the laboratory. Before coming to Shanghai all the science Sal had learned came through the teaching capsules; there had been nothing in the way of practical activity beyond the artfully devised simulations and virtuals. She now began to learn what it was like to set up and carry out real experiments and trials. Instead of predictable results served up in hologram form, now she was shown how to use a neutronscope to study at the sub atomic level, how to set up an old fashioned MRI scanner and interpret the results. There were more modern instruments and methods. It was challenging. While trying to set up and carry out a test she could not switch things off and wander away to pick up the show later exactly where it had been abandoned. This had been normal before. If things went wrong she could not call up a re-run or correction. Working with real materials and instruments, no longer being watched and guided at every instant, she developed a sense of personal responsibility, which she had hardly needed before. As the days went on, Jezzy seemed to find her a good pupil and was prepared to spend more time with her. Sal herself became deeply interested in what was being done and, before long, could justly describe herself as an assistant rather than a mere observer or experimental subject.

Jezzy always called her Rusalka, and occasionally addressed her as *My Little Mermaid*. They became good friends. One day in a moment of exasperation over some error of her own which Jezzy pounced on, Sal swore and called her a horrid old witch. The woman stopped instantly what she had been saying, let loose her long hair, glared at the girl, raised her claw like hands and fingers, screeched 'Hee Hee,' and for a couple of minutes played the part. Sal, after an instant's terror, burst into uncontrolled laughter. Jezzy relaxed and they laughed together. Torva had told her she would come to love Jezzy. This was happening. The thought occurred to her that Jezzy and she were coming to feel as she supposed a mother and child might have felt during the landages. This was the experience that Alicia and Euna were seeking.

Meanwhile, as Alicia had warned her, Sal felt discomforts as her ears changed. There was a swelling behind her lower jawbone and in her throat. Jezzy examined her frequently and was satisfied. The time when Sal would be able to breath under water was approaching. There were more things to learn. The under water code of dots and dashes was one of these and using the terminals for undersea navigation required some study. There were the expected subtle changes to her singing voice.

Alicia and Euna became pregnant within days of each other, a discovery they kept secret from all but Jezzy for a week or so. It soon became obvious to everyone who saw them. They themselves were delighted. Jezzy examined them with close attention. It became clear almost immediately that the developing embryos were going to have efficient gills. The girls were breeding true. There was more learning to do, preparations to be made for the care of tiny infants. Jezzy made it very clear that the babies, when they emerged, would be a collective responsibility for her little tribe of sprites. Everyone, including Sal, would be counted as a parent. Jezzy chose not to tell who, biologically, had fertilised the ova. All the lads must to learn to fill their roles as caring fathers. Any investigation of the DNA codes was prevented. A few robots were set to work preparing a nursery adjacent to the ocean exit. This building work was soon to be much extended.

Beyond the lab, there were developments of a very different kind. The events of Sal's little tribunal in Sydney had been played in simulation over and over again in all the cities. In every ocean, the story of *Rusalka* became well known. There was, as Sistus had predicted, widespread and growing interest among the rafters in what they were doing. Jezzy's researches were discussed and argued over. Not all the reaction was benign. Calpurnia was not alone in her feelings of disgust and outrage.

Jezzy was already a public figure by worldwide reputation. Her prestige was vast. Even landlubbers, it was said, had heard of her and regarded her with awe. Now her fame was even greater. Too important to be ordered to do anything against her will, she was eventually persuaded by the Chief Mandarin to issue some pictures of her group. To make a favourable impression the sea-children were carefully posed to show that they were normal in all respects other than the flowing, featherlike gills hanging gracefully down over and behind their shoulders. The intention was to inform and reassure the worldwide populations. Among the general rafters the pictures aroused greater excitement than anyone, except perhaps Sistus, had anticipated.

Many rafters were alarmed, angry and even afraid. Old superstitions that had been almost forgotten centuries before, surfaced again. People spoke of the sanctity of the human body, the arrogance of geneticists interfering in the natural development of children, the dangers of directing evolution along new paths towards an unforeseeable, non-human or transcendent human future. The stir of controversy was muted, for there were, after all, only a handful of these *creatures*. Nonetheless, arguments were demanded to justify Jezzy's work. Something like an official line began to emerge from the offices of the Chief Mandarin who felt obliged to defend his decision to give Jezzy her freedom

The point had been made in Nemo's court. Everyone on the city rafts was, directly or indirectly, a product of deliberate, intentional reconstructions of the genome. No one, the official statements stressed, could identify with or pretend to represent what some tried to call the *natural human being*. No one now on the rafts was born with unaltered genes. There had been a thousand and more years of the city rafts, with repeated computerised *mix and match* control. The effect over the long term had been to remove all the more obvious but trivial variations between peoples. Variety was retained, no two humans ever looked alike, there were no clones and no planned conformity to any eugenic ideal but neither was anyone revoltingly ugly, deformed or mentally defective. Superficial differences of skin colour that had once created deadly hatreds and persecution had been blended into a nearly uniform shade of light brown skin. Perfect health was the norm.

Terrible injuries could be healed, organs replaced, limbs re-grown. Lifespans had been tripled. In the strictly supervised cities, there was no hunger. Any adult living now should thank the scientists for their work over the past millennia and encourage them to continue new studies and trials. Without this great tradition, everyone living now would be disabled or dead. All had benefited. What Jezzy's team was doing now was only a small and logical extension of what had been done before. It was exciting and should be welcomed. All these benefits and more must be attributed to the advances of biological, physical and social sciences.

Among the many millions and billions on the rafts, there were, nevertheless, some dissenters. There was, for them, as the Captain's and Mandarin's advisers pointed out, always a desperate alternative. Those who objected to what had been done to humankind and what more might still be done could leave the rafts and live on land. Someone dug out of the archives, few knew from where, an ancient saying that was judged to be perfectly descriptive of this possibility. It was broadcast to every screen on the raft.

Living on land as it was now,

In such condition, there is no place for industry and consequently no culture of the earth; no navigation, no commodious building; no instruments of moving and removing such things as require much force, no knowledge of the face of the earth; no account of time; no arts, no letters, no society, and which is worst of all, continuall feare and danger of violent death; and the life of man, solitary, poore, nasty, brutish and short.[1]

This, for the time being, was temporarily effective in quietening the nascent opposition. Sistus, whom Sal was beginning to respect greatly, pointed out to her that this argument, containing as it did the threat of marooning, was not a fair answer to genuinely thoughtful doubters. There remained an undercurrent of honest worry.

In some quarters the view surfaced that the firmly controlled, disciplined but peaceful, if rather dull, almost utopian way of life developed on the city rafts, was threatened.

'Some think,' said Jezzy, acting her role as the evil witch, 'that my children will rise up and take over the cities, rob them of their easy ways of living, drown them in the ocean and feed them to the sharks. What nonsense. If they think like that, maybe that is what we should do. Hee hee.'

'You don't mean it,' said Darien, taking her seriously as he always did, 'the future must be one of co-operation. We cannot live without the support of the cities. They will understand that we remain humans in mutual friendship, different but alike in all essential respects.' Darien, Sistus said, was over optimistic and a little naive.

'Different is essentially *different*. Some day we will be compelled to build our own raft,' he said. Jezzy chuckled and treated him to one of her distorted smiles. Sal became aware that Sistus, when out of the water, was spending long periods with Jezzy. There was more going on between them than she could discover. Were these two up to something? Sal wondered.

[1] Thomas Hobbes, *Leviathan* Part 1, Chapter 13, 1651

'Jezzy,' said Torva, 'is always up to something.' As usual, he did not know what it could be. In Jezzy's realm there was no surveillance. There were secrets.

In Shanghai there was an attempt to organise a protest march, or drive-by, like the one Sal had seen and briefly joined. The demo was ill supported; the procession ragged and untidy. The cars and banner carriers drifted away and dispersed.

Among young people there was a very different response. When news of Jezzy's success spread, she was deluged with requests from youngsters in every city for tests to find out if they were eligible for what was being called *the sea change*. Most of them, like Sal at the beginning, had a juvenile attitude. They wanted to swim like fish for fun, now and then, when it suited them, and only if the water was warm. Most did not imagine much more.

This was something Jezzy had partly anticipated but she was nonetheless astonished at the enormous surge of interest. Thousands, growing to millions of enquiries, with submitted DNA records, poured in. Fortunately, the machines coped easily with the rush. Everything was fed instantly and automatically to the search engines for sorting. In the enormous majority, replies were sent out immediately to explain that the records showed the applicant could not be accepted. Disappointment was the rule. Jezzy, with help from the Mandarin's staff, drafted a tactful public message of explanation. The childish dreamers were put off. Most had not been very serious in the first place.

Some were found who matched. In the global population they were a small minority but in total there were hundreds and thousands. For these, it was necessary to establish a careful and exact procedure. It was essential that they should understand thoroughly what would be involved. The necessary information, images, explanatory discussions, interviews, were prepared and produced, transmitted for hologram viewing in every city. All over the oceans, young people faced the issues that Sal had faced. Most after all decided they would go no further.

Those who did persist were required to visit Shanghai. Jezzy succeeded in obtaining official support for them to travel by air in a series of helicopter relays from city to city across the globe. They would travel by ferry or chopper to a reception point on one of the larger rafts, wait there until a group of a dozen or so had been collected, then hop after hop to another collecting point and thence, at last to Shanghai and the lab. It was a major logistics exercise, organised and supported by the Chief Mandarin's administrators. Small streams rising from a thousand springs flowed together and together to become a river.

The laboratory faced the prospect of scores, hundreds, of teenagers arriving, by air or ferry to join the sea sprites. The regular research work must continue without interruption but new construction was urgently needed. Jezzy's section of Shanghai was already large. Now it must be expanded. The lab could no longer be regarded merely as a place of work, it must have adequate residential accommodation attached. Each addition must be provided with everything necessary for comfortable living, effectively establishing a small town behind the Iris Door, attached to the greater city.

It was, fortunately, not the first time that Shanghai had engineered such growth. Archived plans and instructions were resurrected, recomputed and downloaded to the robot control centre. The main deck was first extended into the ocean. The machines worked to make and equip new recreation halls and restaurants, personal sleeping capsules were put in place; power supplies established, new hydroponic towers set up, food synthesisers, fish tanks, desalination plants below the waterline, nothing was overlooked. The new work was completed in a surprisingly short time, hardly noticed by the vast majority of Shanghai people who were in any case expecting soon to cut their city into three. Jezzy's realm was still shut off from the rest. Sistus, when not in the sea, made himself busy finding out what was being done and, it appeared, inspecting everything. Sal remembered he had told her he was a robot master when she first met the sprites. Robots could not deviate from the instructions they had been given. Sistus whispered to Sal that he was getting to know every part of the Raft on their side of the city.

'I think I understand everything about it,' he said, quietly. 'We could be entirely self-contained, Sal. If we wanted to, we could be entirely independent of the main raft.'

'What would be the point of that?' she asked.

'No point at present but we might need to know how, some day. How are your studies going?'

'I haven't done much lately. Why do you ask?'

'I think you should keep up with them. There's always a need for good navigators. Think about it, Sal.' *Independent of the main raft?* Puzzled, beginning to think Sistus was not telling her all his thoughts, Sal resolved to spend more time studying her professional subject.

As soon as their quarters were ready, the newcomers began to arrive. Once they landed in Shanghai they were moved immediately to the laboratory, which now was becoming unusually busy with people. Jezzy was obliged to set up a department with Torva at its head, to control the admissions, to welcome the newcomers, and, if they remained, to see them through the initial stages of their operation. The existing sea sprites were required to act as hosts, to explain to every newcomer what would happen if they remained. They were all very busy all the time now, their games in the sea had to be curtailed.

Sal herself was growing her new organs and discovering, day by day, that she could, as expected, stay under water for longer. In Sydney a few minutes had been her limit. Now as the gill fronds lengthened she could manage ten, fifteen, twenty. She became acquainted again with fish that swam round the raft. It was crazy to think that some of them already knew her and came to pay their respects, for the Sydney raft was now far away. Even so, She felt, when swimming, that she was among old friends. Out of the water, Torva asked her to meet as many as possible of the newcomers, show them what was happening to her, explaining as well as she could what the work at the cellular level involved, concealing nothing, admitting what she had to admit, but communicating her enthusiasm.

The two pregnant girls also showed off to the incomers but were anxious to do nothing that might upset their own and their children's development. It was well known that a healthy foetus develops a sensory apparatus as it grows. With the senses there comes a brain adapted to interpret the impulses that already, long before birth, stream in for decoding. Sounds from the mother's body and from outside, are heard within the uterus. Alicia and Euna breathed, their hearts beat, their blood circulated, they talked, sang, listened to music. They swam in and under the sea. All was heard by the tiny ones within. When the babies came, they already had the beginnings of understanding. They were mammalian and would be able to survive under water almost immediately after birth.

11

Day after day, more young people arrived. A few departed again after realising that the changes they had contemplated were not, after all, what they wanted. They went home and explained to their home raft friends what they had learned. The cities were waking up to a fuller realisation of what Jezzy was doing.

Most of the new arrivals stayed and elected to go through the process. As the numbers grew it was clear that there was too much for Jezzy alone to cope with. She was still obliged to supervise the other work of the laboratory. She called on Torva and Darien for help with the intake, which they were well able to give. The arrivals had to be accommodated, fed, attend informal meetings where things were explained to them, and meet the sprites who had already been through the genetic processing. Sal was called on to show herself and tell her feelings. Alicia and Euna proudly showed off their expanding silhouettes.

When not meeting the newcomers, Sal spent a little time in the learning capsules but gave much more to the sea, gaining confidence and venturing a little deeper and further out each time, joining the other sprites in underwater explorations and sport. As a group they often ventured far away from the raft. When they surfaced, they were always within sight of Shanghai, for the towers were very prominent. The fish they encountered beyond the immediate vicinity of home were less numerous and, to Sal, in search of colour and variety, a little disappointing. Occasionally there was a vast swarm of one kind, sardines, herring or mackerel, herded by sharks, barracudas or killer whales into a whirling cluster. The predators plunged into the mass time and again. Above, diving sea birds pounced repeatedly and rose into the air with full beaks. The numbers of small fish in the multitudes seemed no fewer after these raids.

Preoccupied with their easy prey, the sharks seemed to take no notice of the young humans, but these were not places to linger. Using the terminals to guide them, the group would swim gently back to the raft together, taking their time. If there was any current, they knew the raft itself would be carried along too, so there was no risk of being swept away.

The times Sal loved most were when, by herself, she descended as far as she dared under the raft where there was an abundance of variety and colour. It became too dark to see anything if she ventured too far under, but around the edges all kinds of life existed. There were extensive growths of barnacles. These creatures, Sal knew, often attached themselves to whales and the raft must seem to them like a gigantic whale. Sea plants were abundant. At certain levels she felt sure there were corals too, though not in any quantity and not, at least not yet, developing into reef-like structures. She wondered if all these growths affected the general buoyancy of the raft. She supposed the engineers made proper allowances. Anti-fouling coatings and paints did not survive long enough to be of any use. There were special underwater robots programmed to keep the skin of the raft fairly clean, but there were advantages in letting the growths accumulate up to a point. The organic matter scraped off was kept and returned to the raft for recycling.

On return to the decks after her submarine excursions, when she was released from the reception procedures she would study navigation and, with or without the other sea children, she worked sometimes in the laboratory. Her occupation was listed officially as laboratory assistant and she was counted as a Shanghai citizen. She wore the usual lab uniform, her head covered. The hood had a large bag into which she could bundle her gills to keep them out of he way when she was working. She had been training with Jezzy for some weeks. When the old woman was too busy or too tired to attend to her, she became Darien's assistant. Under his supervision she too began to administer the injections and implants as new candidates continued to stream in. Darien, she learned, was a gentle and friendly man, anxious always to be kind and understanding, but as he himself admitted, prone to acting on impulse when a little pause for reflection would have been beneficial. Before long Sal could do independently everything that was required. Her theoretical knowledge was limited but she carried out the routine procedures perfectly. When she had time, she ensconced herself in a learning capsule and continued studying navigation, filling in the gaps in her original studies. Jezzy seemed anxious that she should do this and Sistus sometimes asked how she was getting along with it. Would she soon be a fully qualified navigator?

'What does that matter?' she asked. 'Shanghai has plenty of navigators.'

Sistus shrugged. 'Can't have too many,' he said. 'It would be a pity if you forgot it all.'

The numbers of newcomers tapered off quite rapidly. Anyone who had thought of joining, had, by now, decided either for or against. Jezzy expected there would be only a few more applicants. A line had to be drawn, and soon she drew it. No more would be accepted. This was a relief because it was becoming difficult to accommodate those who had already arrived. When the numbers were reckoned, they came to nearly five hundred. Jezzy was delighted, yet Sal could see, she was also somewhat overwhelmed. Despite her wisdom, she had not expected this response so quickly and was not ready for it. No one was very sure what came next.

The rapid influx of so many young people had changed the atmosphere of the laboratory greatly. It had been an intimate working community of a few dedicated researchers and assistants, all of whom knew one another but most of them also had lives outside in the general Shanghai city. The regular staff came and went as any other workers in a city department would. Now the laboratory area, large though it was, seemed filled with strangers from all kinds of different rafts, many of them barely heard of before, all speaking Raftanglish but with slight variations of pronunciation that occasionally caused minor misunderstandings. The atmosphere remained generally positive. A useful and necessary step was to issue name and number tags for each arriving novice to wear so that they could quickly identify one another. Jezzy would not allow the use of the ID numbers they had brought with them from their various rafts. New numbers were allocated and recorded. When it came to beginning the injections and implants, the young people were given appointments and had to hang about waiting for their time to arrive. They amused themselves as best they could in the existing game capsules and the recreation hall. They began to make friends with one another, tending to group more or less naturally. While waiting for their modifications to develop they occupied themselves in ways similar to those they had adopted when in their own cities. They played games, formed teams, set up friendly contests. They could swim but none yet could join the handful of 'veterans' in their sub surface explorations, and no sexual entertainment was permitted for the time being. This caused some tensions but the reasons for the ban were fully understood and there were no infringements.

All the new people had, on their previous rafts, been occupied in work of some kind and had received training in their trade. They were all young and at different levels in their courses but Jezzy urged them to continue learning through the capsules. There was also work for them in Jezzy's realm, which counted as a newly growing department or district, a kind of suburb, not wholly integrated within the city. As far as possible they retained the roles they had before. Some of the existing staff were reluctant to work with the novices and departed without fuss to the main city. Their tasks in the laboratory were taken over by newcomers waiting for their personal changes to mature. The expanded community on Jezzy's side of the enclosing Iris Door functioned smoothly. The small exodus of older staff had some inevitable consequences in the city as a whole. They talked. More and more citizens now were learning of Jezzy's work. Not all were favourably impressed.

Michel was much occupied with his research into sea life. When not swimming he began to compile annotated accounts of his discoveries, making digital images and accurate drawings. His particular interest was tracing the life cycle of the various creatures he found. Often these were well known species but hitherto little had been discovered about how they survived day by day and over longer periods. Previous divers, restricted by their mechanical breathing apparatus and the *Bodner* type gills, had not been able to gather this kind of information. Michel could remain under water for as long as he chose to follow and observe individual creatures for hours. His findings and colourful images were published as presentations through the inter city net. He came into contact thereby with scores of other marinologists and was establishing a growing reputation. He found others with interests like his own among the incoming youngsters. They were ready to help him, expecting to work with him more closely as soon as they could dive with him. More of his fellow research marinologists in other cities learned of his ability to spend long hours underwater. Some of them envied him.

Alicia and Euna became more and more preoccupied as their time for giving birth approached. Jezzy assured them there would be no difficulties. They had ample advice from the inter raft net. Among the newcomers there were a score or more partly trained professional carers who would help them to see the infants through their first few hours and days. The babies, when they arrived, would be very little different from other human children. Their gills would develop very rapidly and they would soon be swimming with their mothers.

Euna was first, by a couple of days. Nothing like this had happened on any raft for hundreds of years, but attended by Jezzy and assisted by too many young specialists who had spent many hours delving into ancient records, the male child arrived and, like any other baby, screamed for a while, was cleaned up, separated from the umbilical cord, and learned to suck and sleep. The gills, like the organs of sex, were vestigial but pronounced by Jezzy to be entirely healthy. When Alicia's time arrived, everything for her little girl also went perfectly. The two young mothers were beside themselves with joy. The babies were passed round a multitude of admiring and excited folk, including the novices. For Jezzy it was an unprecedented triumph. The little bundles were allocated numbers one and two, Una and Secundus for the time being. They would be able to choose their own names later. Sal visited them often and was asked to sing to the babes sometimes.

Sistus and Sal were becoming very close friends. He would often come to talk with her and share his worries. She soon realised that he was not telling her everything; there was something in his relationship with Jezzy that he would not discuss. She overheard the two of them once when they were obviously in an argument. She was on her way through the laboratory and had paused briefly to admire again the great ray as it seemed to fly above her. She heard Sistus saying, 'I am right about this, Jezzy. It cannot, will not go on for ever.' Jezzy's reply was not clear and the conversation stopped immediately when Sal revealed herself.

When she was considered ready, it was with Sistus that she lay. It was a slightly strange and nervous union for her. She was anxious about the likely result. Until now, sex for her had been little more than an idle and carefree game that boys and girls, men and women, played when the mood took them. It had never been important. A minimal physical attraction, which could develop between almost any couple and at anytime, would result in an encounter that might be over within minutes, like a quick snack between meals or a brief entertainment before sleeping. If both felt like it and had time and energy to spare, they could repeat the game a few times, make the pleasure last longer, with hardly more thought than would be given to a VR game or an hour or two on a tennis court.

When Sal and Sistus joined, both knew that there might and very probably would be, a pregnancy. This made Sal self conscious and anxious. After a few intimate meetings she became able to relax and enjoy herself more. Their intimacy extended into their everyday behaviour. For the first time in both their lives, they felt they should not engage with anyone else, at least until the expected result was achieved. The baby, when it came, would be their own; their responsibility. They would know, and get to know, their own child. This would be an entirely new experience for both. It would be part of a great adventure together.

One day, both weary, in each other's arms, Sistus whispered in Sal's ear.

'Sal, do you know Jezzy's birth year?'

'No. It's a secret. She has never said. She is very old, everyone knows that.'

'I can't find her records. She has hidden them somehow. I think she must be the oldest person in Shanghai. Perhaps she's the oldest person in the world.'

'She is an old witch, after all. If anyone is immortal, she must be. She has probably made herself a magical elixir'

'There is no magic. In her serious moments she does not claim to be a witch.'

'Then she is just a very, very old woman.'

'Yes. Yes. There is no elixir. Think about that, Sal.'

'I… I will. You have been spending a lot of time with her. You must know her very well, Sistus, better than anyone.'

'I do know her. She is very fond of you, Sal and she is very old. Not quite what she was.'

'Why are you…' She did not finish the question. Sistus was asleep, or pretending to be. Sal lay awake for a little longer, pondering. Jezzy was always up to something, Torva had said. It was so. And what was Sistus up to with the witch who was not a witch, but an old, old woman? Old. Old. What would happen when…. Sal was overtaken by sleep before she could complete that thought.

Darien, Sistus and Michel, were released from their duties with the immigrants and returned to more normal routines in the lab. They had some time free and would often leave Alicia and Euna attending to their babies to sport in the sea. They invented simple water games, sometimes chasing one another in a kind of tag, playing hide and seek under the raft, and what they called porpoising, which involved swimming as fast as possible below the surface, then leaping out of the water and plunging again, continuing so in undulating fashion, in and out for long distances together, turning at last and finding their way back to the landing stage using their terminals. Sal's gills now functioning perfectly she joined in enthusiastically. One of her dreams was coming true.

She did not mind that the men usually left her behind in their wake. These were not races. If she lost touch altogether, which sometimes happened if the boys forged far ahead, she could find her way back to the dock with her direction finder. In one such game they had left her as usual but she found suddenly that she had caught up with them. They had stopped playing and were together in a group, heads out of the sea, breathing air. She came up among them, cleared her throat.

'What is it? Why have you stopped?'

Darien raise an arm and pointed. 'See it?

Sal at first could see nothing unusual at all, but, lifting herself briefly further out of the water, glimpsed a dark object on the sea surface some distance away, rising and falling with the regular ocean swell.

'Isn't it a bit of rubbish? Flotsam, something washed out from the land.'

'No, Sal. It's a raft, well, a boat, I think, a crude sort of yacht. There's somebody on it,' said Darien.

'There's a sail,' said Marcel. 'There's two, maybe three, people.'

Sistus dived, followed by the others. They could now see the object against the light and swam towards it. From below it was lozenge shaped and appeared to be made of timber, a material they had rarely seen. They had learned that on land there grew trees which could be cut into logs or boards, and which would float. They swum close to the boat, for that was what it must be. Taking another quick look, they could see there were three small human beings on the vessel. Darien surfaced, spitting and opening his lungs, swam forward and grasped the boat's gunwale, pulling himself half out of the water.

'Darien, no,' yelled Sistus, gasping for air.

The small vessel tilted under Darien's weight. As he rose, one of the boat people, open eyes wide, looked at him in astonishment. It was a young male who reacted with horror, yelled and scrambled away. The female child showed the same signs of terror, but the third, an adult man, stooped and picked up a long, thin rod and raised it in a threatening manner, screaming something that made no sense.

'Fok awa yee deil.'

The stick had a sharp, barbed point. He yelled again and thrust down and out.

'Tyek tha yee munster, awa wi yee.' The barb penetrated Darien's shoulder and he fell back into the water and down. The other swimmers dived immediately after him. He was bleeding. All three followed, caught him and drew him as swiftly as they could away from the boat. Apart from his injury, he was in difficulties. He had been struck when he was breathing air. As he fell, he had swallowed water. Sal and Sistus helped him to recover by hugging him to expel the fluid from his lungs. Blood gushed out of his wound. Michel signed to them that they must get help and rose to the surface. His wrist clear of the sea, he triggered an emergency signal. It was not the first time people from a raft had got themselves into difficulties. Michel hoped that the signal would be received and the marines would come looking for them. The alarm call sent, he dived, found the others and helped to pull the struggling Darien to the surface and with them back towards Shanghai. Darien seemed utterly confused and hardly able to swim or breathe but as they made progress, he recovered a little, although the blood still flowed and his arm was useless.

They had lost sight of the boat. Sistus ascended towards the surface to look for it, though he did not let his head emerge fully into the air. He was alarmed to see that although they had swum some distance, the boat was still close and was keeping pace with them. Darien was leaving a trail of blood, which might be followed. Could the man with the weapon see them? Sistus dived and joined the others, signing to them that they must go deeper and move as quickly as possible back to their dock. He tried to check the blood flow by placing his hand over the deep gash. They had nothing to bind the wound and the blood would not clot while immersed in sea water. Darien must be in pain. Sistus signalled with the ancient code, DI DI DI DAH DAH DAH DI DI DI to the laboratory, but heard no reply. Probably no human was listening. Robot boats would not respond without relevant instructions, so no help could be expected from them. The swimmers regretted now that the four of them had taken their childish porpoise game so far out. The emergency signal might have been received but would anyone understand what had happened? The marines might see the strange boat and investigate it, but would they realise that four of Jezzy's sea sprites were struggling below the surface? Were the marines aware that gill-breathing humans existed? Would they even care?

With Darien only half conscious, they struggled on. Sistus signed that they should switch their terminals to emit emergency signals constantly. If the robots did respond and were close perhaps a chopper would be launched. They hesitated to surface fully because the boat had continued to track them.

At last, they heard and felt something immediately above and, ascending, realised that a chopper was hovering over their position, the surface of the water being flattened and stirred by the downwash. Their four heads emerged into this noisy, churning area. The chopper robot saw them. A Sproule rescue net was deployed immediately to scoop all four of them up and carry them in a strange, tangled bundle to safety. From her uncomfortable, but secure position under the tangled weight of the three men, Sal, as they rose could make out, some small distance away, the boat that they had approached too closely. It was hard for her to tell what was happening but she had the impression that the three small people they had seen were standing, amazed, staring at them as they were lifted up and away.

The net was lowered gently onto the deck of the landing pad and marine medics, dressed in sterile garments and wearing masks, immediately surrounded them. There were exclamations of amazement and even horror when it was realised that what the chopper had caught was three altered humans. Every ordinary citizen had seen those carefully arranged hologram images on the screens but no one outside Jezzy's realm had been confronted closely with any such being. Darien was still bleeding badly and semi conscious. The initial, momentary astonishment did not prevent his being attended to quickly. The human medics cleaned and bound up the injury and Darien was taken quickly away for further attention. The others sprites were hastily examined, pronounced fit, and released. Terminals working normally now, they called Jezzy, who knew already what had happened. She ordered them to return at once to the lab, quickly, not stopping for anything and not touching anyone. Darien, she assured them, would be there too, within minutes. She would look after him herself, but they must all return at once. The quickest way was by car and the three hastily left the landing pad and found a couple of the vehicles, instructing them to make haste. Sistus and Sal rode one, Marcel the other.

There was no way the universal, perpetual surveillance cameras could be turned off. This was a highly unusual event and could not be overlooked by the all-encompassing news gatherers. Their extraordinary arrival and unusual appearance was transmitted to every screen. Small groups, soon larger clusters, then crowds of people on cars were gathering and following them on their route through the streets, at times overtaking and jostling for position, threatening to impede their progress. Sal smiled and waved cheerfully to the onlookers at first, but was dismayed to find her friendly greetings were not returned. Dumbfounded amazement and muttered exclamations were general, but occasionally there were expressions of disgust. Some of the curious crowd reached out to touch, hold and even pull hard at her gills, hurting them. They had to be beaten off, repeatedly. Jezzy's orders, not to touch, had not allowed for this but it couldn't be prevented. As she whacked at the persistent hands, Sal was alarmed by the implications. It took longer than she expected to get to the Iris Door. As they left the cars, something struck Marcel on the side of his head, where the gills emerged. His hand over the place, he stumbled through the door with the others. The iris closed swiftly and implacably behind them, hiding an assembly of astonished, angry and some hate-filled human faces. The trio stood, horrified, but thankfully safe, by the fish tanks.

Jezzy, in full medical garb and masked, was waiting with a team similarly dressed from the lab. Marcel was in pain and bleeding but was able with Sistus' help, to walk. In shock Sal followed Jezzy and the medics. They soon found themselves in a ward none of them had seen before. Protesting that they were unharmed, she and Sistus were ordered, by a fierce and angry Jezzy, to stay where they were while she examined Marcel carefully. Bruised, and bleeding, but no permanent harm, was the verdict. Jezzy and her staff left them, the door closing firmly when they had gone. They were locked in, as Sal was first to discover.

Darien, pale and unhappy but conscious, was lying in a treatment capsule, his injury already stitched. He smiled sadly when the others approached.

'You must think me very stupid, Sistus.'

'You are not stupid, but you are too impetuous. What did you expect?'

'I wanted to greet them as a friend, to show them we would do them no harm, that they were welcome.'

'I know that is what you intended. Maybe you will be able to do it properly later. But those poor creatures were afraid of us, Darien, rising suddenly out of the sea like that. They thought you were a monster come to slaughter them. They did the only thing they knew how.'

'Yes, yes, I understand that now. It is a lesson I, we must all learn. We are different. I had forgotten. How stupid. I would not have been there at all if I had been normal.'

12

'Where are we?' asked Sal. 'I've never seen this place before, and why have they locked us in?'

'It's the isolation ward. It's standard practice, when refugees arrive. They have to come here to be examined for infections.' said Darien, feebly. 'I feel such an idiot. I should have anticipated it.'

'We aren't refugees. There's nothing wrong with us. What is Jezzy thinking?'

'For once she is obeying the law. Those people in the boat are refugees,' said Sistus. 'I expect they were out fishing and when they saw Shanghai in the distance they sailed towards us. It happens sometimes if a city wanders into their fishing areas. They were hoping we would accept them and let them stay.'

'That's what I thought,' moaned Darien. 'I just wanted to welcome them. They will have to be checked over, for diseases. It is the usual thing, part of the lab's duties.'

Who better equipped to do it than Jezzy, thought Sal. Anything must seem better than living on the land.

'That makes sense,' said Michel. 'But why have they bundled us in here? We are not sick. We haven't been near them, didn't even touch them. We can't be infected.'

Darien was utterly miserable. 'They touched me. Or that spear thing did, and who knows where that has been? They probably use it for killing things and I don't suppose they ever bother to clean it. You all touched me, my blood. They will check you out to be on the safe side, and the boat people too, when they get here.'

'The boat people? Will they be brought here? They're still in their little boat. Won't they have turned and sailed away again?' asked Michel.

Sistus shook his head. 'I'm sure they will have been caught by the marines.'

Darien, wearily, replied, 'The least that will be done is that they will be given some food and water, and then if they want to stay they will. If not, they can sail back to wherever they came from. Either way, they will be brought here first, and we will all have to say here too till we are cleared. Or cured.'

Sal remembered. 'Oh doldrums. Some of the crowd outside, just now, got hold of our gills and fingered them, pulled us about. I had to hit them to stop it. If we are infected, they may be too'

'Tell Jezzy when she comes back,' Darien replied, wearily. 'Ah, no, I don't suppose you will need to. She will have looked at the outside surveillance record.'

Sistus seemed briefly amused at this prospect. 'Ha. There might be a whole lot of people to be checked. Whoever jerked us about could catch it too.' He paused, suddenly serious. '*Mudfish.* If they have a lot of close friends it could spread through the whole city They will all have to be checked and immunised, or treated or something. We are not going to be very popular after this. Not with anyone. Not with Jezzy, nor the mandarins, nor anyone.'

'They won't find anything wrong,' said Marcel.

'I hope so. Oh I do hope so,' said Sal.

Sistus sighed. '*We are what's wrong*, Sal. That is how they see us.'

They were all feeling tired and shocked and lay down on conveniently placed treatment capsules which were arranged facing inwards on the two sides of the ward. Sal closed her eyes but opened them again almost at once. The door opened and a small procession entered, six or seven robots and several humans in full surgical dress, masks and hoods, looking monstrous. They half carried three pitifully small and emaciated humans, all utterly terrified, weak with fear and hunger. There were two children, boy, girl, and an adult man. It was hard to judge their ages but Sal guessed the girl to be in her early teens, the boy probably a year or two younger. They were taken to capsules opposite and laid down as gently as possible, and, by very explicit signs, instructed to remain there. The man, he who had wielded the harpoon, struggled to sit up at once and would have stood, but was firmly restrained. Giving up, he turned face down in misery.

The medics left except for Jezzy, who revealed herself by raising her hood and lingering for a few moments, glaring at her youngsters and the strangers. All were totally naked.

'These will be your companions while we examine you all and find out what contamination you have brought in,' she said, looking hard at Sistus. 'We have something to learn from this experience.' She turned to go, but paused, turned back and looked sternly now at Sal.

'These people do not speak Raftanglish. They are exhausted and more than half starved. They have had a light meal and water. They need one thing more than any other, sleep. Let them rest. You should do the same. Calm everyone down. I will come back later today with the test equipment. I must be elsewhere for a while.' She walked through the wall.

The sprites looked at one another. Darien seemed to be in dreamland already.

Sistus nodded. 'She is right. We are all tired. Sleep, everyone, the best thing we can do.' He lay back. Marcel followed his example.

Sal remained standing. Jezzy had stared at her as if expecting her to do something. The exhausted face of the girl refugee was turned to her, wide-eyed and afraid. How could Sal reassure this poor wretch that no harm would come to her? She put her hands over her own face, then used them to pull her feathery gills back over her shoulders, hiding them as far as possible. She tried to smile. The haggard child stared.

In a moment of inspiration, Sal started to sing. It was a melody she remembered, an old song that her caremother had played when children were put to bed. She was well into the first verse when the girl, with an astonished expression, opened her trembling mouth and began, weakly at first but with gathering strength, to sing the same tune.

Sistus raised himself slowly to a sitting position, gazing at Sal and the child with amazement, and looked briefly towards Marcel, who nodded, slowly. The two boys knew they must not interfere. When the lullaby ended, Sal walked slowly and carefully, arms out before her, palms upwards, towards the girl, who tentatively, copied her gesture. When they were close enough, they touched hands, held, and sang again.

The man, who had been lying face down in despair, raised himself and turned to listen and watch, then remained still, entranced. His young boy companion was the same. All four males focussed on the girls and exchanged astonished glances among themselves.

Sal, still singing, released the child's hands, reached out carefully to touch her face, gently, on each side. She gave a slight nod. The girl copied her. Sal felt the slight tremor in the other's palms as they touched her. The fingers reached a little further, to where her ears should have been. The young one had an expression mixed between disbelief, fear, and interrogation. She shuddered, but did not withdraw. The song ended, Sal shut her eyes, nodded, several times, making it almost into a bow, then carefully encouraged the child to lie down. She closed and opened her eyes again, nodded, and again. The other responded. Sal released her hands, stepped back, looked at all the males, gestured, palms down, eyes closing. They understood. Sistus and Michel played their part, lay back and closed their eyes. The others did the same. Sal herself tiptoed to her own capsule and lay down. As her own sleep descended, she heard Sistus, quietly, say; 'Sal, that was the most beautiful thing I have ever seen. Or heard. You are the most wonderful girl I have ever known.'

How long they slept Sal did not know. When she stirred, she discovered the others were already wide-awake and eating, their meals having appeared silently on the usual tables. Darien was awake and seemed much better, although his shoulder and arm were bound up, very stiff. He seemed not to feel any pain. Sal guessed he had been sedated as soon as he arrived at the chopper base. The newcomers had evidently understood what was happening sufficiently for them to be eating too. Sistus told her later, they had been alarmed and suspicious when the food appeared. When he and Michel had started on their own breakfasts they cautiously and suspiciously followed the example. The food given to the strangers was very simple and limited in variety, much of it in liquid or semi liquid form. Once started, they had eaten and drunk with a kind of desperation. Sal guessed they did not know when, or if, they would eat again.

Jezzy and her team arrived as they were finishing, the dishes and tableware vanishing automatically as usual. Jezzy was in hospital mode. The old woman was dressed from head to toe in white, with her wild hair wound up and hidden by a surgical hood. She removed her mask to show the three frightened strangers that, though extremely old, she was no less human than they.

'We are going to begin with Darien, because he is the most serious. Then we will look at you three sprites. I want our landlubber friends to see exactly what we are doing so they will understand, when their turn comes, that we will do them no harm.' Mask in place again, she and the attendants approached Darien. Sal waved gently to the three opposite, raised a finger and smiled. She hoped this would be accepted as a gesture of reassurance and friendship.

The routine for Darien was elaborate and thorough. His wound, which was deep and somewhat inflamed despite the previous emergency aid, required deep cleansing and some minor surgery. There were splinters of bone where the spear had penetrated. At last the wound was closed up, the edges carefully glued.

While the work was going on, the sprites were amazed to see the harpoonist, greatly daring, leaving his capsule and, step by step, moving closer to the group round Darien. Jezzy saw him and, after a first automatic reaction to hold him back, thought again, took her surgical mask off, beckoned him forward and allowed him to move so he could see what was being done. She pointed firmly to the spot he stood on, stared at him, pointed down again. The man nodded. Jezzy, a little taller than he was, replaced the mask.

'Could have been a lot worse. There will be a scar for a time but it will fade.' said one of the white suited medicos. 'You must start immediately to use your arm and hand. Swimming will be good for it, even if it is a little stiff at first. Follow this schedule of exercises to keep everything working. The code is here.' He touched Darien's wrist screen, to show him. 'You can call it up, anytime. We have implanted a painkiller which will last a day or two. You won't need any more. If you do as you are told you will be back to full strength in a few days. A complete new shoulder would take longer.' They proceeded with blood samples, made what Sal thought was a more than thorough inspection of the rest of Darien's body, probing, delving into orifices wherever there was one and sending the specimens into the diagnostic machines connected directly to every capsule. If there was any introduced infection it would be found. If special cultures had to be grown, this might take a day or so, they said.

When it was finished, the medical team moved towards Michel. The harpoonist was left where he stood, three metres from Darien. They stared at each other. Darien raised his good arm, and beckoned. The spearman took a step forward, doubtfully. Darien's smile was a little strained, but he beckoned again, holding out his hand. The man stepped closer, they touched fingers, then clasped. The harpoonist pointed to the scar, then to himself. Darien nodded. 'It's nothing much,' he said. 'I don't blame you. I was stupid.' He tried to shrug, but couldn't quite manage it. Smiling as well as he could, he said; 'Let's be friends?' The small man stood a moment longer, reached out slowly with a finger, to touch Darien's scar, so marvellously closed up now. He frowned, shook his head in apparent wonder, withdrew the hand, then bowed.

'Marrers, gadgie,' he said, turned away and walked slowly and thoughtfully back to his capsule and sat, waiting and watching. One of the startled medics quickly wiped Darien's scar with an antiseptic tissue.

For Sistus, Michel and Sal the inspection took less time but was equally careful and thorough. Jezzy directed the team to the spearman, who, barely understanding when they spoke to him, nevertheless moved in whatever way they indicated, and submitted himself to the intimate examination without complaint. He spoke to the children, in reassuring tones.

'Thems ain't gunna hort weh. Dee what's axd. Wor gunna be reet. Tis canny gud.'

The sea sprites did not understand the guttural speech, but Sal thought there was a word or two that might be something like Raftanglish.

The children went calmly through the routine and the white suited team departed. Jezzy lingered.

'You must stay here until we have made sure there is no serious infection. Try to make friends with these people. I will let you know when there is any news, good or bad.' She pointed. 'Sistus, a word.' The young man left his capsule quickly and joined Jezzy as she walked slowly to the door. They stood for a minute or two, speaking too quietly for the others to hear. Then Jezzy was gone again and Sistus returned, looking solemn.

'What was that about,' asked Michel.

'There is trouble. Things are going to be difficult. I can't explain everything but there are to be changes.'

'Because we ran into these lubbers?'

'Not that alone.'

'I don't think we should go on calling them lubbers,' said Sal. 'It seems... I don't know... insulting somehow.'

'Yes, well, whatever we call them,' Sistus said, 'their arrival has brought things to a head. Jezzy had plans but she wasn't expecting them to be put into action for a while. Everything has gone too quickly, quicker than she expected. I did warn her. We will have to bring everything forward. I am not surprised.'

'Plans?' demanded Michel. 'What plans? Quicker than who expected. You and Jezzy?'

'You must wait. There will have to be a meeting, not just us, all the sprites. I did say before, we are not going to be popular.'

'What do you mean? What plans?' Michel looked at Sistus, frowning. The strangers were sitting anxiously, frightened still, watching.

'Popular? Why not? What have we done? We helped them, saved them.'

'Think of the crowds in the street,' said Sistus. Sal began to understand but Michel had not fully understood.

'I think we ought to try to find out more about our visitors. Their names, for a start,' he said.

'Yes, a good idea,' said Sistus, glad to change the topic. He turned to face the three newcomers, took a few paces towards them, pointed to himself and said 'Sistus'. There was no response. He nodded to Marcel, who indicated himself and said his name. Sal did the same, Darien, from his bed, feebly followed suit.

The man stood, called the two young ones to him.

'Howie, bairns.' They left their capsules and joined him, one on either side. He put his arms around their shoulders, pulling them close.

'Ahm Airther, thor faitha.' He looked at the boy. 'Ees me laddie, Towie', turned to the girl, 'Shis me dotter, Becky.'

I'm Airther, their father. He's my laddie, Towie. She's my daughter, Becky.

Sal moved forward, put a hand on her own chest and said 'Sal', then pointed to the girl, the man, the boy 'Becky, Airther, Towie'. The three nodded, the man spoke, pointing.

'Sal, Marcel, Sistus, Dar.. Daren?'

'Darien'.

Aye, Dari-en, reet.'

Sistus moved next to Sal, repeated his own name, Marcel joined them. Airther nodded, held out a hand to each of the four sprites, and touched fingers, repeating each name. His children did the same.

'Air yee see munsters?' This was Towie.

(Are you sea monsters?)

Becky; 'Wos gun rang wi yer hids? Is t'aaful aad hag yeer mutha? Ne, it canna.'

(What's gone wrong with your heads? Is that awful old hag your mother? Nay, it can't be.)

Sal smiled, spoke to the other sprites. 'We can understand them, can't we? They speak something like Raftanglish, it isn't going to be so difficult.' She turned back to Towie, speaking slowly: 'Nay Becky. That's Jezzy. She's air boss, ne air mutha. Our hids are good.' She shook her gills. 'We air not sea munsters. We have been changed, to swim under water like fish. Jezzy changed us.'

There was uncomprehending silence for a moment. Airther spoke.

'Me wiffie is ne wi weh. She's deed.'

('My wife is not with us, She is dead.')

Sal had to think. Sistus whispered to her.

'I think he means his partner is dead.' Sal nodded.

'I'm very sorry, that is sad.'

'Sheh deed in the bo-att. Wi had ne scran. Wi were at say fre fetheradick dees tryin te scape.'

('She died in the boat. We had no food. We were at sea for fourteen days trying to escape.')

'He says they were at sea without food for fourteen days' said Darien. 'That's a very, very old way of counting, ain, tain, tethera, fethera, one, two, three, and so on. Ten is dick, tain is two, fether-a-dick, four and ten, fourteen.'

How did he come to know this, wondered Sal.

'Tryin te scape,' Sistus muttered. 'Escape from what?'

'Ahm sorry Ah dunsh yee wi me airpoun,' said Airther, staring at Darien.

('I am sorry I stabbed you with my harpoon'.)

'Ahm sorry I...Ah frightened, sceered yee.'

"Aye, Ah wez sceered. Yee jumd up so sudnlike. Ah wez 'fraid fre the bairns.'

('Aye, I was scared. You jumped up so suddenly. I feared for the children.')

So began a long afternoon during which the seven of them, struggling at times to understand but gradually learning each other's words, began to make friends. As they continued, the two groups drew closer, finally sitting sideways on adjacent capsules, facing one another. They looked very different. The three people from the boat were small, thin, toughened by hardship. They had never eaten well, their growth stunted from birth. They had always toiled hard in an unforgiving environment.

The refugees, for that is what they were, had escaped from the island where they had been living. They had offended the community in which they had been surviving and had been forced to flee. The girl had been accused of witchcraft and would have been put to death had the family remained with their tribe. They had been forced to sail without provisions at night, dreading pursuit from other boats. They dared not attempt to go back and became totally lost, knowing only that they must leave the land. When, after days, they had seen, far away, the glittering towers of the mighty city, they had steered that way. They knew from legends that there were people living on the ocean, but had little idea what they would find. Whatever it was, Airther felt it could not be worse than what they were leaving. The children's mother had been sick and weakening already. She had not been able to withstand the hardships of their flight. Sea monsters had not been expected but when they appeared, Airther had no alternative but to strike out in desperation.

Opposite them now sat four well fed, healthy and fully-grown humans, but humans with strange heads and growths out of their ears.

Detaching herself briefly from the limping conversation, Sal visited the toilets. As she sat alone for a little, she saw that these three landlivers; she must not call them lubbers; and the sea sprites, had much in common. They were *different* from the ordinary ones with whom they had lived. The unpleasant incident with the crowd pursuing them and shouting, Marcel being struck outside the lab, herself pulled savagely by the gills; had frightened her more than she dared to admit, even to herself. It had been forcibly impressed on her that the sprites too were not accepted as ordinary raft citizens. Sea Munsters? Airther and his bairns had been driven out of their community. Jezzy's sprites too had offended. Did Sistus believe they would be driven out in the same way? Might the sprites, their little gang and all the several hundred new ones now developing, some day be forced to flee in the night? In little cockleshell boats? Not possible. She returned, thoughtfully, to the group. Sistus stared at her as she sat, not with the sprites, but next to Becky. He looked long and hard, nodded fractionally. Perhaps he knew what she was thinking. He had plans. What plans?

The sprites were released from quarantine after a few more days. Airther and his children were held longer. The family needed a carefully devised diet because they were seriously undernourished and did carry some infections, fortunately treatable. Darien undertook to help the refugees to adjust to a new way of living when they too were freed to explore the laboratory area. They were not permitted to leave Jezzy's little empire.

13

While Darien and the others were in the isolation ward, a raft-wide referendum had gone ahead and a division of Shanghai into three had been decided. Robots at once began working everywhere, severing and remaking connections, relocating machines, building new ones. The dissection of Shanghai into three was far advanced.

On emerging from their isolation, the sprites for the first time encountered the Chief Mandarin, Merlin. Jezzy explained beforehand that he had decreed elections must be held soon to find the three new chief mandarins who would be required. He himself would be retiring. His last official act would be to visit all parts of the raft to satisfy himself that the separation, when it was accomplished, would take place without difficulties. Jezzy's laboratory was one of the first departments on his itinerary. Merlin was an impressive figure, tall and upright, his height exaggerated by his headdress and a brilliant, dazzling costume. Torva told them afterwards he had seen a similar ceremonial dress portrayed on an extremely ancient manuscript in the Shanghai central museum. He understood it dated back at least three thousands years showing the Emperor of old China in what had been called the Ming Dynasty.

Merlin spent some time alone with Jezzy, but emerged afterwards to meet the sprites. He was, to Sal, awe-inspiring. When he spoke his voice carried an authority that she felt no one could ever dispute. The only other chief she had ever met was Nemo in Sydney who had treated her kindly and gently and with understanding. Merlin was altogether a larger, more imposing and to her, an altogether daunting figure carrying absolute authority and expecting total obedience. As she saw him striding with great dignity around the laboratory, escorted by a train of minor officials, she felt small, afraid and wanted to run away and hide. The visit over, Merlin departed without ceremony and everyone breathed again.

'I'm just making sure we will lack for nothing,' said Sistus. 'It is to do with our new extension, to accommodate all the new sprites. That's what Jezzy tells the city robot master, anyway.' Sal, judging from his frequent absences and an unusual reticence in his manner, knew there was something he was not saying.

'Is Jezzy up to something?' she whispered.

'Sistus is up to something,' he corrected her, a finger on his lips. 'I dare not explain everything. Things are going to change. We must be prepared.'

Sal went away thoughtfully and spent an hour in a schoolie capsule, learning more about rafts. Afterwards she swam for a while by herself, venturing beneath the city. From below, in the gloom, she could see where robots were working, cleaning, scraping, cutting and patching the composite, boron and carbon reinforced plastic material from which the main body of the raft was made.

The ocean was never still, but the city rafts were so large that even the most severe storm waves, freak waves that had been responsible for destroying even some of those ancient cruise liners she had heard about, did not disturb them. Sal knew that the underwater part of the raft, which provided the necessary buoyancy, was a honeycomb structure, a multiplicity of hexagonal compartments, air filled and watertight. Damaging and flooding a few of these, even a few hundred, would scarcely affect the raft as a whole. The robots could effect repairs within hours, cutting out whole sections and replacing them with prefabricated material if needed. It was hard for her to orientate herself as she quietly drifted below, in the shadow. She had not realised the line of division was just *there*, or *there*. It didn't make much sense to her. The machines moved underwater easily and toiled without interruption, following the plans. The plans. *Whose plans?* She returned to the schoolie capsule.

In other schoolie capsules she found Airther and his bairns. They had been cleared of infections and were looking much healthier, after some weeks of improved diet and friendly treatment from Darien. They were becoming more accustomed now to the transformation of their own lives. The children were more ready for this than their father. He, while knowing that they had done well to escape their former environment, still retained old superstitions and fears. Their fearful bewilderment when they were taken into the laboratory with the new sprites in their various stages of development and the teaching machines, had been obvious at first. These places had been prepared for the anticipated sprite children who would soon need them. All three former landlivers were encouraged to learn Raftanglish, for which excellent programmes were available. Becky and Towie had never seen anything of this kind before but soon discovered how they could play with the touch screens. Darien made sure that they followed elementary language learning games. Airther was at first reluctant but when he discovered Becky talking quite well with Euna and playing gently with her baby, decided he must learn too. The three of them thereafter were often found together in school. When they could talk more fluently they would soon be reading, writing and learning widely. They were highly intelligent.

Sal was impressed, but wondered how this little group would ever be able to fit into city society. In a community as large as Shanghai, she supposed, there must be a niche somewhere they could fit into. There had been refugees before, but she had never met any. What became of them? What would become of Airther, Becky and Towie? What would become of the sprites?

Meanwhile Sistus was constantly busy with the robots. There was an air of urgency in all he did and he seemed to have no time to talk. Sal hesitated to question him.

Although it was no surprise, Sal was startled when she became pregnant. So much had been happening that this likelihood had been pushed to the back of her mind. Like Alicia and Euna, she must now prepare for the whole experience of motherhood as they had done and were still doing. Choosing the moment carefully, she approached Jezzy. The news seemed to revive Jezzy's spirits. The old woman was delighted. Sal knew enough herself by now to follow through, checking the results of the various tests. All was well and she was assured that when the day came she would get through it easily with minimal pain and struggle. If there was thought to be some small difficulty, it could be avoided well before any crisis arose. There were enough qualified and partly qualified young paediatricians, nurses and child carers among the newly arrived candidate sprites to help her if help was needed. Sal was given a schedule of exercises, as the other two young mothers had been. Her terminal prompted her if she ever looked like forgetting or skipping them.

When she told Sistus her news he was at first confused, for in the past rafter men had never known personal fatherhood. The insemination clinics did not record the donor of sperm beyond checking that it was healthy and genetically approved, *mix and match.*

Sistus and Sal had made simple vows to each other and had kept them. The expectant father was now faced with the unfamiliar and rather frightening idea that when it was born, he would know his own child. As he faced this Sal watched him anxiously. She was relieved to see dawning in him a tremendous wonder, and then delight that such a thing could, and would, happen. He drew her to him, caressed and kissed her.

'Sal, dear girl, I am alive, you are alive. The baby will be alive. We were missing so much, we were never fully human. You know, in the old stories and the reality games, we imagined robots taking over and controlling everything, even replacing mankind. I never thought it could happen, it was only a game. But you see, the reality was entirely the other way round. What was really happening in the cities was that we were making ourselves less human, more like machines. Instead of them being adapted to suit us, we were adapting to fit them, becoming creatures like robots. That is what's wrong with us. We were making ourselves into machines We behave more and more like machines. I didn't realize it when I was working with them every day, but now I see that's why

I wanted to break out. I never properly understood myself before. It wasn't that I especially wanted to be like the fish, I didn't want to be a robot. I wanted to be more human, not less *human, not machine.* Do you understand, sweetheart? Now we are more than, not less than, human.'

'Not like the machines. Yes, yes, I understand,' said Sal, 'But I also wanted to be a mermaid, to swim with the fish. I still want that. I want to be a *sea munster*, not just another human.'

Sistus laughed gleefully. 'I love you, little mermaid.' There was nothing robot-like in what followed. Now when she and Sistus lay together, she was carried away into experiences she could never have imagined or dreamed before.

Work on the separation of Shanghai into three was far advanced. Torva, whom now they saw rarely, reported that robots were working everywhere in the city, severing and remaking connections, relocating and constructing new machines, robots building robots. He told them he was expecting appointment as chief of one of the new laboratories on Shanghai Main. It meant he would no longer be with them when the division took place. He was very busy making sure that his lab would be properly set up and equipped. He hoped to continue his genetic work on the human brain.

When she and the others were swimming and diving, exploring the limits in depth and time in the water, Sistus was spending more time then ever working on the computers and talking to Jezzy. She pressed him for explanations. He hesitated.

'Some modifications to the robot's programming is necessary,' he explained. From his manner she knew there was something more than this.

'It is to do with our accommodation for the new sprites.' He hesitated momentarily. 'That's what Jezzy is telling the city Romaster, anyway.'

'But that's all finished, isn't it? Is Jezzy up to something?' she whispered.

'Sistus is up to something,' he corrected her, a finger on his lips. 'The City Romaster is too busy just now to bother about us. I have to take advantage of his preoccupation while there is an opportunity.'

'What are you doing?' Sal was alarmed now. 'Is it Jezzy's idea?'

'I think she guesses. She doesn't say anything. I am giving the robots in this section a contingency scheme they can work to. We may never need it, but if we do, it will be ready. I hope it will never be activated.' He hesitated again. 'Someone has to think ahead and prepare, Sal.'

'You always say that.'

'Yes, and I always mean it. I don't like the way things are going.'

'Going? What things, going where?' Did Sistus have some mad scheme of escaping, like Airther and the bairns? Becoming refugees?

'Sal, Jezzy relies too much on Mandarin Merlin. As long as he is in power he will protect us. But Merlin won't be our Chief much longer. As soon as the results are in, a new mandarin will be in charge. And this isn't much of a research laboratory any more. We have had to dismantle so much; we can't claim to be doing vital work here now. It's just become a residential area for the sprites, a sort of ghetto, if you know that word.' She knew the word.

'You think we will become a sort of sub-race, shut off from everything? They can't do that, can they? I know the lab isn't what it was, but when all the sprites are developed our field will be the ocean itself. The work will go on even more and better. Look at what Michel has already achieved by himself. When we get properly started, people will come to accept us.'

'That's the kind of thing Darien would say, what he would like to believe. I would like to believe it too, but we can't afford just hoping. I doubt we will be able to continue as we are.'

Sal found this very depressing and let Sistus see her reaction.

'I was talking to Torva,' Sistus went on. 'He's finding life in his new job difficult because everyone knows of his former connection to Jezzy. He has to keep on saying that he isn't going to do anything of the kind she has done. What he is doing is likely to cause huge troubles eventually, if he gets anywhere with it, but he isn't letting that become known at all.'

'He says there isn't so much feeling about us where he is, on Shanghai Main, because they are going to part from us soon, but there's a lot of hostility building up here.' He waved in the direction of the Iris Door and the main city. 'Have a look at some of the things people are saying about us on the graffitinet. They are getting quite nasty, Sal. You don't need to be reminded. Just that one brief exposure to the crowds, and they became quite violent.'

'That was dreadful. It was a sort of mixture curiosity, astonishment, fear and hatred.' Sal nodded and went away worriedly to swim for an hour by herself, venturing as far as she dared beneath raft. From below it was hard for her to orientate herself as she drifted below, in the deep shadow. The robots moved underwater easily and toiled without interruption, following their orders. Whose orders?

She drew Sistus away from his self-imposed work a couple of days later. They were swimming some distance out from the landing stage, exchanging a few words by the sign language, and, to see if it could be done, embracing sexually while still submerged. It was not easy, they discovered, although it could be done if they co-operated properly. At climax, they tested the oxygen giving capacity of their gills to the maximum and had to surface, laughing and choking. They felt they had only just got away with this exercise. They would tell Jezzy how it went.

Afterwards they were making their way back to the raft slowly, admiring the colourful ever-changing light filtering down from the sea surface, when an audible code message directed specifically at them, called them urgently to Jezzy. Abandoning their reverie, a few minutes later they emerged to find her waiting, looking anxious.

'What's the matter, Jezzy?' asked Sal.

'The election is finished. I am summoned to meet our new Chief Mandarin. I shall need some support. Darien and Michel are waiting for us. The girls aren't coming, too busy with the babies. Go and get your uniforms on and tidy your heads as much as possible. He's sent a covered car for us, so we won't be seen. Come down to the Iris Door as soon as you can.'

'Who is it, Jezzy? Who was elected?

'Fauvel.'

Sal had no reason to dislike Fauvel. She knew next to nothing about him but she would have felt happier if one of the other candidate mandarins she had met had been voted in. She sensed that Jezzy was much agitated, although doing her best to conceal it.

Two marines were in the front of the vehicle. It was very similar to one she had been in before. They were directed to capsules in the rear. Sal felt very uneasy. This all reminded her too much of her previous arrest. She had not understood what was happening then and once again she was apprehensive. They had not been formally arrested but it felt very much the same to her. Jezzy would say nothing. Sistus took Sal's hand and tried to reassure her with deaf language signs, although he, too, was obviously alarmed.

The Chief Mandarin's apartments and offices, when they reached them, were much larger and more ornate than those Sal had seen on the Sydney raft. Under escort they were shown into a large hall. The two marines halted inside the door, which they closed, standing on either side of it.

Fauvel sat on what could only be described as an ornate throne, raised on a dais. Apparently he had expected Jezzy to be alone. There was a single chair on the lower level some four metres away, facing him. Frowning, Fauvel fumbled with a key on the arm of the throne. Additional chairs emerged from the floor facing him. Jezzy and the sprites took them. The Mandarin scowled. He seemed not to be looking directly at them, but stared over their heads.

'It is required that you stand,' he said, stiffly. 'Bow to acknowledge the Chief Magistrate.' The four sprites obediently stood and bowed solemnly. Jezzy remained sitting and gave no more than a nod of the head. The others sat. Fauvel's face showed his anger. Obviously he had intended them all to stand and remain so until he allowed them to sit. He may have intended to issue a command, but thought again.

'You have been brought here secretly,' he said. Jezzy shrugged her shoulders.

'This meeting is not being recorded or broadcast. Everything said here is in confidence, there are no other people within hearing.' The sprites looked at each other in some astonishment. Sal felt a touch of apprehension. What was to be said that was not fit for other people to hear? *Except for those two marines at the door, she thought.*

'Why?' demanded Jezzy, fiercely fixing the man with her terrible witch eyes. 'Why have you sent for us?'

14

Fauvel seemed to quail, but took several deep breaths and stiffened, not staring at the old woman, but over her head. *He is afraid of meeting her eyes,* thought Sal.

'Madam, it is time for you to retire. You must give me your resignation.'

Jezzy stood immediately and took a step forward 'Why?'

'There is a dangerous situation.'

'What?'

'Despite everything you have done to explain and justify your enterprise, the number of rafters who are opposed to you, and your... your... m-modified beings, increases daily, almost by the hour. Protests and d-demonstrations are increasing, b-becoming disorderly.' Sal thought, *the man is scared. He is terrified, and not just of Jezzy.*

'Violence is threatened. The marines are on the alert but if things continue as they are, they will not be able to pacify the mobs. A serious mutiny, a violent uprising is likely if not prevented. Shanghai Alpha is likely to descend into turmoil.'

Jezzy took two steps forward. 'Is my continuation in office causing this? How will my retirement prevent such a rising?'

'An immediate announcement will g...go part way to c...calming things down.'

'And if I refuse?'

'If you will not stand down I will dismiss you immediately as head of the laboratory.' Fauvel still seemed to be addressing the distant wall of the chamber. 'It is better if you go voluntarily now.'

'Voluntarily? Rubbish. No.' Another forward step.

'Your departure is the first requirement. It will not be enough without further action. It is expected the mob will attack the laboratory, break in and destroy everything, and everybody, within.'

'So how will you prevent this? What are you proposing?' Jezzy demanded, furiously, stepping forward again.

'The sprites project must cease immediately.'

'That is impossible. What has been done cannot be reversed, that was made clear from the beginning.'

'So you claim.'

'So how do you hope to avoid the violence and destruction you fear?'

'There are two possibilities. The first is for everyone in the laboratory to board one of our ferry ships. It can be made ready in an hour.'

'To go where? Another city?'

'You will be put ashore.'

'You mean to maroon us. That would be to put us to death.' The sprites looked at each other in horror. Sal shuddered but listened desperately.

'Not directly, for it is possible to live on the land. There are people doing so as the handful you rescued prove. Some survive. For this reason, if we assist you to escape in this way, there will be a further requirement.'

'Which is?'

'The danger feared by the mobs is that the sprites will multiply and become a rival race to normal raftish humanity. A justified fear of racial rivalry and war has arisen and will not be quelled by half measures. When you are put on land, before you are released all must be permanently sterilized. If any of your females are pregnant, those children must never be born.'

Sal cried out, Sistus yelled 'No,' and came to her, kneeling as she wept. Michel raised both arms in disbelief. Darien could contain himself no longer. 'This is inhuman,' he cried, rising to his feet. 'You are wicked, an evil monster.'

'Return to your place. If there is any question about what is human and what is monstrous, you, yourselves, in your grossly mutilated form, are not an example of true humanity.'

Darien, amazed and at a loss, subsided slowly and put his head in his hands. Sistus ignored the mandarin and remained with Sal, kneeling by her, trying to comfort her as she wept and shook.

'*I won't allow this,*' he whispered.

'You said, two possibilities,' said Jezzy, controlling herself with great effort.

'The problem is of your making. You solve it. You have created a kind of creature that is capable of living in the water. Let them go and get on with it. Take them, all, now, go and jump into the sea immediately,' said Fauvel.

Jezzy stood, silent.

Sistus suddenly left Sal, went to Jezzy and stood facing her with his back to the throne, his hands moving swiftly. Sal recognized that he was signaling as if to a deaf person in sign language. She caught the sense of it. He was saying, *Our plan, another way.* Fauvel came to his feet, lowering his gaze at last to look directly at them.

'What is this hand wagging? What goes on here? Marines, arrest him.'

Sistus turned furiously to face him, taking two or three steps in a threatening manner ready to strangle him, it seemed. Fauvel looked round desperately for help. The two marines were responding, but very slowly. Jezzy turned and stared at them fiercely, shook her hair loose, raised her talons and stepped towards them as they approached. They hesitated and stopped.

'Is this the kind of mandarin you are? Ordering death for unborn babies?' cried Sistus. 'The new sprite candidates are not yet capable of submarine living. You know that. You would slaughter five hundred young, beautiful and enthusiastic people. Do you really mean to go down in the global archives as a mass murderer?' yelled Sistus. 'Jezzy will be remembered when you are nothing but a despised and hated name. You are the only monster here.' He pointed a furious finger at the mandarin on his gaudy throne.

Fauvel was grey faced, shaken by the ferocity of Sistus' speech. He turned to look at the guards.

'Marines, arrest him, do your duty,' he shouted. The men came forward again, but still reluctantly. Sistus and Fauvel glared at each other. Jezzy stepped close to Sistus, Sal too, and then Michel and Darien joined them. Jezzy and her four sprites confronted the Chief Mandarin Elect.

'There is another way,' said Sistus clearly.

'Seize him,' shouted Fauvel. The marines came forward and attempted to grab Sistus but he stepped aside, extended a foot causing one of them to stumble. Sal shoved the man hard as he tried to recover his balance and he went down on all fours. The other tried to grasp Sistus by the arm but Michel thumped him in the belly. Suddenly both marines were on the floor, held down by three strong young men and a girl. The stun gun that one of them had drawn was kicked away by Jezzy. Fauvel, at a loss, teetered on the edge of the dais. Nobody moved.

There was a sudden disturbance as the door was flung open. Merlin in his marvellous robes swept into the chamber.

'This will not do.' He cried. 'Marines get out, guard the door. Let no one in.' The two humiliated men, released, got to their feet and obeyed.

'You have no right to interfere,' said Fauvel.

Merlin pointed an angry finger at him. 'Get off that damn silly stool, get down and go and stand on the deck over there.' Merlin pointed to one side of the dais.

Fauvel, shaking and stumbling, slowly did as he was told. Merlin stood, dominant and implacable. The sprites, overawed, dared not move.

Merlin turned to them.

'Resume your seats.' Jezzy hesitated. 'All of you,' he said, furiously. 'You too, Jezzy. Sit down. Now.' They obeyed.

Merlin strode onto the dais, tall and fierce.

'I am Chief Mandarin of Shanghai. Fauvel, you do not govern here until I relinquish control.'

'Th… tha.. that is a technicality. I have been elected, the result is already known.'

'A technicality? The law is that when a raft divides the elected chief does not take over until the moment of actual separation. That time is still several days off. Until then, I remain in full command.'

'B b b…but there is no such law'

'There is now. As Chief Mandarin, I decree it, establishing a precedent. Refer this *mere technicality* to the council of Mandarins. It will take a few weeks to be decided and by then the Shanghai raft will have separated. Ha. If I choose I can declare your election invalid and have you arrested at this moment. Appeal against that too if you like.' Fauvel gaped, stammered but failed to speak. 'Stay where you are, keep quiet and do as you are damn well told.'

Merlin took the throne. He spoke.

'Fortunately, I have my own sources of surveillance and intelligence. It is true that there are disturbances among the rafters. Firm action is needed, but what you proposed, Fauvel, would make a minor disturbance into a catastrophe. Such actions in your first few days in office are totally unacceptable. There would follow worse than mutiny, there would be general civil strife and I would lead the forces against you. My influence is not small. The Marines are loyal to me. Your first decision would be your last. The mutineers make a lot of noise but they can be dealt with.'

'I will be lenient. Your election was valid. I will allow you to become Mandarin of Alpha. I now make myself *available* to you, Fauvel, *as your adviser*. I strongly recommend, indeed I demand, that you take advantage of this offer and make an announcement to this effect as soon as we have finished here. Together we can get through the next few weeks. We will be able to deal with any mutiny. By yourself, you would lose everything and would, eventually, be the one marooned. If you choose to disobey, I will order your arrest. You can appeal that too, if you wish.'

'Sistus, come here. I must speak privately with you.'

Sistus stepped forward and onto the dais, Merlin stood and turned his back to the others, drawing Sistus to the side. The two talked softly for several minutes, as everyone else remained frightened in their seats. Sal was unable to hear a word, but remembered with growing hope that *Sistus had a plan*. She had more than inkling as to what it might be.

If she had guessed right, and she suddenly felt sure it was more than a guess, the prospect scared her no less.

Merlin and Sistus finished their conversation. Sistus returned to stand by Sal, a hand gently, reassuringly, on her shoulder.

The Chief Mandarin spoke: 'The action proposed to me by this young man, has my authorization and support. He is ready to move as soon as he, Jezzy and his friends are returned safely to their section of the raft.'

He stepped off the dais, came to Jezzy. They embraced; a few words were exchanged in whispers. *He is saying goodbye to her,* Sal thought.

Merlin turned to Sistus. 'Be finished by 24.00 hours. After that, I guarantee nothing.' He smiled, grimly. 'I may be busy for some days in the appeals court. The vehicle is waiting for you. Go.'

The five hastened to the door. As the marines closed it slowly after them, Sal heard Merlin speak.

'Fauvel, you can do more of the clever publicity tricks that got you elected. Say this was all your own idea.'

15

As soon as they were through the Iris Door, Sistus ran to the nearest main computer terminal and began to instruct it verbally, hammering the keyboard and touchong the screen. Dormant robots awoke and began to move. The immediate sound of work in progress was muted but unmistakable.

Darien, after a brief word from Sistus, before midnight issued an emergency call, bringing all the sprites and candidates crowding into the main recreation hall. The place filled rapidly with novice changelings, some with gills almost fully developed, others only partly so. Jezzy's small band of mutineers, as they now thought of themselves, stood with her on the raised stage at one end of the hall. Alicia and Euna, bewildered but beginning to understand what they had hastily been told, were carrying their babes. Sal looked about. Airther and the bairns came in, wondering. Sistus was the last to arrive to join the group on the platform. He signed privately to Jezzy and the small group of sprites with her, *FINISHED.* It was a quarter of an hour before midnight.

Jezzy stepped forward hesitantly. She was tidy in crisp uniform, but seemed unsure of herself and uneasy. Her hair was escaping from its restraints. The crowd was totally silent and listening anxiously. They knew something was seriously wrong. The old woman was very far from her normal, forceful and determined self. Her image was projected onto screens in places all round the hall so everyone could see and hear her clearly, from every angle, as if this were a transmission from the Mandarin's office. Sal recalled her first meeting with the old woman, when, looking like a witch, she had been reflected a hundred times in the glass walls of her experimental tanks. All those tanks had gone now to make room for more young people.

'Sprites, greetings,' Jezzy said, 'There has never been an occasion like this before. It is the first time we have all met together at once. Introductions are not necessary. You know me and you know my friends here with me.'

'I must not conceal from you; we are suddenly in a desperate situation. A hostile attitude to us has developed among some of the rafters. This has alarmed Mandarin Fauvel who has been elected to take charge of Shanghai Alpha, our section of the Shanghai raft.'

'Fauvel's attitude is that of a badly frightened man, in something of a panic.' The audience heard this in dead silence. 'He attempted to dismiss me and presented me with an ultimatum. He wants to terminate the sprite programme forthwith.' This shook the assembly profoundly. There was a rising murmur of dismay, they whispered to one another, questioned, shook heads, several hands were raised to ask questions. The noise subsided when Jezzy indicated that she had more to say. Stumbling occasionally, she went on.

'We will not, *cannot possibly* obey. You are wondering, what is to become of you, of all of us. Fortunately, the Chief Mandarin, Merlin of Shanghai, has intervened. Our programme will continue, but under very different conditions.'

The crowd still rumbled with dismay and doubt. Jezzy was shaking and stumbled over her words. 'I am unable to speak more. Sistus, this boy who has foresight clearer than any old witch, Sistus will explain.'

Exhausted, she turned to Sistus who stepped forward to take her place. He glanced at Sal. She gave him a brave smile, nodded. Sistus gained confidence, faced the crowd. He was nervous and had to clear his throat. The audience was not at first ready. He would not raise his voice. He stared aggressively, glaring, waiting until they gave him their attention.

'Jezzy has asked me to explain.' He coughed. 'She credits me with foresight. I don't pretend to see the future,' he drew himself up to full height, and went on more confidently as the crowd realized they must listen, 'but I have always understood that we are different from ordinary humanity. We will, we must, live differently.' Sistus raised his voice a little. 'Fauvel wants to be rid of us. He ordered us to jump into the sea.' The audience was shocked, disbelieving, horrified and showed it with a rising buzz of whispered and voiced questions.

'I have from the beginning believed that we must make ourselves *independent of the Shanghai raft*. I began to make preparations for this some time ago. Fortunately, we are ready.'

'Shanghai is dividing itself into three. This involves severing all mechanical links between the three segments. Very soon they will cut themselves apart to continue as three separate cities.'

'Sprites, **we are going early and we are taking Jezzy's part of the raft with us.**' There was a sudden hush. 'As I stand here, no material links between us and Shanghai exist. We are on our own, on a separate raft. Beyond the Iris Door, where there was a corridor, there is now a narrow strip of water that widens as I speak. While you have been listening, we have been drifting away from Shanghai.'

After a few moments of shocked, silent bewilderment, the crowd's agitation broke out in a tumult of noise, there were shouts, cries of dismay, groans, anger, a few rather faint and hesitant cheers, some clapping. There was no sign of the racket dying down, the babies were screaming and some of the sprites wept too. Amazed, frightened, confused, angry, they showed it by shouting questions. The noise continued and rose in volume. Sistus and Jezzy could not make themselves heard, signed desperately to one another. Jezzy nodded and turned to Sal.

On their hurried journey back from their confrontational meeting, Sal had learned from Sistus what was to happen. She had guessed correctly but she was hardly less shocked than anyone. She was still trying to work out the likely consequences. They had neglected to prepare her for what came next. Had she known, she would have been too terrified to do what they now demanded of her.

'Sal,' Sistus, coming very close, signed: 'Calm them.'

'What? Me? How can I? What do you mean?' she responded.

Jezzy took her by the arm, led her forward. The front few rows of the assembled sprites, fell silent and watched.

'Sing to them, little mermaid,' Jezzy said, close enough to be heard, 'Sing. Put them to sleep.'

Sal, paralyzed, stared around the hall with its amazing array of screens. Now the images were all of herself, enlarged, multiplied and multiplied. She raised trembling hands, surrendering, unable to do more, palms facing the rowdy and distressed crowd. To her horror, this simple gesture quietened some of the sprites, then more, and she was suddenly aware that they were all waiting quietly, expecting something from her. She lowered her hands slowly, realizing even as she did so, that they took even this as an appeal for silence. They obeyed. The hall became deathly quiet. There was only one thing she could do. Not a lullaby, that wouldn't pass, these were not children or refugees. Not Rusalka's sad song to the moon, wholly inappropriate. What? What?

She had heard it, played it and sung it before, remembered and loved it, another ancient, ancient melody, but passionate and finally optimistic, full of hope. It might, it *must*, bring them all together.

She sang the *Ode to Joy*.

When she finished there was a long silence. Sistus began to clap; the other gang members copied him, the entire audience followed. There were cheers and calls for more. The two babes were woken up by the renewed din and started wailing again. Alicia and Euna tried to reassure them. Someone in the crowd cheered even this, the noise grew louder. The two young mothers took their children away to a quieter place. Sistus gestured to Sal, signed to her: *Again, sing again.*

She sang, and sang until she could do no more, an impromptu program, continuing until she could remember nothing further. In the silence that followed, many of the sprites were smiling through tears. Sistus came to her, took her in his arms, hugged her and kissed.

'Sal my darling girl, darling girl.' Sal, trembling, did not hear the cheers.

'Sistus, how could you... why did you? I wasn't ready for anything like that.'

'Sal, darling Sal, we didn't plan it; everything was done in such a desperate rush. I had to get the decks cut immediately. We didn't know what the sprites' reaction would be and there wasn't time to talk about it. They needed reassurance. You were *here*. You were *here, you are here*, marvelous girl, you did exactly the right thing, the best possible thing anyone could have done. You are the most beautiful and wonderful person and a quite extraordinary singer. That is your personal magic, Sal. You bewitched them.'

'It wasn't fair. I was in panic. What if I had dried up? There was nothing else I could do. It was dreadful. I nearly died.'

'No, it wasn't fair. Nothing in this is fair. This is all criminal. It is a terrible shock for everyone, especially Jezzy. She thought Merlin's protection would go on forever. She isn't infallible, Sal. He can't go on, she can't either. I have been warning her for weeks and months to be ready for something like this.' He held her closely. 'You didn't dry up, I was sure you wouldn't. You knew I was programming the machines.'

'I knew you were doing something.'

'I am so thankful I did. It was a matter of an hour or two, Sal. If we had not cut ourselves loose immediately, we might have been destroyed.'

'Would they really throw us into the sea?'

'Fauvel is in panic, frightened out of his mind, that's why he was so cruel, it was the reaction of a desperate man. It could have been the end of everything. He could have marooned us. Merlin was taking a great risk, intervening as he did. I don't know what has happened now. I hope Merlin has managed to pacify him. I've never seen Jezzy in such a state, Sal. This whole business has shaken her to her roots.'

'And now we have a raft, and we have the communication system intact,' Sistus continued. 'All the usual links have survived. There is no way Fauvel or anyone else can cut us off from the global net. We are independent. We will go on and gradually build ourselves into a full city of our own. The raft-city of scientific sprites'

Controlled, monitored and maintained entirely by computers and robots, the ocean wide net could not be interfered with or disrupted by human agencies. The engineers who had set the system going centuries before, designed it so. Sistus knew what was required and would quickly establish links with the space stations.

'Your old game of Atlantis? The submarine city'

'Not yet, Sal, not yet submarine. We might able to move towards that, eventually. I think it's for a future generation. First, right now, today, we have cut loose. We have all the essentials, adequate power, food production, unrestricted access to the sea, almost all the facilities we are accustomed to. This piece of raft is intact, self contained, independent. We will be able to go on. There is no alternative, we must go on. Remember Neurath's boat? We will rebuild and expand the entire vessel piece by piece.'

'Sistus, you are wonderful. I do like you. No, I think I love you, if I know what that means. Yes, I love you. But don't, don't ever do anything like that to me again. No secrets between us, no secrets ever again.'

'No secrets, my darling.'

'Do you suppose Fauvel will try to stop us? We've stolen his laboratory, well, what was the lab, and all the alterations they have built for us, all that work.'

'The robots did the work, they won't complain. We have Merlin to thank for everything. I think he must have known what I was doing; he has his own sources of intelligence, as he said. Now Fauvel has lost us altogether. What can he do? I suppose he could send a boatload, no, it would have to be a raft load, of marines and choppers to capture us all. That would be a vast stupidity, it would bring the problem right back to him. All he really wants is to be rid of us. Why should he bother to chase us? The robots can soon patch the gap we left. He can build a new lab if he wants it.'

'I hope you are right.'

'I'm sure I am. Merlin still has many supporters, he is a cunning old bugger, Fauvel can't just ride over him. I doubt he will even try. Merlin will keep control of him. Fauvel would not dare to attack him openly. There would be worse than a mutiny if he tried.'

When the sprites in the hall had recovered sufficiently to start thinking clearly, their mood became serious and a little afraid, but calmer, thanks to Sal's remarkable talent and Sistus' charisma. In groups, they ventured onto the open decks. Shanghai was already half a nautical away; they were truly separate, adrift by themselves. It was in many ways a new beginning. It took them more than a few days to adjust.

16

Their portion of the raft was very much smaller than the usual city size and was responding to the motions of the sea in a way that no one had ever felt before. Sal could sense the difference even as she stood. The floor beneath her feet was flexing. In anything other than a dead calm, waves caused the raft deck structure to move slightly. The two tall hydroponics towers, one old and one quite new, could just be perceived to be tilting back and forth slightly, the tops moving inwards and outwards slightly relative to one another as the flexure passed through under them. It was disturbing for a population who had never felt anything like this before. They were not being thrown about as a small boat would have been; Jezzy's empire had been and still was, a couple of nauticals long, broader than a ferry and very stable. It was, nevertheless, much smaller than a city raft and behaved differently.

The rafters could feel an irregular motion of the deck beneath their feet, and were alarmed. Sistus discussed it with some of the young engineer sprites as soon as they recognised the motion. They were not fully qualified but knew enough to understand what was going on without being able to do all the relevant calculations. They gained access to the worldwide linkage of professional engineers, without revealing that they were working from the detached part of Shanghai. They used the ID numbers, modes of contact and passwords that had been registered to them before they left their home raft.

They were soon able to explain to Sistus and Sal. The raft was not big enough to flatten the waves entirely, as the full-scale city rafts did.

The effect of waves on the smaller raft was to cause it to vibrate. The stretched string of a musical instrument, if plucked, emits a certain note. Any structure under repeated tress responds with a vibration of a certain frequency determined by its shape and constitution. The natural response of the raft structure was a vibration never in tune, so to speak, with the oceanic waves. There was a disharmonic resonance. This increased the local strains in the structure and would become worse in stormy weather. Some who could do so went swimming, inspecting the underwater aspect of the truncated raft. There was little to be seen for the light was poor.

Alicia and the engineers quickly created a presentation to put out on the screens and into the capsules so that everyone could understand what was happening. They were moderately reassured. Sal dared to ask, if there should be a big storm, how would the raft respond? If the sea waves became much bigger, was there danger? Might the cleverly designed, airtight honeycomb structures that kept them afloat develop cracks and leaks that would begin to let water in, so the raft would founder. Sistus hesitated. 'No secrets.' She said, fiercely.

'No secrets, Sal, and I don't know. There is something that used to be called metal fatigue but the raft is not made of metal. Composites are different. I will get robots to monitor constantly and make repairs if anything like that begins to happen. The young engineers will help and advise us. We all need to read up on structural fatigue. I'll get a good team together.'

'Meanwhile, you and some of the others who have experience of navigation can help us to avoid dangerous storms. We can still follow the old routines; take the currents that will keep us in safe areas. Sal understood. 'Now I know why you wanted me to go on studying. You guessed this would happen.' He smiled and nodded.

'A hundred other things might have happened and I couldn't prepare for them all. I saw change coming; it came much sooner than I had expected.'

Using the holo screens, Sal asked for sprite navigators like herself, partly and fully trained, to join her in the school area. Only when she had sent this message out did it occur to her that she was acting without authority. Sistus too had been taking responsibilities on himself without any senior officer knowing, let alone approving. The only captain they had now was Jezzy, who had supported his actions, but this should not mean Sal could ignore her. She went looking for her. She was with Michel in the much-reduced laboratory, instructing a small group of the new sprites in monitoring the few remaining experimental tanks.

Jezzy had always looked old. Now she looked desperately weary. Sal didn't interrupt, but Jezzy saw her, brightened, raised a hand, pointed towards the school deck and nodded. Did this mean she approved what Sal was doing? Did Jezzy always know and understand everything, even now, when she was so tired? Perhaps not quite everything.

In the school where a few potential navigators were already assembling, Sal also found Airther and his children occupying three of the teaching capsules, Darien helping them. In the upheaval and change associated with the raft division and its aftermath, Sal had almost forgotten them. The three were able now to converse with some understanding, the children were getting on particularly well. Their language was, after all, recognizably a dialect of Raftanglish. Airther insisted that he spoke the original true Anglish, and what the rafters spoke was dialect. He was probably right, Sal thought.

Airther explained, haltingly, that soon after the crisis and separation, Jezzy had given them the option of returning to Shanghai. It would still have been be possible for them to take a boat and sail to the land, or transfer to the main raft before the segmentation was completed. He believed Torva on S. Main would be prepared to sponsor them and look after them if they chose to leave. They could work for him. Airther said the decision was not difficult. The *sea munsters* had rescued him and his children. They had been treated with great kindness, especially by his new *marrer*, Darien. Jezzy had cured them of diseases they did not know they had. Soon, Airther believed, they would find something useful to do. For example Becky, he said, could help Alicia and Euna and the other sprites with their babies. There was no prospect of Becky ever bearing a sprite child. She had no training at all in modern childcare but could learn. Darien seemed devoted to the little group and was taking care of them.

There was much else for Sal to worry about. When not swimming, or talking and loving with Sistus, she now had more than a full time occupation as leader of a new navigation department.

With the recruits she improvised a Nav office, using some of the regular teaching capsules. She was able to call up all the instructional material she would have expected to study on the way to her full Nav 4 qualifications and picked up where she had left off. The volunteers also continued studying. Sal arranged with Sistus and his robots for the necessary map screens and plotting machines to be set up.

So much, she thought in a quiet moment, for the little mermaid playing with the friendly, colourful fish. No time for that now Later, it must happen.

The raft settled down gradually to a routine not very different from what had been before. As days and weeks followed, Sal began to think that the future was bright after all. Michel was taking Torva's place in the laboratory as Jezzy's deputy scientist. He remarked to Sal and Sistus that Jezzy seemed to be withdrawing gradually from her active involvement, giving him a free rein. He was contemplating further lines of research and study, inspired by creatures and events he observed in his underwater ventures. He gathered round him a staff whose work would be divided between underwater explorations and laboratory time. Very soon now, when they were all completely grown, they would be joining him in the underwater studies. Results, when there were some, would be broadcast to the global net. Jezzy approved. All could study and contribute to the marine biological archives.

Beginning to feel stronger again, Jezzy told Sal and Sistus, 'After we left, I got in touch again with Merlin. His authority over the marines was fully accepted. The severance of the sprites' section took all the wind out of the rioter's sails. Fauvel did as Merlin had suggested, stole the credit.

Sistus was amused. 'Merlin is a wily old wizard. It would take a very brave newly elected chief mandarin to threaten him. Fauvel is not brave; he is a bureaucrat, a jack in office. He would never dare to touch him.' Merlin was constantly at Fauvel's elbow. What might happen when the old man did decide to retire, or when he died, was something no one could predict.

The three rafts that had once been Shanghai were all undergoing a period of adjustment.

'There are enough problems and changes to keep everyone's mind fully occupied with day to day affairs,' Merlin had said. 'They were not bothered much by the departure of the laboratory.' The engineers and their robots were busy healing the wound left when the suburb had been cut loose. Shanghai Alpha would soon have its full, seaworthy elliptical shape again.

Torva was pleased when Sal was able to reach him again and explain what had happened. He was setting up his new department on Shanghai Main. His appointment had been conditional on not undertaking any further structural modifications of human beings.

'I am doing nothing of that kind. Nothing that I am attempting will change people *externally*. You understand what I am saying?' He was guarding his tongue. On S Main full-time surveillance was in force, even in his lab. Sal had no hesitation in taking Torva's hint, conveyed only by his choice of words. Some day, she speculated, it might be possible for Torva to influence the development of human, or superhuman, brains. Nothing would show externally but they would be profoundly different.

'I learned a lot from Jezzy, and not only about genetics. Everything I am doing remains open to inspection. I am making a little progress. Anyone at all can read the net. They might even learn something if they do. Not many seem to bother. I suppose my choice of language is a bit difficult. Someone persistent like you might manage it.

Sal wondered if she should also try to speak directly to Neppy on the Sydney raft again, but decided against it. It would reopen old wounds, she thought. He must by now have made friends with someone else. *Forget Neppy, or forget me*, Jezzy had said. She had chosen, but she could not forget.

Jezzy herself had recovered some of her old energy and became a familiar sight to everyone, moving round the smaller laboratory and into the enlarged recreation areas, watching the youngsters at play and seeing them diving gleefully into the ocean. She encouraged the fully developed sprites to bring forth offspring. No laws were laid down. After some time of abstinence they were enthusiastic to rediscover free sex. It became apparent that most were following the example set by Sal and Sistus. Long before an expected birth the bond between the coupling pair and their offspring was recognized, not least by the couples themselves. There were no formal vows but the idea of true parenthood and family took a firm hold. Fathers and mothers began to take interest in their children.

The old witch wandered about with attention and pleasure, went to play often with Una and Secundus. Alicia and Euna were happy to be the first sprite mothers, honoured matriarchs. They had a place in history that could never be taken from them. The babies flourished, grew and were happy, beginning to swim with their mothers even before they tried to walk. Jezzy often drew the pregnant girls away from their activities to be inspected and tested. It was established that Sal's growing baby was female.

Everyone became so accustomed to the slight instability of the deck that they no longer worried about it. There were times when it virtually ceased, but if the ocean developed waves of any size, the raft still moved uneasily.

Sistus spoke every day with Jezzy. She remained nominally in charge but Sistus told Sal that the old woman was deferring to him more and more as days and weeks passed. She often asked for his advice when previously she had not needed it or not heeded it when it was offered. He became convinced that she was glad to be shedding her responsibilities.

'She wants you to be captain. And so you should be, who else?' said Sal. Sistus shook his head. 'I don't want it, Sal.'

'It seems to me,' she replied, 'that the only person fit to be a Captain is one who does not want the job.'

Sal's navigator group gained experience and confidence, studying weather patterns, constantly watching the ocean currents, learning to bias the drift and plotting courses. It was an elementary requirement to avoid entirely those regions of the tropics and semi-tropics where hurricanes, typhoons and cyclones arose at certain seasons. Sal was confident that she would be able to copy the routes followed by the big cities, as she had been taught. For a considerable time they remained within sight of one or all of the three Shanghais and Sal was able to relax, knowing she was following orthodox practice.

They learned about thunderstorms but they did not learn everything. It was well known that the large city rafts exerted some influence on the weather and often generated their own local weather as isolated islands did. Artificial decks exposed to the sun absorb more heat than the sea immediately around them. Some of this heat is passed to the air, and air even slightly warmer than the surrounding atmosphere rises. In unstable conditions any rising current quickly enters cooler air above and so rises more rapidly making the upward surge stronger. The low-pressure area so created draws more air inwards from the surrounding area and feeds the upward current. A vortex forms. At some level moisture contained in the rising flow condenses and cumulus clouds form. In such a cloud latent heat of condensation is released to the air, making the upward current stronger still. On an unstable day the upward motion of the air becomes more and more powerful. *Cumulonimbus* storm clouds reach the stratosphere and there, at the outer fringes of the atmosphere, they spread out horizontally creating gigantic anvil shapes. The anvils spread and spread, casting their shadows over wide areas, so in the long run, allowing the air under the anvil to cool and settle down again. The great cities could withstand the worst of any storm; even the roughest seas and strongest winds could not shake them. People on the big rafts would retreat below deck and watch with interest as rain and hail swept over, lightning striking the towers with no more effect than brilliant flashes and thunder. It was all very entertaining. At worst there might be an occasional glitch in the gaming screens.

On the day that everything changed, Sal and her team recognized early that the atmospheric temperatures were unstable. Soon after dawn on this day, anvil shaped clouds were seen developing. The *Shanghai First* raft, still distantly within sight from Sal's operation centre, became entirely blotted out of view as the storm it had created developed immediately above and around it. There would be heavy rain there, probably hail and even tornadoes

17

No one was ready for the next three hours. The distant storm, a vortex in the atmosphere, grew and spread. On the outer edges of the vortex the winds, like water draining from a bath or tank, began to circulate round the low-pressure centre in spiral fashion, raising great waves. Sal issued a general warning and recalled all swimmers.

The small raft, for now it seemed very small indeed, was in the worst possible position and it was the wrong shape. The circulating wind raised great waves, sometimes tilting the whole deck one way or another. Sal could see nothing beyond the windows but torrential rain and driving sea spume. There were blinding and crackling strikes of lightning and explosive crashes of thunder. Again and again the lightning struck. Fail-safe and override devices were knocked out repeatedly, wires and cables became instantly white hot and evaporated altogether. There was the smell of smoke. Some wall-mounted connections were blown to fragments; pieces of insulation were thrown violently in all directions like shrapnel. The sprites took cover wherever they could; some were too slow and were injured. Hail came, small at first, then suddenly the raft was bombarded with egg sized balls of ice that hammered and rebounded and were swept along by the howling wind to pile up against every possible obstruction, hammering at windows and sweeping unchecked along exposed decks. The noise was unbearable. Sal and everyone else she could see covered their gill ears in horror and fear.

The hail ceased as suddenly as it had started. Those still on their feet, stared round, the deck still rocking wildly. Unsteady on their feet

they were able to exchange brief, but grim, smiles, as if to say, we are
still alive, still afloat, the worst is over.

It was not over.

The huge masses of humid air that had been drawn up to stratospheric
heights had cooled there. When they met overlying stratospheric air
they could rise no further, so descended. The resulting cold downburst
on the fringes of the main storm came roaring, reached the sea and
spread out with super gale force raising more huge waves and driving
all before it. Jezzy's raft, in such fearsome conditions, behaved like any
other piece of flotsam. It was driven, pitching to and fro, for hours.
Only gradually some stability returned but the terrifying disharmonious
oscillations continued.

Still clutching tables, capsules and anything that gave her a firm
handhold, Sal stood and saw several of her staff bruised and bleeding,
two lay motionless. She and others on their feet stumbled to give
assistance. Those injured were helped and their wounds bound up
with anything that came to hand. A broken arm was hastily splinted
and tied up with someone's shirt. Efforts were made to bring the two
unconscious ones round. One of them came to and staggered to her feet.
The other, a man, did not move, several sprites kneeling round him.

What to do?

Someone small came rushing towards Sal, grasping and hugging
her tightly. It was Towie, the boat boy, clinging desperately, trembling.
Becky was suddenly there too and Airther, the small man, threw his
arms around all three. The family had been in the schoolroom with
the student navigators. There was nothing Sal could do for them at
present but return their caresses. *Where was Darien?* He had been with
the family before the storm but was nowhere in sight now. They stood,
a small huddle, as other navigators, bewildered, milled around, trying
to reassure themselves, looking anxiously to find friends and to seek
more help.

'Where is Darien?' Sal asked Airther. 'He was with you, wasn't he?'
Airther understood, but had no answer, he looked around anxiously,
spoke to the bairns, who shook their heads.

'Weh'l sik him.

'Reet,' said Sal, sithee'int' Rec Hall.'
We'll look for him.
Right, See you in the Recreation Hall

Sal hurried to the fallen man who lay very still, face down. One of
the female navigation team, Perrini 970, was kneeling by him, weeping,
the others standing, horrified.

'Sal, Sal, what can I do? He's dead. It's Conder'

'Is he breathing? We must try to get his lungs working. Is his mouth
clear? Help me push down on his shoulders, try to get him breathing.'

'No, no,' screamed the young sprite. 'It's no good.' Conder's head
was at a terrible angle. Something had struck his neck with great force
and shattered his spine.

'Sal Oh Sal, Sal, it's Conder, my Conder, my boy, what can I do?'

'Perrini, my dear, we can do nothing for him, this is terrible. I am
so sorry.' Sal tried to comfort the girl but knew it was hopeless and she
must not delay. 'There are others who need help.' She stood, shakily, and
looked around. The deck still moved wildly. There was chaos but those
who needed urgent assistance were getting whatever the inexperienced
students could give. Some of the young medics and nurses must come
to do whatever they could with the injured. Call them to the Nav office,
urgently.

Every piece of electronic equipment within reach was out of action.
Nothing was working. The capsule screens were blank, dead. Sal tried to
use her terminal. It was active but there was no contact with anything or
anyone. There was no way of making general announcements or calling
for assistance. Even to escape from inside to the open deck was difficult.
Doors, which had formerly opened automatically, were solidly closed.
She and those who now followed her had to find ways to force the exits
open manually, which was only just possible.

Sal and a shocked group of young navigators struggled out into the
open. There were still great waves; water washed over the deck, clouds
of spray soaked them as they emerged. No one was in sight. Where was
Sistus? Where were Jezzy, Michel, Darien, the girls with their babies?
Where was everyone? Were others badly injured or dead? Was anyone

missing? The raft was utterly alone on the ocean, out of contact with the world and with no hope of external assistance. The *First Shanghai* raft had disappeared, the vast storm cloud still grumbling and sparking in the distance.

The raft responded awkwardly and unpredictably, totally out of rhythm with the oceanic swell. There was also, Sal realized, an asymmetrical tilt that did not go away. There must be some damage to the vital buoyancy structures below.

Sistus, where are you? There was no organization. Sal realized quickly the urgent need for someone to give directions. She told the bewildered group around her to gather in the recreation hall, help anyone who was injured. They should tell any others they found to go to the hall.

Spaces, cabins and capsules on lower decks with no external light would be in total darkness or, in a few cases, dimly illuminated by a few surviving fuel cell-powered emergency lights. People might be trapped in such places.

Sistus? She ventured down alone, using the motionless escalators and companionways, in the dark at times, feeling her way, finding a few frightened people wandering without direction or aim. She guided them upwards to the light and directed them to the Hall.

Jezzy? Must be in the old, reduced laboratory? Sal blundered through gloomy corridors, struggling with ordinary doors that were jamming, sliding doors that would not slide, one or two iris doors that she managed to open without power, and to her enormous relief found Jezzy, stumbling and struggling out as she was going in. They embraced. The old woman was trembling.

'Jezzy, oh Jezzy, are you hurt? Are you well? Was anyone with you? Have you seen Sistus, Darien, the girls? The babies?'

'Rusalka, Michel was with me,' Jezzy gasped. 'He will follow. No one else. He is checking the tanks. Everything there, all our specimens, will die if we have no power.'

'I have told everyone to meet in the Rec Hall. There are people injured, Jezzy, They need help.'

'Get them to the old treatment centre where we did the injections. I will go, there's everything needed there.' Jezzy had a purpose, it helped her.

'Others, to the hall, Sal gasped, 'I can't think of anywhere else. There is a window there, light. Everyone must go there if they can move.'

She found her way to the nursery. To her relief Alicia and Euna were safe and in comparatively good order. The nature of the troubles had not escaped them. Now the babies were feeding at the breast and their mothers seemed less disturbed than the other sprites.

'We were all asleep at the beginning,' said Euna. 'It's quiet here, and sheltered. When we felt everything moving, it woke us, and there was that deafening noise. The power went but we get some light from the windows in here. It was terrifying but we held the babies as quiet as we could, well wrapped up and warm. We shielded them from the flashes. I don't think they really noticed very much. It wasn't funny. I don't think anything will ever be funny again.'

Sistus? Sal left the nursery. As she did so, she chided herself, for she had forgotten her own condition. Was there any truth, she wondered, in the old tales that serious stress for a pregnant woman could cause dreadful traumas for the growing embryo? Her child was no longer an embryo. She was past the eighth week, a foetus, not what she had once thought of as a piece of gristle but a human with organs, a developing nervous system and in the head, there was a brain, already learning. The gill ears would be forming. What had they heard?

Jezzy would tell her what to expect. Oh Jezzy, Sistus. As she searched through lightless corridors, past damaged fittings and windows, she found others and made sure all understood what they must do.

Sistus, Sistus, where are you? She hunted, almost running, stumbling as the decks shifted under her feet, dashing up stairs and down, until, exhausted, finding no one more, she stumbled to the Recreation Hall. It was crowded with terrified sprites, some bruised and bleeding. More were entering.

Among the arrivals leading a small crowd was Sistus. They ran to meet.

'Sal, oh Sal my darling, you are alive Unhurt? What a relief.' He hugged her.

'Sistus, my dear, my dear, I thought you might be dead.'

'No, but there are some, and others are seriously injured. We must help them.'

'I found Jezzy. She is going to the treatment room; she has all her medical things there. Sistus, she is trembling from head to foot, won't be able to manage. She needs helpers, nurses, medics.'

'I'll get some of the sprites.' He climbed to the platform, yelled for anyone with medical knowledge and nursing skills to go to help Jezzy, and anyone needing aid to go there too. People, thought Sal, always listened to Sistus. The rocking motion had eased a little now, but the general tilt remained.

'Please,' Sistus yelled to make himself heard, 'everyone who can move freely, go and search the raft, everywhere, from end to end. Don't go alone, keep in small groups of three or four, but spread out, don't leave any corner without searching. We must make sure no one is lost or trapped. When everyone has been found, meet here again. Search, and then come back. We must see if we can get some food for everyone, but it will be cold. Anyone who can get into the stores?' Several raised hands. 'Go and see what is there, bring it here if you can.'

'I know some people have died. If you find anyone, please carry them here carefully. We must identify them.'

'Engineers, please, gather round here. We must get some power on again. We can't do anything until we have that.' Young engineers clustered round the platform as the others hurried away. 'I'd like you all to go and check the state of things,' Sistus said to the group. 'Do any of you have experience with... let's start with the wind turbines, anyone?' Several hands went up.

'Good, can you go at once and see if any of them are workable, if we can get them running? Come back here when you have done it. We'll keep a record... Go at once, the sooner we know the better. If any of them can be restarted, we must do it quickly. The group moved away. One of the girls, Liy 756, seemed to take charge immediately without being chosen

'You three this way, you go there, some of you this side, the others that,' Liy said. They obeyed without argument.

'Solar panels, who knows about them?' cried Sistus. Hands went up. They set out at once.

'Now, the hydroponics towers. I can see one of them came down, or nearly, but check the other one, is it capable of producing anything? Can we keep the crops growing?' A group set off to look. 'Hydrogen engines, are they usable? And generators? The de-salination plant? Communications centre, satellite contacts, any hope there?' At each word, the engineers, prominent among them one called Vogel 509, sorted themselves out and set out on their mission. Leaders seemed to appear in each group as they were needed.

'Have I forgotten anything?'

'Wiring,' said one of the girls. 'A lot of the wiring has blown out, you can see, but maybe it's just fuses in some of the circuits. We can check and switch them back on or mend them. We may be able to crimp the wires if they are broken. I know where the tools are.'

'Yes, good, Lesley, do what you can. The connections won't be any use till there's some power but they should be repaired.'

'Good. Now, Robots' said Sistus. 'That's my responsibility, but they won't work till they can be powered up. Some of them should have some battery power left. We'll go and look. Anyone else, come with me. Oh, someone must stay behind to keep records.'

'I can do that,' said Sal.

'Good, sweetheart, thanks. Note every report in your termin... Oh no, they aren't working properly. You'll have to write things down. Can you find something to write on? Get them to wait here when they report. We will have to have another meeting with everyone here, organize some repair parties, find tools.'

'I can write on this wall, there must be a pen somewhere. Jezzy's got some in the treatment room. I'll get one.' She sped off. Jezzy used felt tip pens for marking flasks containing samples.

When she returned to the hall Sal was relieved to see Darien with Airther and the children, and Michel, all safe.

The first of the engineer groups came back almost at once.

'We've checked the turbines on the port side. They are all damaged but a few of them have rotors intact, as far as we can see,' said their leader, Liy. 'The blades feathered themselves correctly when the wind got up but they can't turn now because their pylons are distorted. We should be able to get the rotors off. There are some undamaged pylons, we can swap them round. The others are all too badly damaged.'

Sal marked a series of vertical divisions on the wall, and wrote under Turbines, *Liy 756, Some rotors good, some pylons good, Rotors swapping to pylons?*

Other columns she headed: *Solar Panels, Hydroponics Tower, Communication Centre, Desalination, Hydrogen Engines, Generators, Robots, Electrics.* After some hesitation, she marked a final column: *Deaths.* Here she wrote the one name she knew, *Conder 438.*

The solar panel group returned.

'Some of them may still be working,' said the young man who spoke for them all, Shaw 478, 'but a lot have been ripped to shreds. Those thin photosynthesis leaves we were so proud off, they were battered by the hail and then split and blown away. We'll have to make more.'

'There may be some still rolled up in the reserve store,' said one of this group. Sal wrote it up under the name, *Shaw 478.* The various columns were soon filled. *Communications* was the least hopeful.

'It's like a distorted, melted monument,' the leading girl, Peta 334, said. 'Everything has been taken out, no contact with the satellite relays or the space stations. All the screens are dead. Wrist terminals are alive but useless.' They, like the rest, had relied on the communications centre.

The reports came in, the wall filled up with writing. A young woman, Diane 832, had apparently been running full tilt down an escalator when the power cut out, stopping the escalator abruptly and causing her to tumble violently to the bottom and die. Sal sorrowfully added her name to the board. Orao 175, a boy, had been found lying soaked and burned on the upper deck near a turbine. It had probably been struck by lightning, which killed him too. His name went on the wall. No more deaths were discovered. The sad remains of the three were placed carefully in capsules in the treatment room and covered for the time being. The names meant nothing to Sal, but they were mourned and wept over by their friends. Something would have to be done for them later, but there was no time now for this.

The searchers having all returned and the walking wounded, bandaged, splinted, coming into the hall, she saw Sistus in deep conversation with Jezzy. He waved for her to join them. She went to Darien first and encouraged him to come with her. Airther tagged along too, the bairns following. Jezzy was grim and tired.

'Sistus, I cannot speak to them. My voice is not strong enough,' Jezzy was saying, 'and I have no idea what we should do. You must take charge, tell them what you think best.'

'We must get on at once with repairs. Everyone must help.' Sistus stepped up onto the platform alone, lifted his hands. The crowd was immediately quiet.

Sistus raised his voice sufficiently to reach the furthest corners without the usual electronic aids. 'It is obvious we are in serious trouble,' he said. 'How bad things are we cannot tell yet. You can see, Sal has written a list for the engineers. They will start working immediately to get things working again. That's just the beginning. Every one of you can help and *must* help.' Sistus had to think on his, feet.

'Is there anyone still in need of urgent medical treatment? If so, please show by raising your hands.' Mercifully, no more than two or three hands were raised.

'As soon as we finish here, go to the treatment room. Nurses, doctors, please help them.'

'There's an awful lot of minor damage and general mess. Just cleaning up will help. Everyone can start on that. If you can think of anything that needs doing, please do it, don't waste any time about it.'

'Is the raft sinking?' shouted someone.

'Some of the underwater structure has certainly been damaged,' He gestured with his arms and body. The tilt was not very great but was perceptible. 'It will have to be repaired but that cannot be done unless we get the robots going again. Everything depends on the power supply. Anything else?'

'What about getting help from the big rafts?'

'There isn't anything in sight. The one we could see before is over the horizon now. We are on our own. We cannot ask for help unless we have the communications systems running again.' Sal wondered, momentarily, how the cities could or would help them even if they were able to ask.

'What chance is there of another storm? Could it all happen again? There are still storms out there now. You can see the huge clouds.'

Sistus reluctantly, turned to Sal. She feared this question but no one else could reply. Trembling inwardly she stood next to Sistus and attempted to speak. Her voice was too faint and someone shouted 'Can't hear. Speak up.'

'I cannot be sure it will not happen again,' she shouted. 'The conditions producing a storm like that are not common in these latitudes but there is no guarantee. This is a small raft, which made everything very much worse. I think, I hope, the storms will die overnight. I cannot get a satellite image, or even a verbal forecast until the machines are working again. I'm sorry…' She could say no more. Sistus came to her rescue.

'If there is another storm, we must not be in a weak position to meet it. Everyone must work and get things running again. Anything else anyone can think of?'

'What about about Conder and the others?' cried Perrini.

'Ah. That's dreadful,' Sistus replied. 'I'm so sorry. We'll have to do something, we must think about them. There's nothing we can do just now. We must work, there will be a… a ceremony, later, when we have done all these other things.' He pointed to the list.

'Sal,' shouted a voice from the back. 'Sal, sing for us' There was a murmur of agreement and even a few cheers and handclaps, but there was little real support for the idea. Sal turned away, shaking, could not face them. She felt responsible for the disaster for she had not predicted the storm or been able to give proper warning hours or days in advance. She stumbled down a couple of steps from the platform. The crowd murmured in a mixture of disappointment and approval.

'Come on Sal, we know it wasn't your fault. Sing.' someone yelled. Sal shook her head and would have stepped further down but was suddenly confronted by Airther.

'Ne lass, yee canna leave it thare. Yee muss gis them summat. Gissies aal summat, ah mean, there muss be summat more.'

No, Lass, you cannot leave it there. You must give them something, Give us all something, I mean there must be something more.

He almost dragged Sal back up to the platform again, pushed her forward and the crowd fell silent, expectantly. *No, no,* she thought.

'Airther thinks I must give you something more.' She had to shout again. 'I will not, I *cannot* sing now. I cannot. Everyone has so much to do, we must not delay. But I will give you this. When everything is repaired, when we are a living and working raft again, then I will sing. I will sing a requiem for those who died. And afterwards we will all sing. There will be a… great singing…music, a concert afterwards. Now get to work.'

Sistus hugged her, whispered to her, 'Thank you my love, thank you.' He turned to face the multitude again and began to direct the engineers.

When the meeting had broken up, a sad young man came to Sal. His name tag read Ranjit 892. 'I think there is someone else missing, Sal, my friend Moki 371. I've been looking for him everywhere. I think he might have been washed off the deck into the sea.' With Ranjit she made her way to the treatment room where she was relieved to see that Jezzy had let the nurses and nearly qualified doctors take over while she sat, wearily, and let them do the work.

No sign of Moki 371. Were any others missing?

Anyone in the sea would be lost now, gills or no. Sal knew Alicia had kept a register but if it had been stored electronically it would not be accessible. Alicia was there with Euna, helping.

'I have a hard copy of the register,' said Alicia when Sal asked her. 'I printed all their names and numbers on cards and made backup copies I was going to issue them to everyone to wear, but never got round to it. They are in an old box file over there, in that cabinet.' Sal found the box file, a thing she had never seen before, but soon understood how it was arranged. She asked Ranjit and some other sprites to go round getting everyone to check their card and wear it. They were still checking two hours later. Two cards, one of them Moki's, another for Dickon 986, were left in the box. Possibly they had been swimming and failed to come in when she called, or they could have been swept off the raft altogether by waves. Either way, they were gone, would never be found. She wrote the names sadly on the wall. Five sprites had been lost.

They drifted aimlessly and powerlessly for days, running into weeks. Work to restore life to the numerous machines was very slow. Formerly it had been taken for granted that with a few brief touches or verbal instructions to a capsule, any kind of information would be instantly displayed. Circuit diagrams, repair and re-programming procedures, special materials, advice from distant places or experts far away, position reports, anything needed would have been easy to find. Any special tools needed could be made quickly by the robot machines and robots themselves would do further work as directed.

Not now. Even distress calls were impossible. As far as anyone could see, the ocean remained entirely empty.

Sal knew that Sistus had not sought the responsibilities that were now thrust upon him. He had stepped in when it seemed vitally important for someone to take charge. Now all acknowledged him as the man to go to when decisions and advice were needed. Almost in tears of desperation, frustration and self-doubt, he needed Sal's company, reassurance and rest. He confessed to his darling that he was overwhelmed, running out of ideas, but must continue. She supported him as best she could. In public, he was becoming a great man. In private, he wept.

'You must not try to carry everything alone. Find good people to take charge of the various groups. Let them share the work and the responsibility. They can report back to you.'

Sistus nodded. 'They are finding their own leaders'. Exhausted, he slept in her arms.

With little or no hands-on practical experience, even the most qualified engineers and other experts fumbled. New problems emerged every day with no immediate solutions. Potable water was running out rapidly. The desalination plant lacked the necessary pumping power. Food was in short supply. The surviving hydroponics tower required hand and foot work to mix, carry and pump the fluids necessary to maintain nourishment for the growing vegetables. Protein supplies from the food fish tanks and synthetic meat factory were running out. The faithful bacteria toiled in the sewage treatment plant, but power to move the stuff was lacking. There was great reluctance to jettison anything to pollute the ocean but as the settling tanks threatened to spill over, this began to look like the only option.

Jezzy, appalled and weary, blamed herself for everything but could not help. She retreated to her laboratory and, with Michel, struggled to keep things going there.

The first success was to restore a wind turbine. A group of the engineers, led by Vogel, struggled for three days. They lacked even such simple tools as spanners and vice grips. Some help was obtained from a robot with a dying battery. A complete set of rotor, blades, a generator and connectors were salvaged with a struggle from a crumpled pylon. The whole engineer gang managed to carry the dismantled rotor to a mast that still stood. The damaged pieces from this were removed and replaced, piece-by-piece. The rotor, at last began to spin and the generators worked. There were no connections to anything and still no power but the wiring was replaced gradually.

To widespread amazement amounting almost to worship, it was Airther and Towie together who became vital now. Airther showed Sistus, Curtis, Vogel, Liy, Michel and the others how to make soldered joints in heavy copper cables with a minimal acid flux from the lab and a small, rare piece of ordinary lead. They had to make an open fire on the deck to heat their improvised soldering irons. Even lighting this fire required primitive technology. To find some burnable material required a raft-wide search. There was no wood anywhere. A few rags soaked in oil and dry vegetable leaves from the hydroponics tower were the best they could find. Airther made and demonstrated a fire lighting friction bow. The crude joints they managed to make were not good, but they worked. An important step forward had been taken. Taking power from the wind turbine, they were able to run a few machines and charge some batteries. It was little but it was an important beginning. With jury-rigging they were now able to work a computer. Alicia rejoiced. With her baby nestling on her lap she gained access to some limited memory banks. Diagrams, plans and instructions began to appear on screen and made sense to those who could interpret them.

Shaw's group found some stored photosynthesis leaf solar panels. They could now, slowly, fuel some of the power cells in the robots. Liy and Vogel's gang together repaired another turbine and connected it up. Sistus and other engineers dismantled a humble robocar to find some essential parts. They were still far from getting any of the heavy machinery to operate or deploy any advanced tooling, but they could draw on the vast global memory. They were making progress.

Sal still could get no weather predictions or images, and spent anxious hours without the usual aids, trying to work out where they were, which direction they were moving, and where they might be on the morrow.

'Lass, tha needs a *sextant*,' said Airther, the fisherman.

Lass, you need a sextant.

'What's that?' she had to ask.

'T'idee's laak this,' he showed her, drawing on the back of one of Jezzy's file cards. 'Sithee, a quadrant, like this, wi' a sight, tha can use a length of string.. wi a knot, It tells thee t'angle o' t'sun, gis thee latitude. Ne, I canna mak a proper 'un,...'

The idea's like this. See, a quadrant, like this, with a sight. Yer can use a length of string with a weight. It tells you the angle of the sun, gives the latitude. No, I can't mak a proper one...

He came back to her later and tried to show her how to work the crude gadget he had struggled with. It was desperately imprecise but perhaps it was better than nothing. She could not look directly at the glaring sun, could not judge exactly when it was noon, had no calendar, and the raft was still pitching.

18

Sal formed the impression that they were drifting generally southwards. The raft was rotating at the whim of the wind and currents. Some of the engineers helped her with this.

'You see those vanes,' said Liy, the girl who led the turbine group. 'They are there for two purposes. If you rotate all the vanes in a certain way, they act as sails and you can turn the raft this way or that. There's not enough power to move them all yet but we can set the angles manually. We'll do it when we have a bit of time to spare. Give us a day or two, we'll go round them all. That will stop the roundabout. As sails they'll give you a bit of power to drive the raft along. Not enough to make much real difference, though.'

With her little group of navigators gathered round, on the wall Sal sketched a rough map of the South Atlantic.

'When we separated from Shanghai we were in the so-called Brazil current. I guess we still are, and that would mean we are drifting southwards. But I don't know how far we were taken by the storm, or what has happened since.' She sketched in her idea of the current. It swept round in a great loop. 'It goes so far, then divides into branches. The one here up the West African coast is called the Benguela Current, the other goes eastwards. Before we broke from Shanghai, it was intended we would go that way with it.'

'Sal, if we go north, won't we get swept into the hurricane zone?' asked Szigeti 361.

'I hope before anything like that, we will be under control again and we could catch the westward drift and pick up the Brazil current again. It will take months. We must be in good shape long before that.'

'You hope.'

'I hope, and you'd better hope too. We must not get into the Caribbean, nor the doldrums.'

'Before that, though, we might miss the African one and get into the forties. We might go round and round the southern ocean forever in storms and cold wind,' said Jedwab 139.

'That's too pessimistic, Jed. If that happens, the raft won't survive. I am sure the engineers will get everything going again long before anything like that can happen.'

Thump, thump. Her baby was definitely beginning to stir. Over twenty weeks now, or had she lost the count?

There was no question about the tilting of the deck and it was slowly increasing. Sistus, Vogel and several other swimmers dived to discover if they could see anything that would explain what was happening.

'It was so dark under the raft we couldn't see a thing,' Sistus said when they re-emerged, disappointed. 'We tried to explore by touch, but it's hopeless. Everything is thick with barnacles, all sharp spines and edges. We all got cuts and grazes. I guess the whole raft has been distorted. Some of the honeycomb must be cracked or crushed.' How far could this continue before the raft as a whole began to founder? Would repairs be possible, even if they could get all the machines functioning again? Nobody knew. 'There's no way to find out what is wrong down there till we get some limpet robots working. We must get on to that,' he said.

Sistus the robot master and his team now had a few of the simpler machines working. They used these to re-activate and repair others. They were fed the necessary plans and told to examine, analyze and repair or replace whatever was needed. The re-activated machines in turn were set to work restoring normal functions to everything else, especially the damaged turbines and solar collectors and the communications system. Improvements came rapidly. Day by day, the raft was coming back to life.

The names of the five who had died were still written where Sal had put them. It was, so far, their only memorial. The three corpses were still in the capsules where they had been laid. They could not be left any longer.

'We must have a funeral, Darien,' Sal said to him, when she saw him looking sadly at the wall.

'Yes. But we can't do the usual thing. The crematorium is on the main raft. I've looked at the archives. The old navies used to have burials at sea. The bodies were wrapped in shrouds and weighted down with... well, heavy lumps of iron.'

'I know, cannon balls. Everyone would gather and someone would say a few words, there was some sort of music, wasn't there? A pipe, or something, was played. Then the bodies were slipped into the sea.'

'You said you would sing for them.'

'Yes, I can sing a requiem.'

'We'd better ask Sistus about it.'

'Oh, poor Sistus. He has so much on his mind. We can arrange this ourselves, can't we?'

'We have no authority, Sal.'

'Damn authority. I have had too much of authority,' Sal snapped. Darien was startled.

'You know how much trouble I get into when I do what comes into my head. I think we must ask Jezzy. She might want to be in charge of it.'

'All right. Speak to Michel first. Jezzy is so miserable just now. Michel is with her every day, he will know how she is, how she would take it.'

'Right, I will go and ask him, and we'll come back to you about it.'

Michel told them Jezzy would definitely wish to take part in the ceremony and would speak briefly. They worked out a simple programme with her. Work would have to be abandoned for an hour, except for the robots. There would be a memorial assembly of everyone in the hall,

Jezzy presiding. Sal would sing and a friend of each of the lost ones would speak. The bodies, prepared and shrouded, would be taken down to the landing stage on trolleys. This was the only place with easy access to the sea.

There was not enough room on the restricted landing deck for everyone. Those who had known the victims well would go to witness the sea burial. Sal would sing again if it seemed appropriate. They told Sistus of their plan. He agreed without hesitation, relieved that for once nothing devolved upon him.

On the appointed day the assembly gathered. Jezzy spoke briefly, finding it difficult, but the sprites were utterly silent.

'Sprites, my dears, I cannot express my sadness. You are my people and we have lost five precious members. I feel a terrible responsibility but I cannot undo what has been done. Remember your lost friends, and make the future better than the past has been.'

The friends spoke briefly but with feeling, especially Perrini who was much affected by Conder's death. Sal understood there had been more than casual friendship between those two. She knew, now, what love was.

Perrini ended with the words: 'Conder would want me to say; we do not hold Jezzy responsible for what has happened. Some of the Shanghai rafters allowed themselves to be carried away by a few bigoted fanatics. The Mandarin, Fauvel, was cowardly, frightened to stand against them. It is good that we are far away from them now. The future is with us'

The requiem had many of the sprites in tears, Sal herself having difficulty with the last few bars. At the landing stage the bodies slid gently into the waves and vanished. When she sang again it seemed to Sal that there was a mournful echo of her voice going out over the ocean. She and most of the others left the scene weeping. Afterwards came an immense feeling of relief.

Sal had her navigation system running normally. Now she knew where the raft had drifted and could see where it was going. Her guesses had been quite close. She was reassured to find that she did understand something about the oceans. They were out of the tropics now, well clear of the hurricane belt that, at this season, would be in its northern phase. She felt uneasy because the coast of South America was closer than she wished. She would like to get further out if she could, but not too far where there were calms and stagnation.

She still had no way of moving the raft in a chosen direction.

Liy reported now. 'Come and see, Sal.' She took Sal up to the turbine deck where she had a control console. 'See, the vanes are all standing up properly again. They respond to the controls, like this.' The vanes all turned on their pivots together like marines in a drill movement.

'Can you stop the raft turning round and round?'

'Yes, it takes a while but I can trim it for you now and we can adjust it a bit every now and then, to keep it steady. I'll program it in. Do you want anything else?'

Sal felt it would be most favourable if the vanes could be set to edge the raft away from the coast, which she could almost see.

'To use them as sails,' Liy said. 'you set them this way,' she demonstrated 'they will push us along a bit. It will hardly make any difference; the raft is so massive in comparison with the thrust of the vanes. We can try it.'

The tactic seemed to work. The trend of the drift might have moved a little more easterly. Sal would need something much more powerful if it became necessary to drive the raft in some chosen direction for a while. Lacking a fusion power plant they would have to get some kind of propulsion engines running, if possible. Sistus nodded, promised to get some work going on that.

The Nav School was operating again. Sal herself completed the tests at the end of her nominal fourth year, and became a qualified navigator. She was able to enter this success in the intercity navigation data banks. Others of her staff were not far behind, working through the course and gaining practical experience of a kind never seen before.

Airther and his children returned to the teaching capsules as soon as they were working again, Darien helping. He was beginning to pick up their strange language. Airther often left the bairns working and came to look at Sal's charts as the data came in. He understood what was going on.

The baby was kicking. Sistus, amazed and fascinated, was allowed to feel it too, when they were together. Sal, after checking with Jezzy, began to count down the weeks. When the day came, one of the most advanced trainees would have to act as chief navigator for a while.

There remained the problem of the underwater damage. This now was the great issue facing Sistus and the engineers. There were occasional worrying noises, creaks, and groaning, sometimes distinct thumpings, from deep down below in the lowest decks. The tilting was increasing slowly. The solution remained beyond reach.

'There used to be special robots moving under the raft constantly, checking and repairing,' Sistus said. 'I don't know if we took any with us when we cut ourselves away, but if we did they all seem to have been shaken off in the storm. They are not there to help us now. There's no other answer, other than building new machines. We'll equip them for the job of finding the hull damage and if possible, repairing it. It's easier said than done.'

Robots must be programmed to make extraordinary robots capable of making yet more extraordinary robots to carry out the vital repairs. All this was not going to be achieved in a day, a few days or weeks. Meanwhile the raft threatened to list and sink down further and further. Eventually if nothing was done it would slide below the surface. The robot master with his handful of partly and fully trained specialists began the work immediately and desperately. Another severe storm would finish them. Might they, after all, have to survive in the sea? They could call on the other rafts for help, but would there be any response? It could not be guaranteed. How long did they have?

How long did Sal have? Three weeks or so, give or take? Jezzy now was insisting on careful inspections every few days. The old woman was still alert at these times, but Sal saw she was moving slowly, no longer the energetic and sometimes frightening creature she had been.

Sal was reminded by Euna that she promised they would have a concert. They would hold her to this. Everyone had helped; everyone had done their utmost to bring things back to normality. They had shown themselves to be a proper crew; a spirit of community and friendship had prevailed over the crisis.

Sistus, distracted as he was with work, agreed enthusiastically. Now was the time to have a party. He did not say what Sal knew he feared. There might never be another.

'There are other good singers among the sprites too,' said Euna. 'They should be found.'

'We must have a choir' said Michel. 'It will give everyone something to work for and look forward to. I can sing a bit, and I can help to train them.' The entire audience, Sal determined, would join in some well-known songs, and she would end with a solo. She drafted a programme. After the singing, the afternoon would be dedicated to dancing and celebration.

'Dancing?' said Sistus. 'On a tilted floor?'

'Dancing before the tilting gets any worse,' said Sal, 'and before I myself can't dance properly with my huge tummy'

She made announcements, fixed a day, called for volunteer performers. She and Michel held some auditions and discovered more than enough talent. Alicia's registry listed the musicians. Some were prepared to sing duets, trios and quartets. There were instrumentalists who could play and improvise on synthesizers. They used the capsule archives when they needed more music, or wanted to be reminded of lyrics. She formed a group to work out the details. Sal was astonished when Becky and Towie offered to sing a number called Adam Buckham, they said, in their own language.

'Wi can sing, tha kens'

'Wi want t'sing *Adam Buckham* yee knaa. It's in proper Anglish and it's foonny and arl'

'Wad yee leick weh to shaw yee?'

We can sing, you know. We want to sing Adam Buckham you know. It's in proper English and its funny and all. Would you like us to show you?

Sal heard them.

Adam Buckham

It's doon the Lang Stairs,
And strite alang the Cloase,
All in Bakker's Entry,
Adam Buckham Knars

Chorus:

for It's..
O, Adam Buckham, O,
O, Adam Buckham, O,
O, Adam Buckham, O
Wiv his bow legs.

Nanny carries watter,
Tommy cobbles shoes,
And Adam Buckham gans aboot
Getherin in the news

Chorus:

Adam kissed the servant lass,
That'll never do;
If he dissent mind himsel,
The kitty myeks him rue,

Chorus

Adam gat the lass wi' bairn;
That'll never do.
If he dinna marry her
The kitty gars him rue.

Kitty gars him rue, they explained, was Anglish for being sent to jail. Sal agreed they should sing the short piece as a comedy item. Few would understand the words but that wasn't going to matter. Airther's bairns were part of the crew now and deserved to be recognized.

She went to see Jezzy, the first time, it seemed, in weeks that she had been able to talk to her privately without medical examination. Would she come to the concert? She did not look well, spoke slowly but embraced her.

'Rusalka, for you I will come. I will be there. Tell me, little mermaid, are you sorry you joined me? Are my children regretting the day they fell into my clutches?' Sal had heard no one even hint that they wished they had not joined the sprites. Perhaps if Jezzy could be persuaded to come out of her shell, she would be happy to see how all her sea sprites were recovering their spirits. All now had full gills, all now could swim under the sea and for this occasion, all would be happy.

'Jezzy, no. No one has said anything like that. No one feels like that. Perrini said you are not to blame. We have come to life, more than we ever were before. Everyone admires and thanks you for the gift you have given us. Our children, too, will learn about you and respect you. I have found love with Sistus, he is the father of this child I carry here. I would not have known any such wonderful things if I had not come to you. I love you, Jezzy. We all love you. It has been desperately difficult since we were forced to leave Shanghai and being struck by the storm but it has also been a fantastic, exciting, wonderful adventure and there will be more. That is what we all wanted. Come to the concert. They will cheer you. A little of the old Jezzy spirit reappeared, with her crooked grin.

'They will cheer you, little mermaid, you and Sistus. I will be there cheering for the pair of you,' she poked Sal's tummy with an old finger, 'and for her in there too She can hear, you know. Do you understand that? Children in the womb can hear and feel long before they are born. Sing to her a lot, Rusalka, sing to her. She will remember.'

Sistus was reluctant to attend at first, claiming to be too busy. Sal insisted he should at least show himself. If he would not or could not sing and dance, he must at least be present. She spoke to Darien, Michel and the young mothers. While Sistus was elsewhere, they spent an hour together agreeing on a procedure.

Sal opened the afternoon by bringing a timid Jezzy onto the stage. The crowd cheered and cheered. Sal gave them free rein. When they quietened, Michel stepped forward.

'Sal, before we begin,' he said, 'we want everyone to recognize Sistus who has done so much in the last weeks to restore us to normality. He has been an extraordinary leader. He saw what was coming, made preparations. He defied Fauvel. When the storm struck he kept his head when most of us were in panic. His organizing ability, persuasive skills, clear thinking and above all his powerful and infectious energy have brought us through what might otherwise have been a disaster. Jezzy insists Sistus did everything. She gave him all her authority even before the separation. These are her own words, she and I have talked about it. He has been our commander since the day we had to cut loose.' The audience began to applaud. Michel signed that he had more to say.

'He has had no warning of this, indeed, Sal had to twist his arm even to get him up here with us on the platform. He did not push himself to the front. But I know you will all agree with me, that is where he should be and must remain. He is a great man. I propose that Sistus should be made Captain here and now, by the ancient mechanism of popular acclaim Who is for Sistus?'

The roar of approval was deafening and continued for long minutes and a rhythmic chorus of *Sistus, Sistus, Sistus,* developed. They continued shouting and started stamping their feet rhythmically until Sal and Darien took one hand each and pulled Sistus to his feet and forward.

'Now, it's your turn' Sal whispered in his ear. Don't dry up' Sistus turned to look at her, amazed.

'Getting my own back,' she whispered, and stepped back, leaving him facing the crowd alone.

There was immediate silence.

'I am enormously, overwhelmingly honoured. Thank you. I have no option but to accept. But, please do not stamp your feet so hard. We do not know what effect it might have on the structure beneath our feet.' There was grim laughter.

'I accept on a temporary basis. I will ask for a proper, formal referendum when all this is over, and it isn't over yet. There's more to do and we will do it. But first, let's hear Sal. In my new role as Captain, I appoint her Mistress of Ceremonies'

The concert was a great success. Sal and Sistus retired together early. The dancing continued far into the night but wthout any foot stamping.

19

Despite her best efforts, the coast of South America was coming closer than Sal wished. The current they relied on swung about, now tending westwards where it had been more easterly. Airther assured her he could read the signs long before they could see land. The sky, he said, looked different. The tops of distant clouds began to appear in the west.

'Aye, an look at t'wave pattern,' he said 'Sithee, them's two sets, them's coomin this wey, crossin o'er t'other way. There's an island oot theer away.' He pointed, but Sal could see nothing. She didn't doubt he was right, but the information was of little value to her. There were more birds about; different species of fish were noticed by Michel's team on their submarine excursions. His group was excited at the variety of life they were coming across now.

'Aye, an gandie at the pattern o the waves. Tha sees, there's two sits, those comin this way crossing t'others comin t'other way. There's an island oot there sum away off.'

Aye and look at the wave pattern. See, there's two sets, those coming this way crossing over the other way. There's an island out there some way off.

'We are near the edge of the continental shelf, you see,' Michel said enthusiastically. 'Everything changes as we get nearer to the true coast. One of our lot, Zacher, thinks he saw ruined buildings of some sort down there. We can't be sure, it was quite a way off in the murk, covered in growths, and we've drifted away now. It could have been the remains of an old land city.'

The prototype of a new type of limpet robot was completed and was being demonstrated on the landing stage.

'It looks like a huge mechanical spider,' said Sal trembling slightly. There were no spiders on the raft but she had seen videos and read about the ones that could bite and sting. They trapped insects and the females sometimes ate the males after mating. The machine, at maximum extension, spanned about four metres from tip to tip of its claws.

'Could be an octopus, with tentacles,' said Alicia.

'No, a giant crab' said Michel, fascinated. 'Ten legs and efficient-looking mouthparts in front.'

'One difference' Sistus pointed out. 'It can move in any direction, not just sideways. It goes with a walking motion, upside down, right way up, on a tilted surface, whatever it encounters.' Sistus and the engineer sprite team set it going on the deck and all watched as it began to step along, slowly with a menacing deliberation. Little Becky was terrified and Towie ran to hide behind his father.

'It can't attach itself directly to the skin of the raft,' Sistus explained. 'Everything is so heavily encrusted with molluscs and plant life.'

'How does it hold on, then?' asked Darien.

'The claws will grip and it has neutral buoyancy so it won't sink if it comes loose. It can work at any depth. With so many claws, most of them will grab something and hold even if one or two slip. Each of the limbs is tipped with a drill that will penetrate the fouling to make direct contact to establish and hold the location. Then the main probe sends ultra sound signals into the structure.'

'It's echo sounding,' said Fareed 924, an electronic specialist. 'The central receiver here,' he pointed to the carapace, 'gets all the echoes, integrates them and sends the result to the processor which will be up above deck. After each probing, repeated three times to check, it will move one step forward and do another. We can monitor and control it remotely.'

'We are testing this one today. If it works, which it will, we will get a lot more made and set them all going. The pattern of the echoes will tell us where, and what, the damage is.'

The engineers lifted the machine and dived with it carefully, set it on its ponderous crawling path and escorted it for the first hour to observe that it was obeying the programme set for it. The crab crept slowly into the shadow and was lost to sight. The incoming data showed that it continued to work well. It stopped on command, turned, crabbed forward or back as ordered. Within days more robots were crawling under the raft and more were added as the other robots produced them.

Meanwhile, Sal in her jury-rigged navigation centre was still trying to guide the raft away from danger. They experienced some rough seas and she could feel the raft was not responding well. The slight oscillatory vibrations they had noticed before seemed sometimes to change frequency, or tried to do so. The creaking and cracking sounds were much worse at such times and undermined confidence.

'Sistus,' she said, when she had a chance to talk quietly to him, 'There's an unpleasant sense of something being constantly slightly out of step. Is it my imagination?'

'I feel it too. Everyone knows things aren't right. The raft had a resonance at the beginning. It isn't a resonance now, it is getting a little closer each day to breaking altogether.'

'Every time we get a bit of rough weather, it is worse afterwards.'

'We have to wait for more data from the crabs. When we know what's wrong down there, we will know what we have to do. We are working now on the propulsion engines and pumps if we need them.'

'Do we have fuel for them?'

'The solar leaves are back in action. We are getting some hydrogen now. Jezzy's oil bugs are working all the time and there's some methane. When the engines are ready we will be able to run them, but they have to be mounted under the raft first. It's all a matter of time.'

'Suppose we don't have time?'

'We must make more effort. I will get Vogel and his team onto it, top priority. But it isn't easy.'

'I can guess what you are thinking,' he said. If we do begin to sink, can we get help from the other rafts? We might have to ask them. If we have to, we will. Are there any rafts within reach, Sal? Will they be close enough if we need them?'

'I have checked. At present, no, we are by ourselves.' said Sal. We were swept out of the usual routes by the storm and we are out of the main currents. There's no other city within a hundred nauticals now.

The choppers couldn't reach us but they could send a ferry, couldn't they? There would be room on one of those ships for all of us.'

'They won't come rushing. The rafts drift, it takes huge power to get them moving, and then very slowly even with the fusion plants at full bore. I doubt if they would want to save us, anyway. Captains of many cities wouldn't want a whole lot of sprites suddenly arriving. We are *different*. I can imagine what Fauvel would say; *They chose to jump into the sea, they must live or die with the consequences.* Quite a lot would react the same way.'

'Well, let's hope we will never need to ask.' Said Sal. 'We are not sinking yet. If any raft does come close enough we might get a chopper overhead to look at us but one chopper won't rescue five hundred sprites.'

'Even if they wanted to.'

The drift continued. Sal and Liy adjusted the vanes again and again; persuading themselves they were making a difference, trying to edge always away from the threatening land with the grim prospect of being driven onto reefs and rocks. To Michel the coast meant exciting marine life. It was danger to Sal.

Sal found out all she could from the screens about birth and the care of babies. The prescribed exercises given to her by Jezzy and supervised by some of the young physiotherapists in the crew were followed with care. Her navigators often found her stretching and breathing when they arrived for their spells of duty. She remembered Jezzy's instructions; the baby could hear. She sang softly to herself and to the child. Were those internal fumblings a response to the melodies? Sistus, with the engineers almost totally dedicated now to reading data from the busy crab robots, was still able to find time to see her frequently, to talk, kiss and feel the child's movements. She chatted with Alicia and Euna, heard from them what their experience was like. Their tiny children charmed her. They were now recognizing their mothers, smiling, playing, gurgling and perhaps beginning to utter a few nearly recognizable words. The raft limped on.

The Nav School had become a kind of conference room where the engineers met to consider the situation. Sal heard most of their discussions but there was nothing she could contribute. They were being forced to a grim conclusion.

'It's worse than we expected,' reported Vogel, who now had assembled a partial chart of the damage. More data from the crabs was coming in hourly. Confirming his pessimism, the raft structure was creaking and groaning with every slight change of the waves and wind. The group gathered round the chart conferring gloomily. The extent and severity of the damage was clear. Having been cut away from the generally elliptical main raft, the laboratory section was a long and narrow segment of awkward crescent shape. It was not well adapted to the oceanic wave pattern.

'A large number of the buoyancy cells, right across from one side to the other, have been crushed. The raft has a great crease from side to side,' Vogel reported, 'and it isn't even straight. It curves and runs at an angle.'

'The storm broke the back of the structure without actually severing it. There must have been failures when large waves went under us, repeatedly lowering and raising the centre as the fore and aft portions went the other way, and with a twisting motion too.' The machines showed there were small distortions of the higher structures above, related to actual fractures below. The raft was apparently being held together by the upper decks which were constantly bending slightly up and down. Below, the cracks and crushing extended down all the way. On either side of the damaged zone many of the hexagonal cells were leaking, causing the situation to worsen. Cracks that had been narrow were now beginning to open wider, the outer ends of the raft still watertight as the centre subsided. Leakages at first trivial were worsening. The raft was losing buoyancy and sagging.

'We must draw every scrap of information we can from the global net. Work out some way of carrying out repairs, the material that we need and the kind of work the robots will have to do,' Vogel said.

The standard repair routines coming from the data banks were based on the assumption that any leaking cells were few and would be surrounded by intact compartments. Usually, air would be pumped into the damaged areas, driving out the water, and then cracks and punctures could be sealed.

'That's no use to us,' Collin 721 said. 'A whole section of the raft is filling up. Even if we could pump a huge quantity of air in it would bubble out as fast as it entered.'

'We don't have the necessary big pumping engine, anyway,' said Vogel. The engineer group decided it was necessary to stop the leakages, or at least drastically to slow them down, before repairs could begin. They could discover no easy way to do this. An apparently reasonable recommendation coming from the net was to apply an external patch. Airther was interested in this. He understood what was being said and could contribute intelligibly to argument, especially if Darien was within reach to help with the words. It was through Darien that he made his contribution now.

'Aye, a patch. Wot wuh aad fishermen wud dee, west tuh drag a muckle sail owor the lek, tuh keep sum iv the watter yeut. Then weh cud bail and heed fo the shair an beechut an roll it ower an work on the ootseid.'

Yes, a patch. What we old fishermen would do, was to drag a big sail over the leak to keep some of the water out. Then we could bail and head for the shore and beach it and roll it over to work on the outside.

Darien took him to Sistus, who understood after some thought.

'A muckle sail. I think I see what he means. The boat leaks, so you take the sail down and pull it underneath the hull, like a huge bandage. It keeps the water out, or some of it at least. We don't have sails, but a big plastic sheet might do. It would have to be strong, puncture proof to resist the barnacles and the urchins with their spines. Then we could pump. We might be able to get the robo-crabs to move the sheet into place. It would have to be on a great big roller. They could pull it out and down, and under.' He gestured with his hands to show what he meant. Airther watched and nodded. 'Then bring it up the other side and pull tight. Then we could pump some air in. The raft would level out a bit too.'

The groups' momentary hope died immediately. This was not going to be possible. The process, feasible in imagination was totally impracticable.

Said Vogel, 'the plastic sheet would have to be gigantic, to go from one side of the raft to the other across the wound. It would have to be at least two nauticals long, and three or four hundred metres wide, at least. Anything less would be useless. To manufacture such a huge amount of tough plastic sheeting is totally beyond our capacity. It would strain the industrial power of a great city,' he said, gloomily. 'We could find out how to build a plant to extract the required substances from the sea but in the quantities required it would take months. We do not have the time.'

Sistus agreed. 'Even if we could do it, the chemical processing, cooking the mixture, extrusion and rolling of the plastic would require an entire factory and there would still be the matter of getting it into place. It can't be done'

'Even supposing the impossible, repairs would take months at least, even beyond a year. There's no way of doing it quickly,' Vogel said.

No one could think of an answer. They were facing defeat and disaster. The raft was cracking up beneath them, sinking, and there was no way of stopping it. Even a small storm now, or a change of the wave motion, would probably break them in two. Was any other raft within reach? Sal and Alicia using all the resources of the computers and the satellite responders, found they were even further from help than before.

'We forget how huge the oceans are,' Sal said to the engineers. 'Almost three quarters of the globe is covered by sea and always has been, even before the ice melted. There are hundreds of city rafts, it's true, but they are scattered far and wide. Remember, before we broke away, it was a rare event to get close enough to another raft to visit, and that was when we all tended to follow the main currents. We are out of the normal drifts now and there's no way we can get back into them without engines to drive us.'

After this depressing conference, Sistus came in misery to Sal.

'Airther was talking about little fishing boats, like the one we found him in. We have a great raft. It's small against Shanghai, even the separated parts, but it's still enormous compared to a little fishing boat. We just cannot do that business with the sail.'

'He said *beachut*? What is that?' she asked.

'*Beechut.*' He paused in thought.

'I wonder,' he said. 'Oh… I think I do know what he meant.'

'What?'

'Beach it. He was talking about dragging a boat up onto the sands, the beach. They would turn it upside down to repair it. I think that's what we must do.'

'Sistus, no. It's impossible. Drag the raft out of the water? Turn it upside down?'

'Not turn it over, no, but get it where it won't sink, that's possible.'

'We can't drag the raft like a boat, it is far, far too big.'

'No, even if we tried, it would break up completely. It is already almost in two pieces and getting worse. But we can beach it. we must get to the shore, Sal It's the only thing we can do. Beach it.'

'Oh no. I can't bear the thought of going on land,' cried Sal, shuddering.

'There's no choice, darling, the raft is breaking up. If we run into a storm again, it will be in pieces and they will be such an odd shape, we can't even rely on them floating upright. They might turn over in the water. We can't do repairs at sea. It's no good thinking of Neurath's boat now. But we might be able to get to some place where it won't sink any further. We might be able to do that. *Beechut.* Beach it. Get some support underneath. Then the sprites could all get off and be safe on land.'

Sal did not like this at all.

'Marooned. We'll be marooned, just what Fauvel threatened.' Her hatred and fear of the land returned. The baby apparently didn't like the idea either. Sal sat in silent misery for a little, pondering. She might be forced to set foot on the land despite her fears.

Thinking further of Airther's remarks, she had a momentary insight.

'Tides,' she said. 'What are the tides like on the coast over there? How much does the sea rise and fall? Suppose, just suppose, we can find a place where the tides would carry us in when they were high, and then go out, leaving us resting on the solid sea bed. That would help, wouldn't it? At least we wouldn't be sinking.'

'Yes, I see. Some of the water would drain out at low tide,' said Sistus, 'then the next high would float us again and we would be carried in a bit further. When it went out again we would be stranded and more would drain out. It would give us time. We could make repairs. We might even build a new raft. If we have time, anything is possible.'

They stared at each other with a gleam of hope. 'If we got the tide just right, we would be safe. Get onto the beach at high tide,' nodded Sal.

'It ought to work. What do you think Sal, *beechut*?'

'We can go and look at some tide charts. But wouldn't it mean we'd be stuck forever? If we once settle down like that, the raft would never move again'

'Maybe not, but what else is there?'

They looked long and hard at each other. Another realization dawned.

'Sal, maybe it wouldn't matter if we never did move 'We would not live in constant dread of more storms.'

Sal experienced a mixture of horror and reluctant understanding.

'Like a city on the land. Going back, back, back to the ancient Greek cities that Nemo talked about. I… I am so afraid of the land, Sistus.'

'Sweetheart, I know. But we cannot stay at sea with this broken raft disintegrating under us. We must find a place with the right tides and the right sort of bottom and move towards it as well as we can. There's nothing else we can do now. We must get on with building the propulsion engines. To get them running will be quicker than any of the other things we have thought about. It will give us some control.'

'I can bring up tide charts for this coast,' she admitted, doubtfully, 'or any coast.' Another terrible thought came to her. 'Sistus, even if there is such a place, I don't have enough control of the raft to get us there.'

'If all else fails we must get to the land.' *Maroon the lot of us*, thought Sal.

The navigators collectively spent days studying tide charts, looking at under-sea contours, gathering and assessing data from a thousand possible places. All the navigators turned to this task. Frustration awaited them at every step. When the tides were acceptable, the submarine surface was impossible, sloping too steeply, or rocky and irregular. When a good seabed was found, the tides were too shallow, sometimes almost absent.

While the search was going on, the engineers and their robots toiled at fabricating, assembling and installing propulsion engines. All available resources and machine capabilities were turned to the task. The new engines were patched up from whatever was available. This was no time for perfectionists; corners were cut. 'Working well enough is good enough,' became Vogel's catch phrase. The engines were not expected to continue in service for years into the future. Signs of the threatening break-up were becoming evident to the least perceptive rafters. The computers calculated if there were no serious storms ahead, they had a month, perhaps, to save themselves. Any robot not engaged in vital operations was dismantled and parts used wherever they could be fitted into the new machines.

Everyone knew what was being done, what the difficulties were, and that they might, after all, be reduced to swimming. *Go and jump into the sea.* If worst came to worst, some were beginning to think, it might be possible for the sprites to stay alive without the raft. The example of Airther and his family had not been forgotten. A small industry began building lifeboats. Airther was asked for advice, freely given. Pessimists equipped themselves with underwater weapons, spears and harpoons for catching fish. They improvised and learned to hunt for food.

Jezzy understood the predicament. Michel heard her say she wished she could use the magical powers she had sometimes pretended to have. She still confined herself almost entirely to her laboratory, Michel with her. He told Sal, he had to help her more and more now with quite simple things. She could not walk far unaided, needed to rest for some time every couple of hours, and was slow in speech. If the raft had a month, he feared Jezzy had no longer.

Sal herself had a good deal less than a month. She was busy with the tide charts when her waters broke and the contractions began. She was taken at once to the treatment centre. There were plenty of helpers. Jezzy insisted on being present. The search for the right kind of coast continued without her.

Sal's obedience to the exercise routines justified itself. The labour was not unusually long and although stressful, was quickly over. The child appeared headfirst and let out a yell of astonished dismay at the confusing, buzzing world.

Sal soon found herself holding and singing gently to the little bundle. This was her daughter. She and Sistus had made something wonderful and unique; the child was their own. Sistus himself, overcome with anxiety, had left the engineers at work to attend. He was amazed at the rush of profound feelings that overwhelmed him.

'I am a *father*. A father, Sal. We aren't robots. Not monsters either. We are human parents.' He kissed Sal, gently touched the tiny being in her arms, with its screwed up face and wrinkles, and returned to business, rejoicing and even more determined. If this birth were to mean anything, they must get the raft onto the beach, any beach, anywhere. The work on the propulsion system must go on.

As soon as she could, carrying her child with utmost care, Sal was back in the Nav centre. She was satisfied that her crew there had worked consistently during her absence. They had, between them, found two places that looked possible. If they had engines running, they ought to be able to reach one of them but it would be wise to take the nearest.

'See, this is the mouth of a major river, an estuary,' said the boy, Kris 908, who had found it. 'The range of tides is very large. Going with the inflow would carry us up the river until we run aground. Then it will withdraw, leaving us stuck until the next high tide. There will be some draining of the honeycombs so next tide might lift us off the mud and carry us further in. Eventually we'll come to a resting point.'

'What is the subsurface like?' asked Sal. 'Is it flat?'

'It's hardly tilted at all. We'd finish up level, high and dry at least to begin with. There is a snag, though. It's just mud, soft stuff, alluvial. Probably as the tide goes in and out twice each day, it will erode channels around and under the raft. It will settle down more, maybe a long way, Sal, I don't know how much. We might finish up with all the decks awash. We would certainly never move again. There's also the likelihood of floods. If the river rose after heavy rains inland, it might lift us and carry us back into the sea. We would simply have to get onto the land if that was going to happen.'

The baby required feeding before Sal could examine the second option. They became convinced that this would be better if they could reach it, but it was not very close and getting into the right position would be difficult.

'There's this island with a broad channel between it and the mainland,' explained Shih-Feng 557, 'the tides are unusual. The channel would be wide enough for the raft to be carried in with room to spare on each side.'

'The peak tide,' she pointed out, 'comes in at both ends of the channel, north and south, but at slightly different times, about an hour apart. The currents move in to give a maximum high about midway between the ends. When they meet there's a stagnant period before they flow out again.'

'The total rise and fall is about what we are looking for. If the raft is close to the northern inlet at the right time, the inward surge ought to carry us into the channel to meet the convergent flow coming from the other end. That would stop us,' said Shih, 'if we had the timing right.'

When the water subsided they would ground. It appeared from the underwater contours that they would come to rest on a nearly flat, smooth base, probably rock rather than silt or sand. The tides had scoured the underwater surface clean of sediment. Once touched down they would not sink any further. The situation between island and mainland also looked good because they would be sheltered from the worst storms that might occur. After repairs, moving out again would be possible. Would they ever need to do so? That question presupposed success in the beaching process. How were they going to get there? Would they do so at all?

Sal and her team now considered the best route they could to move the raft towards the chosen place. With Sistus and the engineers they worked out a method, resting on the assumption that there would, when needed, be sufficient power to complete the journey. The current they were presently in was steadily carrying them southwards more or less parallel with the coast and in the right general direction although it was not going to be helpful at the critical time and their progress was slow. If they were swept beyond the entrance to the channel they would be doomed. Nothing was certain, everything could go awry. A violent storm, and they would founder.

20

Every sprite on the raft with any engineering knowledge or ability was involved now in the work of driving the raft.

'The engine design is not the main problem, that's done,' Sistus told Sal, but we are going to need a lot of them. The robots are building them. We have to mount them under the raft in a way that's never been done before. There aren't any plans for the kind of thing we have to do. It's not my field. Thank goodness we have Vogel. He's a top class engineer and he's gathered a group of bright designers around him. They are all working like mad.' The motors were going to be housed in separate pods and would be set on numerous pylons in a pattern that would allow them not only to push the raft in one direction, but also to turn it by applying more thrust on one side than the other.

'The pod idea is a good one because each motor will be self-contained unit and independent. They are unlikely all to fail at once. When the plans are ready it will be my turn, getting my robots to mount them all.'

'Have we enough fuel for them?' asked Sal.

'We will have, when everything is ready. They will be electric powered and the current has to come from generators on the raft. The turbines, solar panels, fuel cells, storage batteries, all will be needed. We will have the drill down through the structure to get the power cables to them underneath. That's not going to be too difficult. All the available electric power will go to them when they are running.'

'Everything else will shut down?'

'Yes, except a few things like wrist terminals that don't use current directly and you will be able to use the GPS. You will need that.'

'Will there be enough driving force?'

'Our raft is a lot smaller than a city. With every motor at full power, Vogel reckons we will be able to move at a few knots, single figures, walking pace. You will have some steerage control when it is needed. Drifting with the currents remains the norm, but bursts of power will be available from time to time.'

One by one, the power pods and pylons were completed, carefully lowered into the water and manoeuvred into position by the robots under constant supervision, to be bolted with self-sealing and locking bolts to the hull. In position each motor was started up and tested, then shut down till the others could be completed.

'When, and if, the raft grounds, the first things to touch will be some of the engine pods,' said Vogel. 'We must expect to settle down unevenly. Unless the sea floor is dead flat, which it won't be, when the tide goes out the entire the raft will be resting on the pylons and the first ones to touch and feel the strain will probably collapse. Chances are, the ones remaining will collapse too but not all at once. I am sure they will go one after another as the weight of the whole superstructure rests on them. We might just possibly finish up standing on legs. I can't say what condition the raft will be in afterwards. It might be broken into several parts. One thing is quite sure, we won't be able to move again in hurry, if ever.'

Sal had already worked this out herself. The wind vanes were adjusted again and again, reversing everything Sal had done before to keep them away from the coast, that they could now see directly. It did not look hospitable. There was a chain of mountains sweeping down to the shore with cliffs and projecting, rocky headlands. None of them, except Airther and his children, had ever seen land so close before. The sprites were fascinated but alarmed. Those with nothing else to do stood in small groups gazing, commenting on features they could see, narrow valleys with streams flowing down them, broader river mouths, and inland, behind the coast, steep slopes bare of vegetation, rising generally to a higher level. Sal's satellite images revealed an extensive but irregular and dissected plateau surface inland. All seemed to be barren.

The sprites had all seen representations of land vegetation on their school screens at various times. Some had enjoyed VR games involving adventures in wooded country and on open plains. They had supposed they knew something about it. Confronting the true reality was an entirely new experience. The variety and aridity of scenery took their breath away. They tried to imagine what it would be like to walk among rocks on shore, to climb up those difficult slopes. They knew, as Sal knew, that there were wild creatures lurking, scorpions under the stones, tigers ready to pounce, hyenas waiting to eat their corpses and unspeakable other horrors. These imaginings sent shivers down their spines. They would more cheerfully confront a carnivorous shark than disturb a grazing antelope. Yet they could see no land animals of any kind. This was where, if the navigators succeeded in beaching the raft, they might all have to live in future. Sal, chief navigator, was struggling desperately to take them all to where she herself would rather not be. What had become of her dreams, their ambitions to become sea sprites? They were approaching the land

Hour by hour another position was plotted on Sal's chart. The wind vanes were helping a little. The ocean current so far was proving reliable and in their favour. They edged slowly towards the point where the final and critical moves would be made.

Sal was worried about invisible reefs that might arrest their progress and do further damage. The screens showed nothing of this kind but she was not confident they could see far under the water. They checked again and again. Sal reminded the navigators.

'It is not a matter of touch and go. If we touch prematurely on a reef or hidden sand bar, we will be stuck, or wrecked. If we arrive too soon at the inlet, the tide will be flowing out and we will be carried away. Either means we will never reach the point we hope for.' Nearer to the inlet, the main current was shown on the standard charts as turning away from the coast to pass round the island. At the right time and tide for their purpose it divided into two, a minor branch providing the tidal inflow they hoped to catch. Get the tide wrong and they would be carried away and out again into the main current. They worked with the sail vanes as much as they dared across to the landward side ready for the final push. The drift was slower here, the current being restrained by the friction of the continental shelf. Sal pointed to the chart.

'Here's where we have to be when the tide is low, to ride it inwards as it turns. The current will take us up the channel. Unchecked it would sweep us right through and out at the other end into the ocean again, but we expect to meet the incoming flow from that end. There will be a period of dead water at the highest point of the tides. We should stop there and when the water subsides again it will leave us standing, to settle down onto bedrock.

'If we get everything just right' said one of the boys.

'We will use the engines to make sure we are right, to steer, and then either to push us on a bit quicker, or to slow us down.'

'If the engines are ready in time' said another pessimist.

Sal nodded. 'Make sure we are ready when they are'

She was glad none of them asked her about the likely effect if there was a strong wind, which could so easily slow the current down or even blow the raft itself away. Storms might develop, big waves would be raised. If the raft survived such events at all, which did not seem likely, their figuring would be useless and they would have to start again, trying to find a place to beach and get to it. So far, they had not had to face such complications. She knew they never would. They had only one real chance. The raft would not last long enough for a second try.

Now Michel brought bad news. 'It's Jezzy She will not lie down to rest, Sal, but when she tries to stand she needs support always. Any work she tries to do she has to give up almost at once. She insists on visiting everyone and finding out what is going on. Some of the young ones have to attend her constantly.'

To all the recruits Jezzy had been a rather distant, awe-inspiring figure, the reason they were here as modified humans, part of her project. She was an icon. To discover that she was, after all, an old woman with organs and a body that was almost worn out was desperately saddening.

There was nothing wrong with her brain, although it was working less quickly now. They appreciated and enjoyed her quirky temper and the sense of humour, which had not deserted her. Sal, Sistus and their little daughter spent some time with Jezzy every day to tell her how their work was progressing and to see how she was faring. She must be allowed to hold and croon to the baby, who was called, for the present, *Tertius*, number three. Her delighted parents thought of her as Jezzy Junior, or JJ, because at times her behaviour, screaming angrily one minute, screeching and gurgling happily the next, reminded them of Jezzy as she had been when they first knew her. Her eyes were expressive, too. JJ was a good name for the child. They did not issue her with an official number.

With communications fully restored now, although interrupted when the engineers required a special power boost, Jezzy senior was able to speak sometimes to Merlin on Shanghai Alpha. 'If I am the oldest witch he must be the oldest wizard' she said. She knew she was approaching her end. 'I'm the oldest witch on the planet, hee hee,' she said, gleefully. No one doubted it but she never revealed her birth date. She had a private bet with Merlin as to who would depart first. 'The winner will never know,' she cackled. Merlin's Shanghai raft was now far away, moving steadily eastwards, soon to pass south of the Southern Cape of Africa. Merlin said Fauvel was well under his thumb, and would remain so as long as Merlin himself drew breath. Jezzy had explained their predicament but there was no way he or Shanghai Alpha could help, other than with engineering advice, which they could get from the global net anyway.

Each day now saw them drifting towards the critical area and still the motors were not fitted. The one thing the navigators could not do was to stop and hold the raft in one place to wait for the work to finish. To stand still was impossible. To do so would require an enormous anchor, or more than one, with cables or chains beyond anything they possessed or could make in time. They could slow their progress fractionally by backing off all the wind vanes, or speed up slightly by setting full sail, but this mere trimming was all the control they had and the effects were barely discernible. The current carried them on implacably.

When JJ woke in the night screaming like Jezzy, Sal would attend to the child and could not go back to sleep without going into the Nav School where the night shift were monitoring and adjusting the vanes as Liy had taught them. Sistus usually came with her. Together, eyed now constantly by the child, they recalculated the approach speed and distance, worked out how this fitted into the tide patterns. They returned to bed with the baby calm again.

'I have a plan B, you know,' Sal said to Sistus, one night.

'I can guess what it is. If we miss this entrance, we will be carried round the island. We can try again from the other end.'

'If the raft lasts so long.'

'You know it probably won't, don't you?'

'If we miss that too, there is no Plan C. We will be lost, carried far away.'

'We must not miss.'

Three days later, the last engines were finished and mounted, as ready as they ever could be. Sal recalled all the swimmers. If the raft began to move under power there was a serious risk that anyone in the water would be left behind and lost. Every unnecessary appliance was switched off and full power was ordered. The only things allowed to draw current were the vital instruments in the Nav School.

The motors were started. The raft seemed to take no notice. There was a minute but detectable vibration and a deep humming sound. No other change was detectable. From the deck it seemed the drift had not altered at all. Staring anxiously at her screens, Sal could see nothing new. Sistus, looking over her shoulder, reassured her.

'It can't show yet. The raft is a great mass, with vast inertia. It will respond very slowly but it will respond. Give it twenty minutes, then we will see. Once it is moving under power, it will take just as long to slow down again. We will need to think half an hour or an hour in front of ourselves. Any change we make will take that time to show itself.'

Baby in her arms, Sal watched and waited. The child's eyes were wide open. JJ was watching too. Ten minutes passed.

There was a sudden, almighty bang that shook the entire structure. Then another. Everyone was paralyzed. The raft was breaking up

Smaller noises followed, they felt the raft trembling under their feet. A few more minutes went by as they held themselves in desperate tension.

Vogel came hurrying to the navigator's room.

'We have to expect it. The raft is feeling the strain as the drive comes on. The cracks down below are shifting. It shows that the motors are working and pushing, the damaged area is feeling it. We are beginning to move through the water.'

'Does it mean the leaks will get worse? As the cracks open up?' asked Sistus, the strain evident in his voice.

'Maybe, I can't say. It's equally probable the pressure will tend to close some of them up tighter. 'With any luck, it won't change the total buoyancy much.'

'Luck is what we need.'

'Look,' said Sal. 'Something is happening.' The position coordinates, top left of the screen, began to flick over a little faster. The line on the map image representing their position, lengthened perceptibly, the plotted points each minute were slightly further apart. Sal relaxed, JJ chuckled and smiled. The engines were producing a measurable thrust and it was moving the raft.

'I'm going to let them run for half an hour, Sal, so we can measure the knots. We will need to re-charge the batteries then. We can use the new speed figure for you to work out the approach more exactly,' said Vogel.

'I'd better explain to everyone,' said Sistus. He went to the public address machinery and switched it on, and cursed himself. His own orders had ensured there was no power available while the motors were running. He went outside, gathered a few people around and told them what was happening. The news spread swiftly by word of mouth. Optimism swept through the raft. He promised a general announcement in half an hour's time.

With the motors off and all other systems working again, he made his broadcast about what they proposed to do.

The raft now sagged perceptibly in the middle. They had used the full month they had been allowed by the earlier estimates but those predictions had never been very precise. So far, things were hanging together, but no one knew how near they were to disintegration. Over the next week, the engines were called on repeatedly as Sal and Sistus, with their helpers, worried over the position plots. Every time the motors were started, the raft banged, groaned and creaked and the mid section settled a little lower.

To try to prevent too many people crowding in to the Nav School to watch progress, Sal switched the charts to the public screens. This reduced the crowd but many still wanted to see directly what she was doing. It seemed the main current they were riding was deliberately perverse, always diverting them away from where they wished to be. They would drive the engines at their maximum, correcting the divergence, then the current would swing them too far the other way and the engines had to be used to restore their course. This happened repeatedly. Sal pondered.

'Can it be that the current follows a meandering path? A kind of regular oscillation, from side to side?' she asked Sistus. 'Rivers on the land, on the satellite images and in some of the simulations, often follow a meandering course in great curves. They swing this way and then turn back to go the other way.' She demonstrated with her hands. 'Might an ocean current do that too? It doesn't show on the charts but near the coast they aren't very accurate anyway. The great cities never come here. The charting has been very approximate.'

Sistus hesitated. 'It could be something like that. But we must keep moving in the direction we want to go.'

'Can we try it? Let the current take us where it is going, wandering a little this way and that but carrying us along all the time, getting closer to the inlet. Let's see if I am right? If it works we won't need the engines so much. We can save them for the really crucial time. Let's follow this outward curve we are on for a while. I believe it will turn the other way and bring us back onto course this afternoon or evening. If it does, it will probably wander the other way and carry us off line again, swinging from side to side. We can use the engines to help it along at the best time in each swing, but let it work for us between.'

'Try it once, then. But be ready if it isn't working. Give Vogel good warning if it looks like we are wandering too far and not coming back to the line. Remember there's a big lag in time before the engines can make a difference.'

All watched the position indicators anxiously. Sistus became very restless as the raft seemed determined to take a path well to the left of track, but Sal restrained him, and as she had hoped, the divergence began gradually to veer the other way. By next morning they were, as she guessed they would be, off the line in the other sense, to the right and closer to the coast. Sal's dread of rocks and reefs made her use the engines here for a while. The current soon wandered out again. Sal began to sense and anticipate the twists and turns. They made steady progress, approaching their goal in a series of broad S curves. Tension mounted as the line on the screen extended fractionally, diverted a little here, turned again there, seemed to stall, edged forward again. Small crowds of fascinated and terrified sprites clustered round every available screen.

At last, Sal felt sure they were close enough to the critical point.

'The timing is right, the tide is turning,' she announced to everyone. 'We are very close to the position we calculated. It's now or never. This has to work. Full power now, and keep it going.'

Vogel called for the engines to be turned on fully to drive them into the tidal rip. The raft responded with bangs, cracks, creaks and groans, but the chart showed the move was in the right sense. This was Sal's final throw. If she didn't win, the prospect was bleak. Sistus was with her.

'This is going to work,' Sal whispered to JJ. 'It's got to work, little one.' The baby, open eyed, staring at her, giggled, *hee hee*.

The island and the channel were now fully visible although it took an experienced eye to see just where the entrance to the inlet was. The only coastal sailor among them was Airther who appreciated better than anyone else what was being attempted. With his *marrer* Darien at his shoulder, he pointed out before anyone else could see it, the headland on the right and the low spit of land forming the opposite shore.

'Tha sees ut, Lass? Ye mus kip that heedlan on yer stairbord side and t'other, thas low lyin, to poort. Thas shaller watter there. Steer doon t'channel t'ween em.'

You see it, Lass? You must keep that headland on your starboard side and the other thats low lying to port. That's shallow water there. Steer down the channel between them,

Half an hour later he gestured, with his right arm. 'Over a bit this weh. Reet?'

Reet, thought Sal, *if weh can steer t'all.*

They stared at the screen, Sistus next to Sal with his arm round her shoulders, the baby in her arms, wide awake.

'Work your magic, JJ' Sal whispered. The tide was running and the motors were going as hard as they could. Sal warned that they might have to reduce power on one side or the other to turn if they needed to do so. Vogel and the engineers stood by. They drove now directly for the inlet. After twenty minutes, Sal said that she would do better to con the raft directly rather than trying to do everything via the screen. Truth was, she admitted quietly to Sistus, there was nothing more she could do now. They were in the current. It would take them in, or it would not. She had no control now. Carrying JJ she led the way and found a place on the open decks at the front, where they could see everything with their eyes unaided. Airther was there before them with Darien. Vogel joined them, ready to call orders to the motor engineers. Judging from the only fixed reference, the shore, they were moving quite rapidly. Was the tide going to sweep them in, or would they be baulked in the last hour, perhaps running onto rocks before reaching the inlet?

They were all amazed to see Jezzy, carried by Michel, coming to join them. She insisted on standing but he continued to support her as they all watched intently. The tide was taking them where it would

'Thas reet, Lass. Thas reet' said Airther. Becky held her father's hand anxiously.

'We are in the tidal current, Sal. You can see the inlet is coming closer,' Sistus said.

They watched; willing the raft to go where they desired.

'Shift t'port, Lass, just an inch or tain.'

Vogel called to shut down the left hand motors. The raft slowly, slowly, rotated to that side.

'Now, all full power again, straight ahead.'

'Reet, reet, lass.' Airther was becoming highly excited. Towie was jumping up and down.

The raft continued turning, sluggishly, cracking and groaning, then straightened again.

The inlet entrance was very close, the tide was strong, nothing could stop them, they were moving into the channel. Would it be deep and wide enough?

They missed the rocky headland. The low level spit was passing on the left.

They were within the inlet, between the island and the mainland. There was a muffled cheer from the crowds of sprites who had assembled wherever they could to see directly with human eyes. This was not a virtual reality game. They could not switch it all off and go for a meal, change to another game or take time out for a swim. If the tide should turn prematurely, or a sudden wind blow from the south, they might still be ejected into the ocean again.

Vogel kept the engines on until Sal and Sistus were sure they were well up the channel. Then he closed down the power. The current must take them safely forward now. So it did, but at one point there was an unexpected shock and a rumbling noise. Everybody felt the jerk, and there was a nasty crack. The raft stopped. Vogel called for all the engines. The raft hesitated, then lurched and slowly began to rotate. As it did so, there was another jerk, a long groaning, screeching sound, and it began to progress again along the channel, turning ponderously on its axis as it did so.

'We must have hit something,' Sistus said, 'A rock or a sandbank.'

'We've lost some of the engines,' said Vogel, 'on that side.'

'But we have broken free again. Stop all engines, Vogel' cried Sal.

'Can you prevent us going round and round?' asked Michel.

'I might, with a burst of power on one side, if they still work. But it might be a good idea to let us rotate,' Vogel said. 'When we are facing outwards we can use the motors to stop the drift where we want to be instead of relying too much on the other tide coming in.' The raft continued moving silently and slowly along the channel rotating at about four revolutions in an hour.

Liy came to her. 'Sal, I think we should feather all the wind vanes now. They will only make difficulties if we leave them as they are.'

Sal gave her child to a delighted Jezzy to hold. With Liy she hastened back to the turbine console. With the engines off there was power to release all the wind vanes to float freely round their spindles so that they automatically adjusted themselves to give neutral thrust whatever the local wind direction. It took only a few minutes. She got back quickly, took charge again of the wide-eyed, now chuckling JJ. Still drifting, they waited for the current coming from the opposite direction. It should bring them to a halt. The sun was going down, disappearing prematurely behind the mountains. They were in shadow. Soon it would be too dark to see anything beyond the raft itself.

The change of tide was a long time coming, or so it seemed. Sal checked again and again. Tide charts for such odd corners of the globe could easily be out by half an hour either way. The peak of the convergence was still to come.

It was almost full night now. Everyone felt another shock, there was a loud grating noise, the deck shook and all momentarily lost their balance, staggered, some fell. The rotation ceased. Everyone looked around, anxiously, silently. There was no more movement.

'We have arrived,' said Sal. She and Sistus hugged, gently to avoid squashing Jezzy Junior between them. Jezzy Senior tottered to join them.

'We have *beechtut*,' Sal cried, happily.

'Aye, bonnie lassie, that weh ave,' cried Airther.

The crowd at first did not know how to react. A startled muttering began to grow into a roar, a cheer. The raft was motionless. The tide was flowing past on either side, but was soon replaced by the counter flow, not so strong, but enough to shift the raft a little. Vogel called for the engines to check any drift, but this time only some of them responded. Many pods must have been dislodged or torn loose. Once again they touched bottom solidly. The tide had turned and the raft did not shift again.

For the next several hours the raft groaned and creaked as it settled further onto the solid seabed. The sagging mid section had been first to touch. There were many loud bangs from below, a regular cacophony of noise which died slowly away. As time wore on it became a creaking and that, too, at last ceased. There was silence, broken only occasionally by another muffled crack or muted thud.

With a sense of shock Sal realized she had not been in the water for weeks. A little mermaid? Soon she must teach JJ to swim.

21

Sal and Sistus, exhausted, slept. When the baby woke them the sky was lightening. Sal was feeding JJ when an excited Darien came hurrying to them, with Airther and his two children running behind.

'Sistus, Sal, there is a light.'

'What light? What do you mean?' demanded Sistus, half asleep.

'On the shore, there is a light, someone is there, with a fire. There are people on the land.'

'Aye, well mi lad, what did yee expek?' said Airther.

They hastened to the viewing deck. On the mainland side was a pinprick of reddish light. The news spread rapidly round the raft and soon the whole crowd had gathered to stare. *Landlubbers.* The word passed around in whispers.

Sal and Sistus had been so utterly preoccupied with getting the raft to this position, that they had not given a thought to what they might find when they arrived.

'Who are they, Airther? Will they be friendly?' asked Darien, anxiously.

'Thems airn't me fowk.'

'But you will be able to talk to them'

'Ah doot them spik Anglish at aal' They stared at him in dismay.

'Over there' someone in the crowd shouted. 'On the island.'

All ran to look. Not merely one solitary light; half a dozen had appeared on the other side of the inlet.

As the sun rose, the lights were no longer visible but plumes of smoke were rising from where they had been.

'Whoever they are, they will see us, as we see them. We must be ready for whatever they do,' said Sistus.

'We should take a boat and I can go across I will go and meet them,' said Darien, 'Or I could swim, it isn't very far.'

'No, no, Darien, remember what happened last time you came suddenly out of the sea? Don't rush into things until we have thought it all through.'

'But I … I only want to… I want to be friendly, show them we mean them no harm. And… and see how well I get on with Airther now.'

'Next time someone sticks a spear into you,' Sistus said, sternly, 'there might be no chance for you to make friends afterwards. Stop, think, carefully. It's further than it looks. You wouldn't be able to swim so far, and the currents can be severe in this channel, as we have found out.' The channel, in the middle of which they were grounded, was about two nauticals wide.

'Darien,' said Sal, 'of course we all want to be friends with whoever they are. But can you imagine what our arrival here, out of nowhere, must seem like to them?'

'We know nothing about them at all. They may regard us as terrible invaders from a frightful, alien world, out to destroy them,' confirmed Michel. 'I guess they didn't see us arrive last night, when it was getting dark. They must think we came down out of the sky, or from nowhere.'

Jezzy had her say too. 'Likely they will think us all evil spirits, want to burn us all as witches' She cackled. Becky hid her face. Airther held his child close.

'What shall we do,' Alicia said, 'if they come out to us in boats, large numbers of them? We can't let them get onto the raft to swarm all over us. Think of what they might bring with them, and what they might do? I don't mean just spears. Think of contamination, diseases. We used to quarantine land people, like they did with Airther. We can't cope with them. We have to keep them off, if we can. Can we do that if they attack us?'

One of the young engineers spoke up.

'I don't believe they can swarm all over us. They won't be able to get onto the raft at all, except at our landing stage. That is the only place where anyone could get out of a boat. All the rest is just vertical walls. A group of us swam all round it, before the storm hit us. It's because of the way Sistus had to cut the raft away in the first place. There is only that one way in. We can close that off easily. We can sit tight behind our walls.'

Sal remembered Nemo and the ancient Greek cities, confined, autonomous, but constantly at war. The sprites had their protective walls. Full circle?

'Yes,' Sistus agreed. 'I believe you are right. I had to make the cut along the edges of corridors and walkways. The Iris Door is shut, they can't get in there, they won't even be able to see it. We must close and lock the landing stage too, at least until we find out what they will do.'

'There's no sign of any boats coming,' said Sal. 'Can we get a better view of what they are up to? The sky is clear. Let's bring up a satellite image, it might show us what's going on.'

'Let's do that, Sal. I'm sorry, sprites, you can't go swimming till we work out this problem. When we can, we'll try to make friends. Darien, can you and Airther work out ways of approaching them that won't terrify them, or us.'

Sal succeeded in getting an image. Her team of navigators clustered round the capsule to watch with her. They saw the raft as it appeared from space, stuck as it was, an odd crescent shape at an angle to the inlet. She moved the focus to the island and enlarged the image. The plumes of smoke had vanished.

'Those small dots. They must be people moving about,' she said, pointing. 'There aren't very many. It's nothing like a swarm. I doubt if there are more than a couple of dozen.' The dots were gathering in a cluster among what she guessed were round huts or houses.

'Them thaar's booats, said Airther, pointing to one side of the image. 'Them's tethera boats, three, ah means, stanning oot of the watter on t'sand.' As they watched, the group of dots began to break up and move. An irregular and broken line which Sal thought must be a track or path led from the village, if it was a village, inland.

'They aren't going to attack us,' said Sistus. It appeared that the people were moving on the track away from the huts. The dots formed into a straggling line and moved along it away into higher ground.

'They are running away,' said one of the navigators.

'What about the other side of the inlet?'

Sal shifted the image. Search as she might, she could not pick out the place where the first light they had seen might have originated. It looked as if whoever had been there had fled.

'Good, it gives us time to sort ourselves out and decide what to do,' said Sistus. 'I would like everyone to go over the raft and find out what is working and what isn't. We must get the robots going again everywhere, make sure food and water supplies are sufficient and if they aren't, get things running properly again. See if all the pipes and cables are intact. When we are in good order ourselves, will be time to make contact with the land people. Let us not, ever again, call them *lubbers*. They may be able to help us and we can help them. Airther and his family will probably be able to advise us, even if there is a language difficulty. We have a lab here and all possible medical expertise and treatments. If they understand this, we ought to be able to get on with them.'

Clouds began to move in from the ocean. The satellite image was cut off.

'We need to keep an eye on them all the time, if we can,' said Sistus.

'We should built a robat,' said Vogel.

'Yes, that's a good idea. Can you get on with it? Two or three would be useful, I think.'

'Sure. I'll get plans off the net. I expect it will take a few days. Once we've checked everything else we'll start on it'

'What is a robat?' Sal asked.

'It's small robotic flying machine. It has cameras and sends pictures of what's going on all round us,' said Vogel.

'A sort of little chopper?'

'It's more like a big bird, you know, with wings spread out on either side. It has a motor with a little rotor at the front to pull it along, and it can be stuffed full of electronic gear. It can fly around under these clouds faster than a chopper and can even work at night with infrared detectors. It will give us a lot more detail than the satellites.'

Sistus announced to all the sprites that they could go swimming as long as they chose their time wisely and kept a keen lookout. They could not afford to let the tides sweep them away out of reach. Rescue apparatus was not, at present, available. Some of the lifeboats they had started building should be finished; a task for the robots when he could get them all working and programmed.

The rafters were safe. To be fixed in one place was a strange experience, but they would become accustomed to the idea. Towards the end of the afternoon the engineers were able to report that nearly all the electronic equipment was functioning, the wind turbines were spinning faster than when they had been at sea, and the solar leaves producing hydrogen for the fuel cells. Robots were working, their first task being to repair and rebuild anything that had been damaged, including other robots that had been dismantled.

Sistus and Vogel together dived to inspect the raft under water. Their underwater exploration showed that the raft was lying almost level on a base of rock. Instruments showed that the structure as a whole was slightly distorted, the sagging mid section now lifted slightly higher than the ends, but no one above could detect this as they moved about.

'All the power pods have been crushed onto the rocks,' they reported. 'There's nothing to be done with them at all,' said Vogel. 'They are irretrievable. It might be possible some day to move again but it would entail months, even years, of work. It will probably be easier to build what is really needed, a completely new raft.'

The word was now whispered more often, why should they move at all? It seems they had arrived at a good place to stay.

'Sal, what do you think? What will the other rafts do? They will soon realize we are stuck here. They might think we want to be rescued.' asked Euna. 'Or destroyed.'

'We don't want rescue. We are all right where we are now, at least for the time being.'

'But you hate the land, don't you?'

'I think I will have to get over that, Euna. I must.' They would be on an artificial island and would probably remain there for a long time.

'But if they decide we are undesirable, there might be trouble,' said Euna.

'We must convince them that we can be useful, can contribute to human understanding, despite our differences. No, not despite it but *because* we are different, said Sistus. 'We will have much to offer to the cities. We should teach them they can live in their way and we in ours with benefits to both and without conflict.'

'The same with these land people,' he added. 'We don't know if they will be happy with us here. We are different.'

Sal was secretly a little amused. His manner now was becoming that of a commanding officer, a Captain, far-sighted, honest, conscientious, solemn, sometimes a little pompous, not daring to reveal indecision or weakness. She loved him no less, for she knew he was her dear Sistus, full of secret self-doubt, inclined to weep privately in her arms when things went wrong. He was above all the father of their daughter.

'Sal,' he said now, 'it is time for a song.'

Once again, Sal was put in charge and a programme was put together. No one had been able to practice anything very new or different. The singers and musicians who had grouped and rehearsed before prepared to perform again. The Bairns were ready to sing their comedy item about Adam Buckham *'wiv 'is bow legs'* again despite the incomprehensible dialect. Sal wandered through the archives to find some new, old, songs to add to her substantial repertoire. She and the choir would enjoy singing some items that were new to them all. Little Becky offered a sad song which, she explained in her improving Raftanglish, was about a girl who wished to cross a wide, dangerous river to reach her lover on the far side, but could not find a boatman to ferry her over. To hear her sweet, childish voice brought tears to Sal's eyes. There had been a time, she reflected, not very long ago, when she would not have understood this song. That two young people could ever feel so strongly about one another had seemed beyond belief to her. When she lived on the Sydney raft and heard, for the first time, Rusalka singing to the moon, the music had entranced her but the words, in translation seemed almost ridiculous. Since meeting and loving Sistus she had changed. She was singing very differently now, with feelings expressed that she had not had when she was younger.

When the concert took place she was applauded in a way that astonished her. She could not judge any difference in her own voice but Sistus told her it had developed a bewitching tone that had not been there before. Evidently the modifications to her ears and throat had improved it as Jezzy had expected. She wondered if the sprites would want more concerts. She didn't think they were going to need navigators in the foreseeable future. She was no longer indispensable, if she had ever been so. She would have time on her hands. Would she now be able to swim as she had dreamed with the beautiful fish under water?

Vogel was ready now to test the robat. With an electric motor driving the front rotor, which he called a propeller, he launched it by hand from the raft. It climbed swiftly to a height that astonished Sal and the rafters who watched it. Once airborne it was nearly silent and at height could easily be mistaken for a bird. The example pictures it relayed to the raft were excellent and full of detail. It steered itself perfectly to touch down in a net spread on the uppermost deck in a small clear space between the turbines.

The robat added details to what they knew already but Sal and her team also scanned the satellite images as frequently as possible. There were no consistent signs of life on the shores. They searched the island and the nearby mainland. There were, they discovered, several small settlements at intervals around the shores of the inlet, on both sides. There were round huts, boats on the beaches and sometimes, at the further ends of the inlet out of direct sight from the raft, boats in the water, presumably fishing. They discerned small, irregular patches of land, different in colour and texture from the rest, which they thought must be cultivated fields. Of the people nearby they could see little or nothing. More detailed scans and enlarged views led them eventually to believe that there was a place on high ground where someone watched the raft constantly. Faint tracks appeared leading to this point on the island side. Airther, when asked, came to look and said he was sure this was a footpath made by sentries who walked up to the viewpoint daily.

'Them's watchin weh, wor watchin them. They divvent knaa what wor and them's skeered. The fowk hev run away hidin. They wud leik weh to haddawy same as wi came. Vanish in the neet, laik.'

'Well, we cannot vanish in the night,' said Darien. 'We must try to make friendly contact with them. What's the best way?'

He and Airther, always with the bairns, talked for hours, and, at last, came to Sistus and Sal with a scheme. The Captain's reaction at first was negative.

'It's too risky, Darien, for you and the bairns especially. I can't allow it,' said Sistus.

'There is risk, yes, but we can do everything very slowly, in plain sight, and make sure they see there is no threat to them. The bairns are important. Airther and I talked to them and they are ready to help,' Darien insisted. 'They do understand. I will go with them but I will wear something to hide my gills. I know, I will look like a giant to them, I'm a quarter metre taller than Airther. But if we do everything in plain view, and leave them a gift behind, I think it will work. One little step at a time. We must try it. We must have a good, fast boat in case we have to run for it. I don't think we will but we can have it ready.'

Sistus talked it over with Sal and everyone else he could think of who might have advice. 'Darien is always too optimistic,' was Sistus' opinion. 'We cannot expect too much from the strangers. When they see us properly, and understand what we are, *different,* they may react with fear and hatred, whatever we offer them.'

'Darling, we must let Darien try,' said Sal. 'If he fails, it must not be because we refused to support him.'

'We will help, yes. We will do that. But it should not be simply giving them whatever they need or whatever we think they need.'

'Sistus, if Darien is going to do this with Airther and the bairns, I want to be with them. With JJ.'

'No, Sal, No, Never. Never. I can't possibly let you do that. With our lovely daughter? No, it's madness. No.'

'Yes, yes. JJ will show them more than anything else could, that we mean them no harm, that we are friendly, no danger to them. They will be none to us if we do it right. A little at a time.'

'Sal, my love, you frighten me dreadfully. What if they turn out to be diseased, savages, cannibals?'

'Infections we can deal with, if they happen. Cannibals? We can run. Airther will be with us and he means to take his bairns. I will take JJ and look after her. I can keep an eye on Darien, stop him doing anything silly.'

'You mean,' Sistus laughed incredulously, 'you would leave Airther's children behind to be eaten'

'Oh that's too horrid. You know I don't mean that. I'm not joking

'Nor am I. I can't allow it'

'You must come too.'

Sistus was totally taken aback.

'I…. *Poseidon, Neptune, Prometheus.* All the bloody gods, Sal Is this really happening? Are you actually saying these things?'

'It's what I want us to do. It is what we must do.'

Sistus stared at her in silence.

'It's what I *must* do.' You know I hate the thought of being on land, but if Airther and his bairns can do it, I can I will.'

Still no response.

'If you join us, you can protect us, and help us.'

'*Poseidon.* I do love you Sal. *Bloody Prometheus,* I don't want ever to lose you, or JJ. Or Darien and Airther and his bairns for that matter.'

'Let's go over the idea again, carefully.' he said.

There was a long pause.

'Very well, then. We begin with some very simple and harmless excursions. We can use one of the new lifeboats with oars, but with a motor in case we need it. Four adults, with some fishing gear and room for a basket of stuff to eat and drink. Every day for a week or ten days someone goes rowing about pretending to fish. They will understand that.'

'We, WE go rowing about and fishing.' said Sal. We might even catch some. Airther and Towie are good at that. We choose the best time of day for the tides. We are seen eating and drinking like any other humans.'

'For about ten days.'

'Very well, a few days, see how we get on. If things seem all right, we go ashore for a little while,' Sal insisted.

'Just for a few minutes. Then get back in the boat and drive like hell for the raft.'

'If nothing goes wrong let the bairns play on the sand for an hour, a harmless family group. We leave some gifts behind; food, something anyone would be pleased to get. If all is well, we row gently back to the raft and do it again, and do it again every day till someone comes out of the hills to see us.'

'And if they come with spears and knives and arrows?'

'We'll keep our eyes open, and the rafters can look out for us too. If necessary, *then* we run like hell for the raft. I don't think that will happen, but if it does, we won't have lost anything. We can use the motor in case we need to get away fast.'

'So you hope. There must be some protection against diseases too.'

'We know how to do that. We've got lots of medics on the raft.'

'And if this works, what then?'

'Then we may be able to make friends with the landlivers. Beyond that, I don't know. Play it by ear.'

It took Sistus all day to make up his mind. Sal said no more, but was not surprised when he agreed to the scheme, on condition that indeed, he would be with them.

The first rowing excursion was entirely successful, with a difference. Their little boat was escorted by a few underwater sprite swimmers, invisible to anyone on the shore. The sprites with telescopes on the raft confirmed that there had been someone spying from the high spot above the beach.

'Well,' said Sal, as they rowed homeward, 'we caught some fish. That went well, didn't it.' Sistus agreed.

'Even so, we must be vigilant.'

Another outing followed, and several more, with no apparent developments except that Airther and Towie caught more fish. The telescopes reported that a sentry and sometimes a small group of landlivers was present every day on the viewing point.

At last they landed on the beach. Sal hesitated, needed Sistus to help her with JJ, put a foot out of the boat carefully, touching the beach with a toe, startled to feel it sink into the sand, shocked when she withdrew it to see the impression she had made filling up immediately with water. She tried again, feeling the gritty, wet substance under her foot, daring to put some weight on it, finding there was support there, bringing her other foot over the gunwale, and the other. It was a totally new experience. Letting go of the boat, she took a tentative step forward. Standing on a beach was not, after all, so very different from standing on the deck of a raft She took her first steps, retrieved JJ from Sistus, who was no more familiar with the land than she was. Together, they walked carefully after Airther and the children up the gentle slope of the beach, Sal wondering at the feeling of sand between her toes, sensing the uneven surface where the sea had made small ridges. She saw no savage beasts about to attack, no nasty crawling creatures. There was a fly. It didn't sting, but buzzed about her ears and settle momentarily on JJ's face. She moved a hand, and it was gone, a mere irritation. Was this what had so terrified her when she had thought of it before?

A cloth was spread and they sat. The bairns played with the sand, Sal fed JJ at the breast. They settled to eat their picnic. Nothing untoward occurred. Before leaving they put some of the fish they had caught that day, some bread and hydroponic vegetables in a basket, and invented a little ceremony. Becky carrying the gift walked away up slope from the group, placed the basket carefully on the ground, stepped back, looked up to where they knew the watcher was stationed, held out her hands palms upward, then the party withdrew and Darien rowed them, gently, back to the raft.

Next day they were disappointed that their basket had not been touched. The picnic was the same. They replaced the gift with the same ritual as before, and returned home.

On the third trip, everything was as before except that Sal was beginning now to enjoy the feeling of being on land, the sensation of sand under foot and seeing the bairns making little mounds roofed with seaweed, digging small ditches to let the sea water flow in a little way. With JJ in her arms, she walked with Sistus for a few metres along the beach, dabbled her toes in the water, and sang quietly to herself and the baby. She began to think that life on shore might be almost tolerable after all.

There was no visible reaction from the high ground. Another gift basket was left untouched.

'Perhaps they don't recognize what we are giving. We don't know what they eat, and our hydroponics vegetables are probably quite unfamiliar. We can't wonder if they are suspicious,' Darien said,

On returning on the fourth day, what they had left had gone. In its place was a small offering of fish. Becky picked it up happily and waved to the distant spy, leaving another gift as before.

22

Next time, as they were preparing to leave, a solitary man, apparently from hiding, showed himself and moved cautiously towards them. Darien signed for the sprites to remain seated. Airther got to his feet carefully. The man, small, paler of skin than Airther, was naked save for a necklace that hung down in front of him to waist level. He was pitifully thin but walked upright and proudly. He came to stand near. Airther stepped slowly towards the stranger, held his arms out, palms up, then extended one hand. The white man hesitated, then, slowly and tentatively came forward and, took the hand in his own.

'Howie, bairns.' The children came to stand with their father. Airther pointed to himself with his free hand. 'Airther.' He indicated the girl, 'Becky', and the little boy, 'Towie.'

'Airther, Becky, Towie,' said the man, releasing Airther's hand and holding his own out to the bairns, who responded solemnly. The man bowed from the waist, touched his own chest with his hand, and in a deep voice said 'Basco'.

'Basco,' replied Airther, bowing, his children copying him. The white man turned a little to one side, and stared at Darien, Sistus and Sal, who were still sitting. He pointed a finger, glancing again at Airther with questioning, doubtful eyes.

Airther said 'Darien'. Darien stood, slowly, revealing his true height. Stepping forward, he towered over Basco, but bowed deeply, then extended his hand. There was a long moment of doubt and fear in the newcomer's eyes as he stared up at the rafter, but he held his ground bravely and took Darien's hand.

Sistus stood. Airther pointed to him: 'Sistus'. Basco bowed. Sal stood. 'Sal,' she said, speaking for herself, and proudly showing her child, saying 'JJ'. Basco bowed once and a second time to the baby who watched him with wide eyes, giggled and smiled. Basco, grinning with apparent delight, bowed a third time very low.

'*Marrers,*' said Airther. The white man bowed again. Becky went to the gift they had brought, a bowl of mixed fruits and vegetables. She laid it at the feet of the visitor, took a couple of steps back, bowed, and smiled. The man took the necklace he had been wearing, stepped forward and suspended it round her neck, turned, picked up the gift and walked away.

This was the first of many careful meetings.

After several more encounters, Basco came one day with two children, a boy and girl, and encouraged them to meet, and play, with Becky and Towie. The implications were obvious. The watchers on the raft after this reported that the round houses of the village were occupied. The three boats that, till now, had been lying unused on the beach, were once again seen on the water.

Reporting everything in detail to the sprites, Darien now had great plans. He had a vision of a new kind of world in which the land and the sea people could come together and develop a common culture. It was, he maintained, the beginning of something entirely new. He resolved to devote the rest of his life to nurturing the peaceful and respectful relationship been land people and sea sprites. He hoped to be recognized by Basco and all the other land people, as one who would bring the two cultures together.

'It was very significant, wasn't it, that they tried to meet our gifts with gifts of their own, fish, and the precious necklace?' he said.

'Precious?' Michel laughed. 'We could get a robot to make a dozen in five minutes.'

'The necklace was important. How many hours of handwork did someone put into it?' said Darien.

'It must have great significance to them,' Sal answered, 'and it isn't at all worthless to Becky. She loves it.'

'We must treat it as precious. They can teach us how they survive, their ways of getting food, how they live on land. None of us have any experience of it. If the raft had collapsed, even if we had been able to swim to the shore, we would have perished. We came very close to marooning ourselves. Some disaster could still strike us even now, for all our machines. We have much to learn and we should not sneer at what they have.'

'There are three kinds of human now,' said Sal. 'The city rafters, the land people, and the sprites. Will we be able to live in the world together without strife?'

'We will have a damn good try' said Sistus, 'For the sake of JJ, Unus and Secundus and all the others who will come soon.'

Darien, with Sistus' approval, began to go on shore regularly with Airther and the bairns. They became confident of their welcome from Basco and his tribe. Darien was eventually taken to the village. His visits became more frequent. He observed the tribe's way of life, and met many more of the people. He could not understand everything they did, but developed great sympathy and admiration for them. He made copious notes and talked of putting his findings out on the global net.

'I am constantly in doubt about their words and ways of speech,' he admitted to Sal. If you and I nod our heads we mean *yes* and if we shake side to side it is *no*. These people don't do that, they do the opposite. If I am with Basco's little boy and we are looking at one of their animals, he points and says 'gavagai'. So I say *'gavagai'* and write it down. It looks like what they used to call a goat in our ancient times. So I put *gavagai* = *goat*, but next time I see one when I am with Basco and I say *gavagai*, he laughs and nods, which means *no*. So I cross out my note. He points to the animal and says *ziege*. What is going on? Does the boy mean, *gavagai* is the animal's pet name, while to Basco himself *ziege* means the species? Or is *ziege* the name and *gavagai* means goat? Or what?' At least when they point they mean the same as we do. But what are we looking at? He might be pointing to the animal as a male, or a female, or it could even be he means *'that's our dinner for tomorrow.'* Darien expressed his bewilderment with arms and hands.

'I am called Sal, but my real name is Rusalka, and then I have a number as well. For me, you can write: 2405263, or 263, or Rusalka,

Sal, or sprite or little mermaid, human being. They would all be correct. But not dinner for tomorrow.'

'And the next thing,' said Darien, 'I see Basco's partner, his wife, milking the animal and she says *kais.'*

'Is that her name for milk? Or milking?' suggested Sal. 'Oh, if you soften the *k* sound it could be *ch*. Perhaps *kais* is *chaise,* meaning *cheese.'*

'Yes, that's very likely, so maybe *gavagai* is *the kind of animal from which we get cheese.* Or maybe *kais* just means goats milk, or maybe the word changes according to the sex and age of the person speaking I can't even point to some commonplace object and be sure to get the right name for it Even *Basco.* Is that his name, or does it mean *great chief, high priest,* or just *man*? I'm having trouble, Sal.'

'Well, don't give up. We do need to understand these people if we can.'

'The one thing they do not want is to come to see us on the raft. I think it is so far from anything they have ever experienced they simply dare not approach.

The sprites now were beginning to explore their new environment. They went swimming cheerfully, venturing a little further each time, returning with descriptions of marine species and beauties they had never seen before.

Michel and his team were becoming vastly excited. Every day he had things to report on the web that no living marine biologist had seen before.

'The rafts always move, so it is impossible for them to study a particular coastal location in detail,' he said. 'It is wonderful to be able to return over and over again to the same place.' he said. 'I've been delving deeply into the archives. The ancient folk knew these things, but the coral reefs they studied don't exist now. We find new ones growing.'

'All the same, I would like to be able to move around a bit, you know, compare one stretch of coastline with another. This strait between the island and the mainland may be quite different from the coast just a few nauticals north or south. We can't reach them from here, not yet, anyway. We'll have to get a laboratory boat, one day.'

Alicia and Euna often took their children with them into the water but were not sure yet how the babies would get on below the surface. Jezzy, in her lucid moments, told them the children would behave instinctively.

'Let them show you, you won't have to teach them anything.' she chuckled. Sal was also gradually initiating JJ to the wonders of life in the water. The baby seemed to enjoy the experience, swimming came naturally.

A few of the more adventurous sprites organized their own brief excursions to the shore. They had no problems. They were not approached by the land dwellers, but Darien said he was sure they would, ere long, find they could make friends with them. Sal with JJ began to accompany these small groups and sometimes persuaded Sistus to come too. Her under water explorations now were beginning to delight her as she had always hoped they would. Rusalka, she thought, was returning to her proper place. Her dream was coming true. She began, at last, to feel like a mermaid but of course, not a maid any more. A *merwoman*? There was only one small doubt. With no navigators required, what was she going to do with her time?

All was suddenly overshadowed by the discovery, first on the satellite images and then on videos from the robat, of large numbers of people on the mainland. On their first night in the channel the rafters had seen a single fire on that side. After it vanished they had paid little attention to that area until one night a few lights appeared on the shore that side. The next night there were many more. At dawn, boats were visible with large crews paddling them. These were not fishing boats but long, narrow vessels that Airther identified as war canoes.

'Them's ratts,' he said, 'tha nars, py-ratts.' Sistus at once forbade all further shore trips and insisted that no one should swim, under or above water, anywhere near the landward side of the inlet.

Something was certainly happening. 'I think he means they are an army. They are not Basco's people. They haven't made any attempt so far to get in touch with us, to ask who we are and what we are doing here. Airther insists they will attack us. They mean to come at us in large numbers, he says.' Sistus said. 'Even if he is wrong, we must prepare for it.'

'How can we defend ourselves? We don't have any weapons,' said Vogel.

'I doubt they can do us any harm if we keep everyone inside the raft. There's only the one way in, from the landing stage, and the entrances there can be locked. The rest is just high, vertical wall all round, like one of those ancient city-states. We must sit tight and see what they intend. I don't want a fight, that is the last thing we can afford.'

'We must get the robots to work at something to defend ourselves with in case the worst happens. I'll get the robat flying and make some more,' said Vogel. 'It won't take long. They will be useful now.'

An aerial surveillance flight at night revealed that the canoe people were apparently performing mysterious rites. There were large fires and crowds of people around them. It was Jezzy who suggested they were worshipping the moon.

'I am a witch,' she cackled like her old self for a while, as if the tension revived her spirit. 'I understand these things. They are waiting for the moon to reach a propitious phase, the phase that will favour their warriors. When the gods are on their side, they will come. Hee, Hee. *O, moon high up in the deep, dark sky, your light shines on far distant regions.*'

'Hear that, Rusalka?' said Sistus, smiling grimly.

'You need not think I can get the moon on our side. And I won't be singing to that army either.

Sistus kept the sprites up to date with developments and preparations.

'We don't know their intentions, but we may be compelled to resist them. We can't see any sophisticated weapons over there. I don't think they will have any explosives or firearms. I hope not. I am sure they will not be able to break into the raft. Above all else, we must not harm anyone if we can possibly avoid it. We want to make friends, not enemies. If we do have to defend ourselves, Vogel has ordered the robots to manufacture some stun guns. They can also be programmed to use them. We can make firearms too, if it seems we need them. None of us knows how to shoot, but the machines can do it very accurately if necessary.'

Darien came anxiously to Sistus. 'Sistus, we should ask Basco about them. He probably knows who they are and can advise us.'

'Do you know his language now?'

'No, not yet. I'm making progress, every time I go on shore. I think I can communicate enough to explain. I don't know if he can see far enough to make out what is going on.'

'Take a motorboat, then, by yourself, and don't be too long. Find out what you can.'

Darien returned after more than two hours. He was downcast.

'He wasn't there. I waited and waited. Nobody came at all. The huts are all empty and the animals they kept around them have gone too. I think he, his people, have run away, as they did before, when we arrived. They probably expect an attack from across the inlet.'

'Then we must expect they will attack us too. Us first, probably.'

'But why? We aren't doing them any harm. We don't take their fish. We don't pollute the water or anything.'

'I don't suppose they see things that way, Darien,' said Sistus. 'And those long boats do not look like fishing boats to me. We can't tell what they think. Maybe they see us as evil spirits. We must wait to see what they do, and be ready for whatever it is. I suppose they might be prepared to talk to us, but from only from a position of strength, as they see it.'

Michel was angry. 'We want to get on with our work. They won't even know we are there if we stay under the water.'

'The water is very clear. They might see you and they probably have harpoons and things like that for killing big fish and seals. You must stay in the dry. Everything might be sorted out in a few days. We can't afford to lose, you Michel.'

'I didn't know you cared.'

'Well, I do and you know it now. Don't do anything stupid, and the same for your team.'

There was a hiatus, an anxious waiting time of several days.

Predictably, on a night of full moon they came. The robats gave ample warning and, knowing that the landing stage doors were fully locked and barricaded, the rafters assembled at every available viewpoint, high above the waterline, to see what happened. The boats came swiftly through the darkness in rough line abreast.

'There's twenty canoes,' said Michel, 'and about ten small men in each, so there aren't more than two hundred altogether. It's nothing like as many as I had expected. What can they hope to do with two hundred men? We outnumber them, and we are all so much bigger.'

As the fleet came nearer, the watchers could see that each had a frightening figurehead, a monstrous creature with gaping jaws and staring eyes. Above each head was a blazing torch casting a flickering light, making the heads seem alive. Standing behind the paddlers on each boat, with a flaming torch on each side of him was a figure in elaborate costume with strange headdress, face and body painting.

'Them's priests' said Airther. 'Thems bring t'spirits. Towie, Becky, Awa wi yee.' The little family ran below decks. A heavy drumbeat was audible. The drummer sat in the extreme stern of each canoe. The paddles kept in time and all the crews were chanting in unison.

'They are hoping to frighten us,' said Darien. 'With the monster heads, magic spells repeated over and over, and the moon in their favour.'

'Airther and the bairns are hiding down below,' said Euna. 'I wouldn't mind joining them. It is scary, isn't it? I'm glad they can't reach us.'

The line of boats turned into a long line and began to circle round the raft. It was a long way for them, probably more than they had expected.

'I think they are looking for a weak spot,' Sistus said. 'They will be unlucky' The raft, two nauticals long and about a third of that distance wide, presented a high, dark, almost featureless and impenetrable wall all round. The decks loomed high over the canoes. The boat formation became ragged. It took the leader two hours to travel round, by which time all the paddlers were obviously tiring. The attack that had seemed so impressive began to look puny and ridiculous.

The first vessel stopped opposite the landing stage, turned to face the raft and waited until one by one, sluggishly, the others came and formed up next to it, so that all twenty vessels were bow on to the landing stage.

At a loud collective shout, all the canoes came forward together, as if to ram head on, but as they came closer, apparently realizing that they could achieve nothing other than slamming into a high and solid wall, most slowed and stopped before getting close. Three, side by side, ran their bows up onto the landing stage. Their leading crews scrambled forward and leaped onto the deck, carrying spears and clubs. More followed. The watchers could not see directly what was happening but a carefully placed surveillance camera transmitted an image to the screens. The limited deck space became full with a crowd of painted warriors. They tried to break in through the closed doors and walls but made no impression. Soon they could hardly move because of the press of others scrambling from more canoes.

From the boats that could not find room to get to the landing stage a few spears were thrown, hitting the vertical wall with a thud and falling into the sea to sink immediately. One or two of the vessels paddled up and lay alongside the wall. After a few useless thumps with clubs, they backed off. One at last turned away and began paddling back slowly towards the beach they had come from. Others followed. The warlike chanting had stopped. The attack had been completely futile and the long boats paddled away.

Sal watched the canoes as they receded. They looked, she thought, like some kind of nasty animal with ten legs on each side of their long, narrow bodies. There was something familiar about this. She had seen, in her schoolie days, pictures of some nasty land creatures with many legs. The boats seemed to walk over the water.

There were no more attacks on the raft but the canoes and their people did not go away. The robats made many quiet reconnaissance flights, monitoring them constantly.

Eventually the canoe fleet set off in the night. The robats revealed what they did. The warriors landed at dawn near one of the small villages on the mainland side of the inlet. Everything useful, tools, food and stored crops, was stolen. They slaughtered, skinned and butchered on the spot any animals they found, though few of these had been left behind by the villagers. The houses were set on fire. Leaving total destruction behind they paddled back to the beach they had come from. A bleak and deprived site awaited the villagers on their return.

Everyone watched as the war canoes came back from their destructive excursion. Fires that had been damped down were evidently stoked up again, and even from the distance of about three nauticals noises could be heard. A robat launched quickly returned images of a crowd gathering around one main blaze.

Airther did not need to look at the pictures.

'Them'ill rosst the biff they took, stuff themselves wi scran. They's ganin tuh kick thems heels up, thall be ravin aaal neet lang. Nivvor mind the racket. They won't stop till they aal fall doon.'

They will roast the beef they took, stuff themselves with food. They are going to kick their heels up, they will be raving all night long. Never mind the noise. They won't stop till they all fall down.

'Fall down? Why?' Sal asked.

'Them'll be tippling,' said Airther, as if it was obvious. 'Them'll be 'ungovor in the morn. Then they'll get ready fre another raid.' Sal was no wiser.

They will be tippling, they will be hungover in the morning. Then they'll get ready for another raid.

'I have no idea what he is saying,' she admitted.

'We've not found out anything about those people,' Sistus said. 'Where did they come from? Are they from a city on the land somewhere near? We ought to know.'

'I suppose they are celebrating their victory in the village,' said Michel.

'That's not much of a victory, it was just cruel,' said Sal.

'Fo' them, tuh hev won sum scran an' brew that will keep their bellies full an' their brains screwed fo' a few hoors, is a victory,' Airther laughed, grimly. 'What for shud the' care abyeut daft peesunts?'

For them to have won some food and ale that will keep their bellies full and their brains screwed for a few hours, is a victory. Why should they care about daft peasants.

At dawn, as Airther had predicted, humans could be seen by a robat spotter lying asleep near the remains of the fire and scattered almost at random in ungainly postures over a fairly wide area.

Sistus asked for all the robats to be dispatched on a series of high altitude searches along the coast and inland to the maximum of their range. The screens throughout the raft carried little else for a whole day. The engineer and navigator groups studied the resulting mosaic map closely.

'There's no sign of any settlement like a city, but along the coast north of here there is a whole series of burnt out fishing villages,' Sistus concluded after watching and playing back the images repeatedly, Sal and others crowding round to watch. 'This tribe, if that is what they are, seem to have been moving down the coast from the north leaving devastation behind them, never staying anywhere more than a few days. I think they are nomadic robbers.'

Airther looked at the maps, waved his arm in the direction of the long boats.

'I've telt thee afore. Them's pyratts,' he said.

'They won't make fools of themselves again trying to get at us. That is too difficult and there are no rewards for them in it. When they've plundered all they can from the villages around the inlet here, they will move away down the coast. We shall see the last of them,' Sistus declared.

Next time another village would suffer. Darien was particularly upset to think that Basco, his little family and others in his village, might be robbed and slaughtered.

'Are we just going to sit here and watch?' he demanded, angrily.

'What else we can do. We have nothing to fight with and they won't change their plans to suit us. Basco and his people have escaped, they must have faced this sort of thing before and survived.'

'There something I have just thought of,' Sal said. 'When our crab robots had finished the damage survey, what became of them? Did you jettison them all?'

'No, certainly not. They went for recycling like everything else.'

'They've all been dismantled, then.'

'Well, no, not yet. They were brought back on board and taken to the scrap yards down below. They are still waiting there for reprocessing. Why?'

'Do you remember when you tried out the prototype, how little Towie was so frightened?' Sistus nodded. 'Those machines are quite scary, I felt it myself. I was thinking, just now, if we got all those crabs out of store…how many are there? Twenty, thirty?'

'More than that. We made more than we needed, some in reserve. What are you saying?'

'Set them to walk across the inlet under the water, to climb slowly out onto the beach over there, all at the same time.' Handing JJ briefly to Darien, she gestured with her ten fingers to indicate the step-by-step gait of the ten-legged machines advancing. 'That would be a very scary thing for those people… pyratts wouldn't it? If they tried to stand and fight, they wouldn't be able to do any damage, would they? Those machines are tremendously strong. They would just walk over anything in their path.' She finished with an imitation of Jezzy playing the witch.

'Sal, that is a brilliant idea, said Darien. 'It might work Nobody would be really hurt. It would cost us nothing.'

Sistus paused in thought for a short time. 'We may not need it,' he said at last. 'The pyratts may decide to move on anyway. Or we might be able to make friends after all, once they see they can't destroy us. But if the canoes look like setting off on another raid I'll send the crabs and the robats out. We'll give them some of their own treatment, bullies that they are.'

'Will the bats be armed?' asked Vogel.

'They could carry guns, but I'm not going to do it that way. There isn't enough time. The crabs have claws, they can grip things. We can capsize all the canoes and then sweep the beach and capture what we can. At least we will give the men a ducking.'

'We can give the plunder back to the villagers. Perhaps there will be a chance after that for us all to settle down,' said Darien, enthusiastically.

'It is worth trying, isn't?' Sistus replied. We can thank Sal for the idea I think it will work, don't you? If not, we won't have lost anything.'

23

The pyratts showed no signs of leaving. For the next few days they could be observed moving about again. It appeared that the canoes were being made ready for another attack. The crab robots were brought from the scrap yard, checked over, the work being done as usual by other machines. One by one they were lowered carefully into the water. When ready and viewed from the high decks they could be seen dimly under water as they began to move ponderously into the formation that Sistus thought would be most effective. Fifty of the sprites wearing VR helmets, one for each crab, volunteered to manage their controls. They practiced the trick of walking under water and tried using the claws.

As expected, a few evenings later the canoes and warriors were seen to be assembling again. The crabs were started on their crawling journey but to the rafters' dismay the boats were already well on their way before the machines could intervene. Their target was evidently another village further south, beyond the previous one they had destroyed.

'We were too slow to realize what was happening. Never mind,' said Sistus. 'We'll catch them later. We'll deal with their camp first while the men are away.'

The canoes were out of sight when the crabs began to emerge from the water, giant and menacing monsters with deadly looking sharp claws and projecting spines in front that might be deadly weapons pointing ahead. In the gloom they presented a terrifying sight.

The effect, as viewed from the robats using infrared sensors was even greater than the sprites had hoped. Within minutes, the people on shore, several hundred of them were in total panic, running for their lives, taking nothing with them, running and running and, it seemed, unlikely to stop until totally exhausted. The watchers cheered for a total victory, yet no drop of blood had been shed unless some of the runners had fallen in their haste to get away. The beach was entirely clear of people within minutes and the crabs began to collect and stack the multifarious objects that had been left behind. There had been a large number of crude shelters made from timber and animal hides. There were stores of food and tools, probably all stolen, and some crude pieces of furniture. A couple of their canoes were on the beach too, under repair or abandoned.

Sistus, mindful always of the likelihood of contamination, sent robots in boats to save the foodstuffs, tools and utensils.

Tents and the two abandoned canoes were stacked on the beach and set on fire. The blaze was spectacular in the night.

Sistus turned attention to the raiders who, still paddling, had not yet reached the targeted village. The robats were sent over them to make a series of alarming low level passes, buzzing angrily. To everyone's delight, the canoe fleet hesitated, broke formation, and turned back.

'They've seen the fire.' The crab operators withdrew their machines under the water and waited. The raiders had been out for a couple of hours and had the same distance to come back. As dawn began to break they swept in hurriedly, with nothing awaiting them but the smouldering fire. As they approached, one by one, the canoes were seized from below. Long arms with snapping claws came from the water, gripped the gunwales, tipped the boats over, rocking them violently, dumping the men, weapons and all, into the sea. Chaos was complete. The warriors swam and stumbled, panicking, in ones and twos to the land. The crabs kept their grip on the canoes and towed them away. A few of the men held on but, when they realized what was happening, let go and escaped to the beach. The watching sprites could only speculate as to what the disorganized warriors were thinking and saying when they saw the deserted camp that a few hours before had been crowded with people and stolen goods. They, like their victims, were left now with nothing.

The canoes were set adrift. The peculiar tidal ebb currents of the inlet would carry them out to the ocean before any hope of salvage could arise.

'It was our turn for victory,' Sistus said 'We have taught those villains a sharp lesson.' The sprites cheered.

'They probably won't survive at all,' Michel said. They have nothing to eat now and no way of raiding any more villages.'

'We have marooned them. Serve them right' said Alicia.

Sal had no sympathy for the pyratts. They had survived by preying mercilessly on other people. They deserved what they got. Life on the land, *nasty, brutish and short.* Yet she felt sorry. To Sistus, she whispered, 'We made ourselves into brutish *sea munsters* to defeat them'

He looked at her seriously. 'To fight someone, you have to make yourself as evil as the ones you are fighting'

As the long, narrow boats drifted away, Sal, giving them a last quick glance, thought she saw a movement on one of them. Looking again, she realized that not all the warriors had escaped to the beach. One was apparently struggling to his feet, staggering as if injured. The canoe he was in was swept steadily away by the tide.

'There's a man on that boat,' she cried. 'Look, he's trying to stand up.' Sistus followed her gaze.

'Get a scope' he said. Someone handed him binoculars and he quickly confirmed. 'Yes, there's a man there. What is he trying to do? Paddle the thing? It's too big for him.'

'Can we rescue him?' asked Darien.

'Why bother?' said Alicia.

'We should do something,' said Sal. Sistus agreed.

'Yes, and we want to know more about those people. Get a motorboat, Darien, and some helpers. Go after him and bring him here. Be careful, watch out for his spear. No, no Sal, you mustn't go. You stay here with JJ. Darien, be quick, or he'll be swept out to sea for good. Take Airther if he will go with you.'

Darien was soon on his way with two other sprites and Airther, who had emerged from hiding.

'They will all have to be decontaminated,' said Michel. 'I'll set up the ward.'

The motorboat came back half an hour later. The single pyratt was bound and had to be carried to the treatment room. He was dark skinned with long, wild and filthy dark hair and beard, but apparently well nourished and strong, with broad shoulders and muscular arms. Clearly terrified he babbled incoherently. He had a belt, which had probably carried weapons, for there was a long sheath and a holster that must have carried a truncheon or club.

'He doesn't seem to know who we are or even where he is. He kept falling down all the time and vomiting. He didn't resist at all. I can't see any injuries.' said Darien. 'We had to tie him up just to carry him.'

'E's sozzled,' said Airther. The little group of sprites stared at him with total lack of understanding. 'Hev none of yee ever seen a drunken gadgie before? Deed drunk he is'

'What do you mean, Airther? What's wrong with him?' asked Sistus.

'Ah, ne yee divvent kna aboot ale, dyer. There's ne intoxicatin likker on the rafts.'

Airther's explanation took some time, the sprites having to stop him repeatedly with sceptical questions, Darien translating where he could. Airther told them how land people made and consumed beer and spirits.

'Eftor thor portee, raand the foyer yee knaa, that's why the' aaal lay flat yeut on the sand. The' weor aal deed drunk, that neet. Yee cud hev picked them aal up an droonded them, the' wouldn't evon knar.' It was difficult for the sprites to follow this speech, but they understood the general drift of it.

After their party, round the fire you know, that's why they all lay flat out on the sand. They were all dead drunk, that night. You could have picked them all up and drowned them, they wouldn't even know.

'I have seen something about this in the archives,' admitted Euna. 'In the land age, people used to make all sorts of poisonous drinks. They contained ethyl alcohol. It made them ill, like this pyratt.'

'Aye, yee feel happy at first, ye knaa,' said Airther, 'all t'gether wi yer marrers, like. This'n overdid it a bit It catches up wi yee later, what's caaled a angover.'

Aye, you feel happy at first, you know. All together with your mates, like. This one overdid it a bit. It catches up with you later, what's called a hangover.

'You've actually drunk that stuff?' asked Sal, horrified.

'Oh aye, lass What did yee spose? Not here. In your bars ye have only sweet cat's piss'

Oh aye, lass, what did you suppose? Not here. In your bars you have only sweet cat's piss.

'Some of them got to like alcohol and drank it a lot, but they often died of it,' said Euna. 'It's addictive.'

'Oh, yes, they called them drugs, didn't they? There's a lot about drugs in the history videos,' said Marcel.

'Them pyratts have to be pickled oot of their minds afore a fight.' said Airther.

Those pirates have to be pickled out of their minds before a fight.

'Well, we've seen what it can do' said Sistus. 'It renders you totally helpless. Airther, Darien, and the others who handled him, check out for diseases, clean him up a bit and then I'll need your help when we question him. We don't know if he speaks any language we can understand, but we must try.'

'Yee will get nothing useful frem him till the morrer. He will hev a shockin' heeadake an he willna be ower tha fre a dyah or twa.'

'What will we do with him after we've talked to him?' asked Darien.

'Put him ashore, I suppose,' said Sistus, hesitantly.

'Maroon him,' said Sal, shuddering.

'What else, love? We can't keep him here, and Basco's people won't want him.'

'We don't know what Basco's people want,' said Sal. 'What do you think, Darien?'

'They're hiding, but I think they will come back soon. I'll try to make contact again. If you really want to know, maybe you should come with me and see what they can tell us.'

'I will. I will do just that,' Sal replied. 'I'm curious, and it's time I saw that village a bit more closely.'

Darien was pleased. 'The bairns are learning the language much quicker than I can. They play with the other kids, and pick it up quickly and they are teaching Airther. But when he talks to me I can't understand him all that well either'

When Sistus, with Airther and Darien, tried to question the pyratt, they made no progress. There were translation services available on the global net. These, however, were rarely used except by historians trying to decipher ancient documents from the land age. Their captive could not, or would not, write anything for them. He spoke neither raftanglish nor the local language of the villagers, which Alicia, after a good deal of research, said might have come from ancient Spanish or Portuguese.

The pyratt was clearly horrified by the sprites with their conspicuous gills, but refused to take any notice of Airther. Attempts to communicate by signs met with no response.

Among a jumble of primitive tools, bowls and what Airther called bottles brought back by the robots, Sal found a strange, crushed and broken box with a tangle of fine strings and an extended handle or post, broken off but with strings attached at one end of. She showed it to Sistus.

'I can't imagine what this is,' she said, unless it is some sort of thing to make music with. You see, if these strings were made very tight, you could get twanging noises out of them.'

'Yes, maybe. What about it? We have our synthesisers that do all that sort of thing for us.'

'May I show this to the pyratt?' she asked Sistus. 'It might mean something to him.'

'Well, you can try, sweetheart. I doubt you'll get any sense out of him. Sing to him if you like. Who knows, you do wonders with your voice.'

With Darien in close attendance, she took the box with its tangled strings to the prisoner and put it on the table in front of him. The man stared at it, nodded, hesitated, shook his head and pushed the ruined object away.

'Does that mean yes or no?' Darien muttered. 'Both, I suppose. He seems to recognise it, but won't have anything to do with it'

Sal took up the bits and tried to put them together. The man watched her with what seemed to be contempt. She persisted, untwisting the long stick until the strings seemed to be in line, though broken. She began to hum quietly, concentrating on trying to see how the shattered box could have fitted together. Darien, watching her, saw two pieces that he thought might go together, pointed to them and made a tentative fit. They continued for a few minutes with their joint efforts, without much success.

Suddenly, as if exasperated beyond bearing at their fumbling, the pyratt grabbed the broken thing, laid the parts out in what was, they saw at once, the obvious way they should go together. He then withdrew, waved his hands and made no further attempt on the reconstruction. Instead, he adopted a pose, his left hand and arm extended to the side gripping something, his right hand moving briskly up and down, demonstrating how his fingers might have been able to pluck strings.

'*Flamenco*' he said at last, then folded his arms, said no more, withdrawing from any further attempt to communicate. Try as she might, Sal could get no further with him, but she thought she knew now what to look for in the ancient music archives.

Giving up after several futile hours on different days, Sistus decided the man must be released. He was taken to the shore where the pyratts had camped. There was nothing there at all now but remains of the fires. It seemed the raiders had left for good. The man was given food and water in a backpack, enough, with care, to last for a week or two. As the boat withdrew, he set off with apparent purpose to walk south along the coast.

'He seemed to know where he was going,' said Darien. 'I suppose he thinks he can catch the canoes. A robat launched to keep an eye on the stranger showed that he climbed the high ground above the beach, reaching the plateau, and was not seen again.

Sal put the smashed instrument aside for later study. She must remember to hunt for flamingo music in the archives. There must be records of it somewhere.

Darien re-established contact with Basco. The villagers had seen the arrival of the pyratts and witnessed with joy their defeat. The looted goods were distributed as far as possible fairly to those other villages who had lost them. Darien hoped that all the small struggling communities around the local shores would come to regard the rafters as friends.

Airther and Sal together carrying JJ, with Darien spent a long time with Basco, trying to find out more about the pyratts. They did not learn much. The villagers' attitude was comparable to people bothered by occasional destructive storms or plagues of hungry animals. The pyratts were true nomads, working their way along the coast to no particular plan, plundering as they went, rarely meeting serious resistance.

The coastal people survived by fishing and some farming. Apart from their round houses, built with mud brick walls and wooden framed roofs thatched with locally grown reeds and plants, they had few possessions. The raiders gained little or nothing from the island people and they were usually left alone. Villages on the mainland were more prosperous and more vulnerable, but even for them, to run away and hide when the raiders approached was thought better than trying to fight.

All the screen images now were operating, the robots were fully functional, the routines of normal raft life were fully re-established, sprites every day were swimming and diving into the inlet without fear. Michel was continuing the thorough survey with his team. This would be what he called a sample study, a careful and exact account of marine life in a restricted area. This kind of thing had been done before, as he knew from the ancient archives, but since the rafts had put to sea little or nothing of the kind had been attempted. Every coastline in the world was different. Much that was wholly new remained to be studied. 'What,' he asked, 'would we find just beyond the inlet, on the far side of the island, a few hundred nauticals away down the coast?' Places out of range. 'We need a new boat, a laboratory boat, he said, one we can move along the coast.'

More of the sprites now ventured on shore, Sal and JJ among them. Sistus came occasionally, Alicia and Euna with their children, and others. JJ loved being in the water with her mother and father. Sal herself at last was playing with the fish as, it seemed so long ago, she had dreamed. She was Rusalka now, at least, some of the time. She expected to be pregnant again soon. She knew Sistus would probably find some of the other sprite girls to his liking. Old habits, she thought, will not disappear. Even so, she wanted him to be the father of any further children she had. She avoided other males and, she suspected, he approved.

Airther alone was troubled. 'What is it, Airther,' Sal asked him. 'I can see, something is worrying you. Tell me.'

''Tis Becky, Sal. Sheh has tyaken a likin te one of those villij lads. Sheh wants te stay wi him. Sheh doesn't want te live wi us any more.

It's Becky, Sal. She's taken a liking to one of those village lads. She wants to stay with him. She doesn't want to live with us any more

'Oh Airther That... that's very worrying. Not just for you. Becky is like one of us now, everyone loves her. But I think I understand how she feels. She can never have a sprite boy friend, can she? And she's just at the age when that's very important.'

Sal thought for a little while Airther waited anxiously.

'Well, there's an easy answer. Let her go and live in the village. Why not? There's much to be said for that. The raft will still be here. She will always be welcome and can visit you whenever she wishes. You can go to see her every day.'

'Aye, Ah see what tha means. But... but'

'But what. Airther?'

'Ah fear fer Towie. He's thinking like his big sister. They divvent fit in well heor, they knaa they will nivvor be leik the others. Thys don't want Jezzy to get at them tha knas. They want te be ornery fowk.'

I fear for Towie. He's thinking like his big sister. They don't fit in well here, they know they will never be like the others. They don't want Jezzy to get at them, you know. They want to be ordinary folk.'

'Ah, yes, I see. Well, the same thing for Towie. Let him go, Airther'

Aye, weh could do thet, but, tha knaas... Ah.. divvent want te seem ungrateful, but ah will nivvor be much use heor. Ah think wi three should aal move ower there an settle doon wi Basco's lot. They are canny good fowk. They waad be glad te hev weh. An Ahm a fisherman, ye see. That's whar Ahm canny gud at.'

Aye, we could do that but you know, I don't want to seem ungrateful but I never will be much use here. I think we three should all move over there and settle down with Basco's lot. They are very good folk. They would be glad to have us. I am a fisherman, you see. That's what I am specially good at.

'It's a hard, hard life, Airther. It's a constant struggle for the tribe.
You've seen how we live, how strong and healthy we are. But of course,
you and the family could come to us for anything you need, the
villagers too.'

'Aye, aye, that's true noo. But will yee always be heor ? Isn't the idea
tha yee will rebuild t'raft an sail away agyen as soon as yee can? Ah knaa
that's what the captain wants te dee. Yon scientist gadgie tu, Michel, he
won't be happy stook heor fre ever. He will want te gang off an sample
some other playeses.'

'An yee, Sal, divvent yee want te be a navigator agyen ? Yee are a
lass whee always wants te dee summat. Stay heor an there's nothin fre
yee te dee at aal.'

Aye, aye, that's true now. But will you always be here? Isn't the idea that you will rebuild
the raft and sail away again as soon as you can? I know that's what the captain wants to do.
Yon scientist fellow too, Michel, he won't be happy stuck here forever. He will want to go off
and sample some other places. And you, Sal, don't you want to be a navigator again? You are
a lass who always wants to do something. Stay here and there's nothing for you to do at all.

Sal felt tears spring to her eyes.

'Airther, Airther, you see too much.'

'Doan't tek on, Lass. I didna min t'upset yee'

Don't take on, Lass. I didn't mean to upset you.

'Airther, if you and your family wish to live on land, no one will
stop you. Our love will go with you. Live the way you choose, hard
though it is. I will tell Sistus. He will not try to prevent your going.
While we are here, and I think we will be stuck for years, come to us
for anything you need.'

'I know,' she continued, 'Sistus and all the engineers will never rest
until they can get the raft going again like it used to, or a build a new
one even better. Sistus hasn't said anything yet, but I am certain that is
what he wants to do. This is a temporary resting place. We will move,
one day. We will have choppers again, we will explore the deepest ocean.
We will, some day, have a city that can swim under water. Sistus even
has a name ready for it, *Atlantis*. That is what he truly wants to build
and if he cannot do it in his lifetime, he will want his children, our
children, to do it. All that is in the future, I don't know how far. We

will meet it when it comes. For now, Airther, we are here, and while we are here, you will be one of us, Becky and Towie too.'

Airther, Becky and Towie invited the sprites to a farewell celebration in the recreation hall. Basco himself was invited but dared not come. The family left amidst sorrow and tears but their departure was made less upsetting by the knowledge that they would be able to return as visitors whenever they wished. Everyone was conscious of their absence and many went to see Airther and the bairns in the village. Darien spent as much time with the islanders as he did with the sprites. He was becoming a *landliver*; must not say *landlubber*, even in jest. But he could swim under water when he wished.

Sal, as Airther had seen so clearly, was short of an occupation. The navigation department that had been the focus of so much of her life was redundant now and would be so until the raft moved. *When the raft moves.* Would that become a standard catch phrase, like *When the ocean freezes,* she wondered? The raft was a raft no longer, merely an artificial island.

She had introduced JJ to the water, spent long periods with the child singing gently, trying the effect of a few words, feeding, and cleaning. But when her beloved JJ grew older, became independent, what was she to do? Children, when grown up, should live their own lives. Many of the girl sprites were pregnant now. Alicia and Euna were going to have more babies. JJ, Sal thought, will have a brother or sister before long. You are and will be a mother. Yet that is not all you are, all you can be. You will know your children and love them. If she herself had normal lifespan, perhaps as long as Jezzy, most of her life still lay before her. What would she do with it?

The young team who had worked so well with her to get the raft onto the rocks, would be like her with little to do. Now they swam a great deal, exploring the inlet around the raft, using their terminals to get home again when the tide caught them. They danced, dined, and loved. They did not seem to feel, as she did, the need of something more.

Michel and his team of marinologists had enough to do to keep them at work forever. Should she join them? She felt none of their enthusiasm for the minutiae of crustacean and algal life.

You, Sal told herself, have many decades ahead. Will there be nothing to do but looking after children, gaming and playing with the fish? Not enough. How could it be enough for anyone? No one could or should build their life around their growing children.

Why was she restless again as she had been so many months ago when she was a Sydney rafter? Sal the child had dreamed of being a mermaid. As far as it could ever be, her childish dream had been realized but she now was a grown woman, a wiser person who had known fear and danger, had taken grave responsibilities and had come through. A woman of experience. So what was wrong?

Would she never be satisfied? *What more can you wish for?* Who had said that? The hated Calpurnia. Well, damn Calpurnia, Sal still wished for something more.

She wondered if she could train as an engineer to be of more direct help to Sistus. Sistus, as Sal had been told when she first met the sprites, had ambitions. In her long and loving talks he made long term plans with her. His notion of a submarine city for the sprites had never left him. Here, on this very site, was where it could begin. They must start building an entirely new kind of raft, one that would be properly seaworthy, capable of driving itself with powerful engines.

'What used to be called a *cruise liner*,' Sal nodded. 'There were people in ancient times who lived all their lives cruising.'

'It would be possible, almost easy,' he said, 'with robots doing the heavy work, to build a truly mobile, steerable, navigable ocean city. We must start to collect and manufacture the necessary materials as soon as possible. Michel will guide us in the biological methods of extraction and refining. Vogel will help with the design. Some day, Sal, we will need navigators again but it will be a different kind of navigation. Our cruiser, *Atlantis,* will be submersible. You will navigate beneath the oceans as well as on the surface.' Some day.

'There will be many such vessels. Sprites in vast numbers will live on and under the ocean, which covers three quarters of the globe. So much remains to be done' Sistus said, enthusiastically.

24

'Sal, Sal' One of the young Sprites came hurriedly to find her in the Nav School, or what had been the Nav School.

'Sal, Sal It's Jezzy She's asking for you. Come at once.'

They hurried, almost running, to the infirmary where Jezzy was reclining in her capsule, attended by her anxious carers. The old woman, after the raft finally settled, had been carried here, for she would no longer even try to walk. Sal and Sistus had visited her and knew she was weakening. Sal feared what she was going to find.

'Does Sistus know?' she gasped.

'He knows, he will come, everyone will know very soon. They will all come.'

They reached the chamber where the nursing staff were gathered round the capsule. Some were weeping. They stood aside when Sal approached. Jezzy's eyes were open, she reached out a hand to Sal, who took it in both of hers, gently.

'Rusalka, little mermaid' Jezzy whispered.

'I am here, Jezzybaba, old witch,' said Sal.

'My time is come, Rusalka. I am nearly finished. This is the end.'

Sal nodded. There was nothing she could say. She too was shedding tears. Sistus came to stand opposite. Jezzy looked at him and moved her free hand, which he took.

'You are a good man, Sistus,' said the dying woman. 'You have a fine woman here. Take care of her and your children.'

'I will, Jezzy. Thankyou, thankyou for everything, for giving us such opportunities.'

'Do you think I did wrong? I have changed you and so many others. Was it for the better? Or did I do it... do it only because I thought it was possible? Did I do it just because I knew it could be done? For fun? Only because no one had done it before? Was I wrong, irresponsible, wicked?'

'Jezzy,' he said. 'You did right. You knew it could be done and you wanted to do it for very good reasons. For all of us. We are better for it, you have made us better, the Earth itself has a new dimension now. You have opened up a new world for humanity.'

'There will be others like you, Jezzy. We will take charge of our own evolution, to develop humanity still further. People will look back on you as a great pioneer, a great.... a great... great witch,' stammered Sal.

The old woman gave her last crooked grin.

'And you, Rusalka, what will you do now? You feel lost, don't you?'

She can read thoughts, she still, she has always been able to read my thoughts. A witch indeed.

'What are you going to do?'

'I don't know. Have some more babies I suppose.'

'You must sing, Rusalka. You will make music. That is your gift and will be your gift to others. It is a great gift, you must not waste it. There is no limit to music. You will grow further as a singer, you will become the best, the greatest singer the world has ever known. All your extraordinary experience, your developed understanding, will appear in your singing and the great music you will compose and perform. This what lies ahead for you. Work at it, little mermaid. There is much to be done. Music is timeless. Sing now, as you sang to me before.'

The infirmary chamber was crowded now with mourning sprites.

'*Rusalka will sing to the moon,*' said Jezzy, with her last strength.

Rusalka sang. When the song ended, Jezzy's eyes were closed. Without thinking, Sal sang a requiem.

Sal, my dear Sal,' said Sistus when she finished in tears as many of those who heard her were, 'this is not the end, this is the beginning.'

The Author

Martin Simons was born in Derbyshire, England in 1930. After national service in the RAF he trained as a teacher at Borough Road and Goldsmiths Colleges. While teaching full time, in the evenings he studied geography with ancillary geology at Birkbeck College, London University. He graduated with First Class Honours in 1959 and subsequently became a university lecturer in London and Adelaide. He completed Masters degrees in Education and in Philosophy.

He has had lifelong interests in education, philosophy, aeronautics, especially the sport of gliding, and has written extensively about these and other subjects.

In 1954 he married Jean and they had two daughters, Patricia and Margaret. The family moved to Adelaide in 1968. After fifty happy years, Jean died of pancreatic cancer in 2005. Since then he has lived alone in suburban Melbourne but remains fully engaged with his writing and other activities.

In recent years, while continuing to fly and write non-fiction, he has written three very unusual novels, *Jenny Rat, Cities at Sea and The glass ship*.